MW00917233

PRAISE FOR *FRACTURED LIGHT*

"What I thought was going to be another *Twilight* wannabe turned out to be so much better! Rachel McClellan's *Fractured Light* is a paranormal thriller that could easily become the next overnight blockbuster. Her characters are so lifelike, her prose is so smooth, and her story is so captivating that you'll be held spellbound from page one!"

—**Gregg Luke,** Covenant Communications best-selling author

"McClellan weaves an enticing, supernatural tale of a reluctant heroine born with a gift that sometimes feels as much like a curse. Unexpected twists and turns in the story keep the reader guessing what's going to happen next to disrupt this teenage girl's life. Llona is a hero worth cheering for. Strong, determined, independent, and compassionate, Llona will do anything to protect those she loves, even at the cost of her own life. *Fractured Light* is a must-read for fans of paranormal—or fans of any genre, for that matter. Don't miss this exciting book from newcomer Rachel McClellan, the new force to be reckoned with in paranormal YA."

—**Cindy C Bennett,** author of *Geek Girl*

"Rachel McClellan weaves a new kind of paranormal YA tale fraught with intrigue, danger, and believable romance. Not easy to put down with a spunky and intelligent female lead, *Fractured Light* will find its place on every teen reader's bookshelf."

—**Ellen C. Maze,** best-selling author of *Rabbit: Chasing Beth Rider*

"The second I opened *Fractured Light*, I was drawn in by the unique concept and the complex heroine. In many ways, Llona Reese is just like any other teen girl: she has an affinity for sports, a complicated family life, and sometimes she just wants to be invisible. But in one very remarkable way, Llona is very different: she is gifted with the power of Light. McClellan's gift for the haunting and the heartbreaking shine in *Fractured Light*, and her pitch-perfect descriptions drew me into Llona's world, making me never want to leave. You won't want to miss this debut by a bright new star in the urban fantasy genre!"

—**Elodia Strain,** author of *My Girlfriend's Boyfriend*

"A talented writer can convince a reader that fantasy is real; a gifted author makes it look easy from the opening scene. Such is Rachel's brilliance and readers have been granted another great storyteller they can follow for years."

—**Wallace J. Swenson,** *Morgan's Pasture,* Three Muses Press

"The forces of darkness and light collide in this tale of forbidden love, sinister threats, and ancient battles. Llona must delve into the shadows to discover who is trying to destroy her as she learns to wield her power. You won't want to put this one down until the final scene plays out."

—**Marilyn Bunderson,** author of *The Mark*

"Llona is just trying to stay alive—to blend in and be normal. But nothing about her is normal. As she struggles between a normal life and control of her unique powers, a force greater than herself plots her undoing—but not in the way she could ever imagine. Every reader who loves original, powerful paranormal and fantasy YA will be absorbed by this compelling read."

—**Kimberly Kinrade,** YA author of *Forbidden Mind*

"*Fractured Light* is a creative story that simply doesn't stop. Intense action sequences, along with some wonderful twists, makes this book a must read for lovers of young adult fiction. MeClellan creates vivid characters that are able to generate real emotions in the reader. A great addition to the young adult genre!"

—**Heather Frost,** author of *Seers*

"*Fractured Light* is packed with suspense and mystery that will keep you guessing. Reading Llona transform into an extraordinary heroin had me turning the pages."

—**Jenelle Maloy,** author of *Forbidden Skull*

RACHEL McCLELLAN

A NOVEL

FRACTURED LIGHT

Sweetwater Books
An Imprint of Cedar Fort, Inc.
Springville, Utah

This is a work of fiction. The characters, names, incidents, places, and dialogue are products of the author's imagination, and are not to be construed as real.

ISBN 13: 978-1-59955-942-1

Published by Sweetwater Books, an imprint of Cedar Fort, Inc.
2373 W. 700 S., Springville, UT 84663
Distributed by Cedar Fort, Inc. www.cedarfort.com

LIBRARY OF CONGRESS CATALOGING-IN-PUBLICATION DATA

McClellan, Rachel, 1977-
Fractured light / Rachel McClellan.
     pages cm
 Summary: After her parents' death, Llona decides she wants nothing to do with the gift she inherited of manipulating light and transferring its calming energy to others.
 ISBN 978-1-59955-942-1
 1. Bereavement--Fiction. 2. Grief--Fiction. 3. Man-woman relationships--Fiction. 4. Supernatural--Fiction. 5. Fantasy fiction. I. Title.

 PS3613.C3582F73 2012
 813'.6--dc23

                        2011041592

Cover design by Brian Halley
Cover design © 2012 by Lyle Mortimer
Edited and typeset by Emily S. Chambers

Printed in the United States of America

10 9 8 7 6 5 4 3 2 1

Printed on acid-free paper

Acknowledgments

A SPECIAL THANKS AND A HUGE DEBT OF GRATITUDE to the following:

All those at Cedar Fort who played a roll in turning *Fractured Light* into something wonderful, specifically Angie Workman, who said, "We want it." Emily Chambers for making it shine, Mariah Overlock, Laura Jorgensen, and Josh Johnson for telling the world about it. And Brian Halley for a book cover that rocks.

The Idaho Falls Chapter of the IWL for telling the truth. Their honesty helped me become a better writer, especially that of Gary and Wally, the Godfathers of writing.

My beta readers whose excitement and sound advice kept me going, specifically Jan, Jenelle, and Michelle.

Liane, Valerie, and Anna for making me believe in myself.

My sisters Stephanie, Alana, Liane, and my brother Michael for not laughing at my ideas.

My father for his wisdom, and my mother who passed on her love for writing.

My husband and children who remind me daily of what's important in life.

PROLOGUE

"SIGMUND FREUD ONCE SAID THAT THE GOAL OF ALL LIFE IS death."

I paused from getting into the now-empty hearse, looking from the black-gloved hand gripping my arm to the woman who'd spoken the depressing words. She wore a frumpy hat with white feathers that looked like they'd been glued on by a kindergartner. I tore my eyes away from the feathery concoction and stared at her. Like a typical adult speaking to a teenager, she most likely thought her words profound—a small, passed-on piece of wisdom to make me feel less miserable about suddenly becoming an orphan.

"What are you saying?" I asked, wiping my wet, snow-colored hair away from my cheek. Rain at a funeral meant something, but I couldn't remember what.

The woman tilted her head and gave me a sympathetic smile as if my simple brain couldn't reason. In actuality, I knew full well what Freud meant, but I simply thought it was a stupid comment. Why would life's goal be death? Unless life was on Prozac and lying in bed all day watching the Soap Network, I highly doubted life's goal included death. Anyone living life shouldn't be concerned with death at all. My mother had taught me that. Sure, her life ended tragically, just like my father's, but all those who knew her knew that dying was the last thing on her mind. Maybe that was the problem—and the problem with my father too.

The woman began speaking again, no doubt explaining the rationale behind the lame quote, but I wasn't listening. I wasn't even staring at her papier-mâché hat anymore. I looked beyond it, back where my father lay stuffed in a casket. Only my uncle Jake remained, staring into my dad's grave. He would be like the rest of my family and wouldn't avoid death if it came for him.

But I would.

I made up my mind right then and there, while nest-head rattled on about the necessity of death. Death would never claim me. I would blend in with society and not try to stand out as others of my kind always did. Inevitably, that was always what got them killed. Even my mother, who insisted she was safe, died—in spite of the fierce, almost obsessive protection of my father. She could've lived a lot longer if she hadn't been so boisterous and colorful. Of course, that is why everyone loved her—she brought joy to their normally depressed lives. This, she told me, is the Aura's purpose: to use our gift to comfort the heavyhearted and provide light to those who are lost. At the time she told me this, it sounded as wonderful as pink lemonade and cotton candy in summer, but now the thought of being someone's raggedy Kleenex was unbearable.

I ignored the lecturing woman and jumped into the front seat of the hearse, shutting the door behind me. The driver asked, "Did you want to wait for your uncle, Llona?"

"No, he'll come when he's ready. Please just take me home."

As we pulled away from the cemetery, I didn't look back. My mind was on the future and on my survival.

ONE

"EVERY LIVING THING WILL FIGHT FOR ITS PLACE ON EARTH," Mr. Yazzie, my science teacher, said. He stood in front of the class, chalk dust smeared on the front of his blue polo shirt. The blackboard behind him contrasted with the yellow walls, but his polyester pants matched the mustard color perfectly.

I leaned forward, chewing on my pen while he continued. "But if their environment changes and they don't learn to adapt, then they will inevitably die. Nothing can save them."

I lowered my gaze to the desk, wondering if I'd done enough to adapt. I hoped so because I was sick of moving. Since my father's funeral five years ago, my uncle Jake and I had moved four times, finally settling in Bountiful, Utah.

I liked Bountiful. It had a rural feeling to it and lots of tall, mountainous trees, but at the same time had all the amenities of a big city. I couldn't complain about the weather, either. Utah wasn't as cold as Wisconsin. Gratefully, I only had to endure the Wisconsin cold for a few months before I decided it was time to move again.

A bell sounded, interrupting my biology teacher just as he was about to reveal who he thought would win in a cage fight—protozoa or flagella. His face fell when students jumped up and rushed to the door.

"Don't forget about the assembly," he called after them.

I let the classroom empty before I stood to relieve my stiff joints. Because of my delay, I caught Mr. Yazzie contorting his body into what looked like a dance position—elbows bent, hands outstretched. He shuffled his feet a few times before he finally thrust his hips forward and left the room. I felt confident he wouldn't have done such an uncharacteristic move if he'd realized I was still in the room, but alas, I often go unnoticed. Being invisible is, after all, my priority.

I gathered my books and followed Mr. Yazzie out the door. He didn't attempt the awkward jig again, but I had to wonder what caused this sudden break of character. Perhaps he had a hot date tonight, a lady friend he had met on the Internet.

Walking in front of me, Mr. Yazzie suddenly reached behind his back and tugged at an invisible wedgie. Okay, so maybe not a hot date. Maybe it was the season premiere of some new sci-fi series involving flagella and cilia battling one another to the death. This theory made much more sense.

I veered to the left and down a long hallway to my locker, where I dropped off my books. I considered skipping the morning assembly. It was just a mini pep rally put on by the principal to get us excited for the new school year.

Behind me other seniors had the same idea, but they bravely acted upon their desire and disappeared out a nearby door. I decided not to follow in case someone saw me. I might be considered "cool" if caught and thereby labeled. I was comfortable with my current label of "weird-girl" or "who?" and I didn't want that to change.

I followed the sounds of noisy students down the hall and toward the gym. Highland High was like every other school I'd been to: light tan brick exterior, white interior walls, and short-weave blue-speckled carpet. The schools even smelled the same: sweat and chemicals, masked occasionally by a squirt of fruity perfume.

I moved into the gym and was about to cross to the other side when I heard, "Llona! Up here!"

I looked up and saw May sitting at the top of the bleachers, holding a bag of chips. Today she was sitting with the goths, and actually blended in quite well. She wore a baggy, black sweatshirt and gray sweatpants. Her dark, shoulder-length hair may have been combed earlier, but now looked a mess. Her whole appearance looked unnatural, masking her true beauty.

I maneuvered my way up to her, careful to avoid stepping on anyone. About halfway, two freshman boys began wrestling, and one of them bumped into me, knocking me off balance.

Afraid to reach out, I fell forward toward a girl with red hair. She had a metal clip of a grasshopper or a dragonfly—I couldn't be sure—sticking out of her hair. I closed my eyes and waited to feel the bug's sting when arms suddenly encircled my waist and pulled me back up.

The grip was strong, the motion skilled, and I instantly pictured a Navy SEAL. They were the kind of men that, despite extreme conditions, lack of sleep, and dangerous quests, still worked hard, knowing a job had to be done. They were a dying breed of real men—or so the commercial goes.

I turned to face my SEAL to thank him for saving me from being speared by a metal bug, but when I looked into his eyes, I couldn't speak. They were the shimmering blue of a dragonfly's wings.

"It's Llona, right?" the boy asked, smiling.

I flinched when he said my name. He was the first person besides my parents to pronounce it correctly. Most people say my name the way it's spelled—Lona, but in actuality, it's pronounced E-o-na. I never corrected anyone. I'm used to it now. Even Jake didn't call me by my real name; with him it's always, "How's it going, Tink?" I'd had a thing for Tinkerbell when I was little, and used to love it when he called me that.

"It's Lona," I corrected, barely above a whisper. It felt awkward, like chewing on water, but I couldn't have him pronouncing my name the way my parents had.

The Navy SEAL tilted his head of brownish-blond hair. "Llona it is," he said. "Are you all right?"

I gurgled something unintelligible, making him frown. The frown looked awkward on him, unlike his smile, and I wished I could've told him so, but I suddenly became aware of his hands still touching my waist.

"Hey, Llona! You coming up here or what?" May barked from above.

I looked past my SEAL. Behind him, May stood, hands on hips.

"Gotta go," I said.

I slid past him and quickly took the next step up the bleachers, barely finding room for my big foot between two students. Finally, I sat next to May, my head down. I didn't dare look up for fear of meeting the SEAL's eyes again.

"What was that all about?" May asked.

"I almost fell. That guy saved me."

"Who is he?"

"Is he looking?"

"He's way good looking."

I elbowed her. "Is he looking at me?"

"Um . . . nope. Who is he?"

"I don't know."

"Give me to the end of the day. I'll find out everything there is to know about him." May sucked a chip into her mouth.

From the center of the gym floor, the principal, Mr. Wilcox, began to speak. "Welcome, students. Thank you for coming to this exciting assembly this morning," he bellowed into a microphone. "We have a great program today and a wonderful speaker who will share her valuable experiences with us." He pulled up his pants—his signature move. He had a belly that made him look like he was pregnant with triplets, and beneath the bulge were exceptionally small legs. This odd combination must've made wearing pants extremely difficult.

Mr. Wilcox opened his mouth to speak again, but a sound to his left distracted him. On the far end of the bleachers, two boys argued, their voices growing louder with each passing second. A few teachers hurried over to break it up, but before they could, the taller of the two boys shoved the other into a group of nearby students.

Suddenly the entire area became like a mosh pit at a Linkin Park concert. Teachers swarmed the area, trying to take control of the situation, but because of all the students, they couldn't get up the bleachers. All they could do was yell, which was as effective as a soccer coach for three-year-olds.

Everyone, including myself, stood to watch the mayhem slowly spread across the bleachers. Fights broke out everywhere. I watched in horror as a girl who looked like a sophomore, accidentally got punched in the face. Blood spurted from her nose.

I glanced at the wide, circular florescent lights hanging from the ceiling. I could end this fight, but should I? A teacher fell to the ground and screamed.

There was only one way to end this brawl quickly. I stared at the lights and thought hard. It was a lot to manipulate, but I felt confident I could do it. Turning lights on and off was the only part of my abilities I could reliably control.

I concentrated on the bright lights until I felt Light's energy surge through me, turning my insides hot. Sweat broke on my forehead and my knees went weak. Suddenly a burst of energy exploded from me like juice squeezed from a lemon. Then there was darkness.

Two

When I was a child, my mother would tell me a bedtime story. At first I loved the dramatic tale, but after hearing it night after night, I grew bored. I often asked for a different one, a book even, like other children, but she always insisted on telling our Auran history. Sometimes she would introduce new characters or change the scenery, but the plot remained the same:

"Once upon a time, thousands of years ago, Light lived among man as intelligent beings. Their presence brought equality and harmony to the humans, and the world was at peace. There was no sadness, pity, or pride; it seemed the righteousness of the people had banned evil from the earth. But when an older prince became jealous of his father's love for his younger brother, he murdered the young prince in cold blood.

"This deliberate evil brought the once-forbidden darkness to the prince's heart where he allowed it to remain. There he entertained it, fed it, until the darkness overtook his thoughts and mind. Eager to corrupt others, he spread the darkness to those whose minds were open to greed, power, and lust. These new dark ones, Vykens as they were called, were unable to stand in Light's presence without feeling unbearable pain. Hidden within the shadows of night, the Vykens hunted and attacked the Light-filled beings at their weakest moments, almost to the point of extinction.

"To preserve themselves and maintain balance between good and evil, Light hid within the DNA of human females. These women passed Light on to their female offspring and became known as Auras. Auras protected their identity for many years, and even learned to use Light's power to fight against the Vykens. But then the Vykens made a terrible discovery. They found that if they drank the blood of an Aura, they were no longer bound to the night. Not only did the sun no longer pose a threat, but the Vykens learned they could manipulate the Auras' power, and they used it to grow stronger than ever before.

"For this reason, Auras gathered from all over the earth to learn how to protect their human form. They created a council to oversee their safety, and to ensure Auras appeared no different than others."

I'd heard this story so many times that when my mother reached this point, I was usually asleep. I never knew why she had insisted on telling me the same story over and over until I had it memorized. Even my father had asked her once, "Can't you tell her a different story, Ella?"

"No," my mother answered. "Llona needs to know Light's history. The truth."

"She will know the truth because she has us."

"Let's hope so."

Their hope had been in vain.

*　　*　　*　　*　　*

Cries rose in the darkness, but they were no longer the angry voices of a mob; they were cries of surprise. The doors on both sides of the gym opened, spilling light from the hallways into the blackened gym and onto the basketball court. This time when a teacher yelled to exit, students listened.

"Was that insane or what?" May asked.

I didn't answer. Mentally shutting the lights off had weakened my body.

May touched me in the darkness. "You okay?"

"Yes," I mumbled.

Students on our bench stood up to leave. "Let's get out of here," May said.

She followed the Stoners out, but I remained still, allowing some time for my strength to return. A tall male form stepped up the bleachers. He looked like a muscular shadow, floating gracefully toward me. His movements seemed so fluid I was surprised to hear the bleachers shake from the weight of his footsteps.

"Are you all right?" a voice in a heavy English accent asked.

Suddenly my weakness returned tenfold. Apparently I had a thing for men with accents.

He touched me on the shoulder when I didn't immediately respond. "Do you want help down?"

I shook my head, unable to speak, but I did manage to stand. Just barely.

"Can you see okay in the dark?" he asked beautifully and perfectly.

"I think so."

"Good."

I followed him down the bleachers as if walking a tight rope. When we entered the crowded hallway, the man, probably a teacher, turned from me and disappeared into a sea of students. I never saw his face, but judging from the back of him, I knew he had to have a nice one.

After a few deep breaths, I turned the opposite way and slowly headed toward my locker. Like always, I kept my head down and followed the steadily moving line of students. All of a sudden, for a reason I couldn't explain, I glanced up. Standing against a row of lockers was the same boy who had saved me earlier. My SEAL. He stared at me with a confused expression, probably just noticing how strange I look.

I knew my appearance was different, shockingly so. My ghostly pale skin appeared to melt into my blonde, almost white hair, making my eyes stand out like the blue of an Arctic wolf's. The only half-compliment I'd ever received (other than from my parents) was from one of Jake's friends. He said I was really pretty, in a freakish, Tim Burton sort of way. I guess there are worse things than being compared to a ghoul, but I couldn't think of one.

Just then his brow furrowed and his mouth turned down. What was that all about? I'd done nothing to him. I quickly looked away, but when I thought I'd walked far enough past him, I turned back around. The boy still stared, appalled, like I'd killed his dog or something. Was it possible that he could've known what I'd done back in the gym? I thought about it the whole way to my next class and well into Mrs. Simmons' lecture on Shakespeare. Impossible. No one could have known. He must be mad for some other reason; maybe he was upset I'd fallen into him. I shrugged it off. Oh well. One more person who thinks I'm mentally deranged.

Mrs. Simmons, who always wore too tight of clothing for her bulging frame, said, "Shakespeare wrote, 'So, ere you find where light in darkness lies, Your light grows dark by losing of your eyes.' Can anyone tell me what you think he was trying to say?"

For the third time in my school career, I raised my hand. I couldn't help it. This was one of my favorite quotes.

"Yes, Llona?" The whole class turned and looked at me.

"It means you can't find light in darkness, and if you keep

looking for it, you'll lose your soul."

Erica, a popular girl, maybe even a cheerleader—I couldn't remember—laughed "Are you for real?" Her nostrils flared, contorting her pretty face.

A couple of students snickered.

"That's a good question, Erica," the teacher said.

I looked up, shocked the teacher had sided with an obviously rude student.

"Is Llona's answer real?" the teacher asked. "Do you think it's possible that if a person goes to, let's say a party where there are drugs, with no intention of ever using, inevitably their actions will ruin them? They're not going to partake of the drugs, just go and have fun with friends. Is there anything wrong with that?"

The room was silent. I could practically here the grinding sounds of a faulty engine as their brains searched for an answer. Finally the silence broke when another kid I didn't recognize raised his hand.

"I think her answer is real and happens all too often. Though a person's intentions seem good in the beginning, if they allow themselves to be a part of an environment that obviously ruins lives, they will first endure it, then pity the people involved, and eventually embrace the lifestyle themselves."

"Exactly. Thank you, Matt," Mrs. Simmons said. "I see you know Alexander Pope's work. I agree entirely."

Matt bowed his head as if a subject to a King in an English court. His long fingers swept sandy blond hair behind his ears. He looked to be a little taller than me and skinny, not gross skinny, but lean and muscular—the body of a runner.

After the bell rang, I gathered my stuff and moved to stand up. I practically ran into Matt, who was suddenly standing directly in front of me.

"I like what you said about Shakespeare," he said. "Not

many people understand what he's all about."

"I'm not sure I do either. He's the master of cryptic."

Matt laughed. "Very true."

I stepped to the side of him and threw my bag over my shoulder. Matt moved to block me. "Listen, I'm trying to get a group together to study the writings of the great ones, sort of like a book club. You interested?"

I shuddered, and I think I grimaced. Not because Matt bothered me, but because I'd never done anything like that before: read literature in a small group. It sounded so intimate.

Matt noticed my reaction. "It's okay if you can't. I was just asking." He turned around and walked away.

The Light within me leapt, wanting to go after him to apologize. It was not in Light's nature to be deliberately cruel, and I felt it course through me now, anxious to relieve any sadness I may have caused him. But I kept my feet firmly planted and closed my eyes. Survival first. It was my mother that would've gone after him. Of course she wouldn't have had such a violent reaction to begin with. She loved being with others in any setting and they loved her in return. Then she was murdered.

I finally moved when the teacher asked me if I needed something. I shook my head and left the room.

Trig class was next. Earlier that morning, I'd overheard a few girls talking about the new math teacher, a *Mr. Steele*. By the way they were talking him up, I was anxious to confirm the hype.

At my locker I replaced my English book with my math book, and then quickly zipped up my backpack. Most students didn't take their bags to every class, but there was something comforting about having it on my back. Without it I felt naked.

The bell rang just as I closed my locker. Shoot! I was late. I speed-walked down the almost empty hallway to where I thought room 204 was. After a couple of left turns, I finally found the classroom at the end of the hall. Before I turned the handle, I took a deep breath and mentally prepared to be the center of attention. I pulled open the door, and like I expected, heads turned my direction. I hurried to the nearest vacant desk at the back of the room.

"Try to be on time, please," the teacher said, in a familiar English accent. The man from the gym!

"As I was saying . . ." Mr. Steele continued to speak. His mouth moved up and down, but I couldn't hear a word. From the corner of my eye, I saw pages turn as students responded to whatever he was saying, but I was frozen. Literally unable to move or think.

He was the most gorgeous, perfect man I'd ever seen. His thick, short hair was blacker than a moonless night, and his full, arched eyebrows hung above deep-set green eyes, shading them as if they were treasured emeralds. He was tall, almost towering, or maybe it was his overpowering presence that made him seem so. He wore a black silk shirt tucked into gray trousers and whenever he moved, disrupting the air around him, the thin material pressed against his stomach, revealing a tight six-pack of bulging muscles.

As far as I was concerned, this man had only one flaw: he was my math teacher. Mr. Steele. His name couldn't have been more perfect, like a shiny metal gun sculpted for my hand. I shivered and continued to stare.

He looked to be in his midtwenties, making him only seven or so years older than me. Society would definitely frown upon any type of relationship between us—as if that were a possibility. I shook my head. At least I think I shook it. I couldn't believe I was having these thoughts about a teacher.

I sighed and continued to watch his mouth open and close as he explained some complex math problem. Occasionally his eyes met mine and when they did, my cheeks grew hot and my breathing quickened. I swallowed hard. This must be love at first sight. I always thought it would happen when I was older and with a guy more my age, but I guess love has no age restrictions. Too bad my infatuation is for an off-limits man. I sighed again.

Mr. Steele walked by me, and the faint smell of his cologne sent my head spinning. My knees weakened, but gratefully I was sitting down so I did nothing but slump further into my seat.

I removed a pen from my backpack and attempted to write, but when I looked down there was nothing on the paper. I shook the pen hard and began to write again, but still nothing came out. I stared at it for what seemed like an eternity, with Mr. Steele's soothing voice in the background, until I realized I hadn't been writing with a pen at all. In my hand, I gripped my mascara.

I looked around and saw Mike Miller staring at me as if I'd just shaved my head. He rolled his eyes and looked back toward Mr. Steele, who had returned to the chalkboard to continue his math dance with a piece of chalk. I quickly shoved the mascara back in my bag and felt around for a real pen.

My fingers grazed something soft, yet stiff. Wondering what it could be, I took hold of it's small form and pulled it out. It fit in my palm like a lucky rabbit's foot, but there was nothing fortunate about it. My teeth clamped down on the inside of my cheek until I tasted blood. It was all I could do to keep from screaming.

THREE

THE BELL RANG. I BLINKED ONCE. MY BACKPACK STILL SAT IN my lap, squished between my stomach and the desk. I tried not to think of what was lying dead inside. Gratefully, Mr. Steele left the room first, followed by the rest of the class. As soon as they were gone, I pushed my bag away, jumped up, and rubbed my tainted palm against my jeans.

A familiar head poked into the room. "What are you doing?" May asked.

"Trying not to freak out." I inspected my hand for blood.

"Why? What happened?"

"I found a dead mouse in my bag."

"Oh no! Let me see." She opened my bag and began to search it.

"You like dead mice?"

May frowned. "No, I just want to make sure it's really dead. Maybe it's just knocked out."

"It's definitely dead. Why do you care?"

"I kept them as pets when I was younger."

"Is that sanitary?"

"Sure. My mom bought them for me. It was the only pet we could afford." She pulled out a white mouse by its tail and held it up. Its head had been almost severed. A bloody string of skin, or maybe a spinal cord, kept it from falling off. "What happened to it?" she asked.

I looked away. "I don't know, but it's disgusting."

May dropped it into the garbage. "It's probably been in your bag since last night. Poor thing didn't have a chance."

"Yeah. Poor thing." I felt real sorry for it. "Let's go wash our hands."

After I scrubbed and rescrubbed my hands, we left the bathroom. "You ready to go to lunch?" May asked.

"Aren't you having lunch with Sean?" Sean was the pothead she'd been sitting by earlier.

"No. Maybe tomorrow. Of course Cindy wants me to hang out with them, so we'll see."

"Who's Cindy?"

"You remember Cindy, don't you? She was Lady Macbeth in the play last year."

"Yeah, I remember." The drama crowd.

"Do you want to go out for lunch or eat here?" May shoved her books into her locker.

"I don't care."

"Let's leave then. I hate school food." She eyed my backpack. "Do you want to put your bag up?"

"No, let's go," I said and followed her out.

I was lucky to have a friend like May. I wouldn't call her a best friend because both of us had an unspoken agreement that we couldn't get too close—to anyone. Where I masked my desire for anonymity by being anti-social, she did it by being everyone's friend. She knew everyone in school, but not one person could call her their best friend. And though she did spend more of her time with me, it still wasn't enough to make someone think we were close.

Our connection was a strange one, but it made more sense to me than most people's relationships. When I'd first moved here last year, May had been my lab partner. We'd only known each other for a few weeks before that day when we both realized the other was different.

May, who always smiled, sat unusually quiet and somber. I noticed right away, but because we weren't really friends, I did nothing beyond asking her how she was doing. If I'd been my mother, I would have immediately pulled her aside and found a way to help her. But I wasn't my mother. My mother's outgoing compassion is what got her killed. That wasn't going to be me.

When Mr. Allen had handed out our experiment involving a liquid-filled beaker, I passed it to May while I read over our assignment. I became vaguely aware that the beaker in May's hand had begun to boil on its own. I quickly glanced around the room to see if that was what was supposed to happen, but all other beakers remained still. I looked back at May who was staring out the window with a serious expression on her face, oblivious to the boiling solvent.

When I leaned over to get her attention, the beaker suddenly exploded into a round ball of fire. My long hair immediately lit up, followed by shocked screams from everyone in the room. I slapped at my head to put the fire out, ignoring the pain as flames licked my palms. The teacher rushed over to help, but through all the commotion I couldn't tear my eyes from May. She was staring at her hands with pure horror and I had no doubts that, somehow, she had caused the beaker to explode.

When the teacher began to escort me to the nurse's office, May finally snapped out of her trance and insisted on following us. I jerked away from her when she reached for my hand. Not in anger, but because I had to keep my hands on my head to prevent anyone from seeing what I knew was about to happen. Even as I moved away from her, I could feel the hair beneath my hands growing.

Of all the strange things about me, this one was the most difficult to explain. For no matter what happened to my hair, it always grew back and always remained the same shocking blonde. I'd tried everything from dying my hair to shaving it off, but nothing worked. My mid-back-length, crazy hair refused to be anything else.

Once inside the nurse's office, I convinced Mr. Allen to return to class, but when I tried to get May to return too, she refused. When the nurse came in and asked me to put my hands down, I did so hesitantly. From under my hands my long hair spilled down past my shoulders, completely unscathed.

May gasped. "How is that possible? Your hair was on fire!"

I shook my head, hiding my burnt palms in my lap. "Nope, I'm fine. It just looked like it."

The nurse examined my head. "You look fine to me. I don't know what all the fuss is about. Do you feel all right?"

"Actually, I have a massive headache. Can I go home?"

The nurse glanced at a clock on the wall. There was only twenty minutes left of school. "I guess it will be all right. Will you be able to drive?"

"I'll take her home," May said.

My eyes flashed to hers, and I could tell she hadn't bought my story. On the way to her car, she suddenly grabbed my burned hands and turned them over.

"I knew I wasn't crazy." She stopped. "So why does your hair look fine now?"

I looked her square in the eyes and asked, "How did that fire start?"

She looked away, and I continued walking toward the parking lot. She caught up to me a moment later. "My car is over here."

We didn't say a word to each other the entire way home, but the next day I suddenly had a new friend, a strange one, but a friend nevertheless. We never spoke about that day again, but that bizarre occurrence had bonded us.

I was about to hop inside the passenger seat of May's beat-up Plymouth Colt when I heard a whistle. Passing directly in front of us drove Adam and Mike in a sporty-looking red car. The new kid who had saved me earlier sat in the back.

"Hey Adam!" May waved.

Adam waved his hand out the open window. Adam and his gang were jocks. May occasionally hung out with them too.

"By the way," May said after starting the car. "I found out who the new kid is. His name is Christian Knight. He moved here from Portland. Apparently, he was the star quarterback there. Coach is really excited, but Alex is super annoyed. It means he'll have to be second string, and he hates not being the center of attention. Know what I mean?"

"Yeah," I said, trying to be interested. I hadn't grown up with these guys, so I didn't know them like May. But I didn't point that out.

"The new guy's pretty cute. I bet Erica makes him her boyfriend within a week. She thinks just because she's a cheerleader she can get whoever she wants."

"Isn't Erica your friend?" I asked, knowing May spent time with her.

"Not really. We had a class together is all. She's too fake for me. Know what I mean?"

I shook my head no, but May kept talking. "Leah asked me if you were trying out for the basketball team again."

This got my attention. "Yeah, I'm trying out."

I liked Leah. She was one of the few girls on the team who still spoke to me. She, along with a few others, participated in every girl sport Highland offered. These were the ones who knew my athletic abilities, and either thought I wasn't a team player or was simply lazy. For the most part I was a good player, if not the best. But when the moon disappeared, I could barely walk, let alone play basketball. How could I explain my "condition" to them? They'd never understand.

March twelfth. That's when it happened. I was barely fourteen. I thought that was kind of late; my mother had been twelve. I wish I were talking about my period. That would've been much easier to deal with.

Other girls knew nothing about real change. Sure their bodies might change, and their tummies cramp, but whooptie-stinkin'-doo. So they've become a woman. They knew nothing about transforming. But I did, and believe me it went well beyond the side effects of puberty.

The day of my transformation, I'd never felt so alive and full of energy. I was on point, on fire; I could do no wrong. We'd played soccer during P.E., and I swore the ball and I were one. I scored nine goals, surprising everyone in my class, including the teacher who happened to be the varsity soccer coach. She begged me to try out, insisting she'd never seen anything like the way I played. Neither had I. It just came so easy. My body moved faster than ever before, and my movements were precise. It was an incredible feeling.

Because of my sudden, amazing soccer skills, some of the older girls invited me to a movie that night. Feeling on top of the world, I accepted without question, something I normally didn't do. But on that day I didn't analyze. I embraced my decision even to the point of suggesting we go rock climbing before the movie. They seemed surprised as I'm sure they thought me a weak, shy freshman who bent at the slightest breeze. Not that day, though. Like I said, I was on fire.

At the community rec center, I schooled the girls on rock climbing and afterwards engaged in a conversation with a much older boy. I could see awe in the eyes of the girls. I wasn't used to being looked at with admiration. It was a good feeling.

During the movie, I couldn't sit still. My body refused to be motionless. Without saying good-bye, I rushed from the theater and away from my new friends. As soon as my feet hit the pavement, I ran.

I felt the full moon rise behind me. Its light tingled my skin, but I didn't stop to wonder how that was possible. Instead, I ran harder and faster, my eyes on the forest ahead. The muscles in my body began to vibrate and pulse with new life. It was the life my mother had told me to prepare for: the day I became one with Light.

But I wish she would've told me how much the moon would affect my body. When the moon was full it wreaked havoc on my muscles and only exercise helped relieve the painful sensation. That's why I played every sport I could. Of course, the vast amount of energy and heightened abilities came with a price. After the full moon disappeared, my body was useless. My teammates couldn't make sense of my strange behavior. Half the month they loved me, the other half they wished I were dead.

"When are tryouts?" May asked, bringing me back to the present.

"Um, in a few weeks, I think."

"I'll have to come to the basketball games this year. I heard you were something else to watch." She turned left into a Burger King.

"Whatever. I'm sure you heard a lot more than that."

She glanced at me sideways. "I heard you were either sick a lot, or angry and wouldn't play." May turned off the ignition and jumped out of the car. The rusted metal door vibrated when she slammed it shut.

"What do *you* think the reason was?" I asked, trying to close my door.

"You have to slam it, remember?"

I slammed it.

"I think," May began, "that it was a combination of both."

"Do explain?"

"I think sometimes you get sick of everybody's crap. Sure they love you when you play great, but the second you mess up, they offer no sympathies. I'd probably miss some games too, just to make them mad. Show them how much they need me."

I laughed as I opened the glass door leading into the restaurant; a breath of air conditioning ruffled my hair. "I would never deliberately miss a game, and I would never play a game unless I was giving it my all, which I admit doesn't look that great sometimes."

"I saw you play soccer a couple of times last year. You were incredible one game: fast, shifty, but then another game you just stood there. You wouldn't even run. What was that all about?"

I shook my head. "I didn't feel good."

We moved to the front of the line. A pimple-faced cashier with red curly hair stared at us expectantly.

"You didn't look sick," May said, staring up at the menu.

I was about to order but turned around, suddenly defensive. "I don't lie. I don't pretend, and I'm not spiteful. I didn't ask you to be my friend, May. If you really feel the same as others you can walk away right now."

May frowned. "That's not what I meant. I'm sorry, really I am. If you say you didn't feel well, then I believe you. Friends?"

I took a deep breath. "Of course."

"Hey, May," a male voice called after we placed our order. "Come eat with us."

May glanced behind her. "Be there in a sec." She turned to

me. "Go sit with Adam when you get your food. I'll be right there."

"Adam? As in Adam who was riding with Christian?"

"Yeah, I guess," she replied nonchalantly.

I looked for an empty table by the window. "Actually I'm going to eat over there."

Pimple-face dropped my food on a tray as if it were a case of nails; several fries slipped from the greasy fry bag. May let out an exaggerated sigh. "You can't be serious? Just go over and sit down. It's not a big deal."

"You know how it is with me. Let's keep it that way."

"Do you want me to sit with you?"

I looked back to the lone table I'd found. Sunlight spilled in from the window, encasing the two-top as if it were in its own single world. "No. I'm cool."

"All right. If you change your mind, you know where I'll be."

After we split ways, I set my tray down and slid into the seat. I really didn't mind eating alone; it was something I was used to. I closed my eyes and let the light from the sun warm my skin.

"Why don't you come over and join us?" a gentle voice asked.

I opened my eyes and blinked once, twice, three times. I stared at the boy standing across from me as if I could see right through him. *Christian.* His eyebrows arched slightly, almost hopeful. I looked down.

When I didn't answer, he said, "I'm Christian," and held out his hand. His skin was light bronze like a perfectly baked cookie right out of a hot oven. I didn't reach for his hand, as appetizing as it looked. Instead I took a sip of water.

Christian cleared his throat and shifted his weight. I wasn't making this easy on him, but I wasn't deliberately trying to be rude. I just couldn't figure out why he was talking to me.

He asked again, "Will you join us?"

I swallowed. The cold liquid slid down my throat and hit my stomach. The shock of it helped me find my voice. "I appreciate the offer, but I'll just eat here in the sun."

He nodded, as if thinking. A red car blaring rap music drove away from the drive-thru window; the bass shook the glass. He waited for it to pass before he asked, "Can I join you?"

"Why?" I blurted before I had a chance to think how that might sound.

Christian didn't miss a beat. "Because I like it here too. There's something about the sun's light." He looked up and out the window toward the sky. "It's peaceful, like lying in a boat in the middle of a perfectly still lake."

My jaw dropped. I'd never heard anyone speak about light that way. I didn't know if I should be impressed or frightened.

Christian frowned. "That sounded stupid. Sometimes I say lame things. Adam's always giving me a hard time."

"Have you known Adam long?"

Christian looked back to where he'd been sitting. "Hold that question. Let me get my food." He walked away.

I started to tell him I hadn't said he could eat with me, but stopped. So I eat lunch with a boy? Big deal. He probably wouldn't talk to me after this anyway. I took a bite of my cheeseburger and tilted my head so I could hear what he was going to say.

Ultra sensitive hearing is another trait I'd inherited, but not from my mother. My father had joked that it was the only useful thing he'd given me. Whenever I asked where he got his good hearing, he'd simply shrug and give me a mischievous grin.

"Later guys. I'm eating with Llona," Christian said.

"Why?" Mike spat with a mouth full of food. I practically

heard hamburger chunks spray from his mouth and hit the table.

"She seems cool," Christian said. The sound of his tray sliding against the table echoed over his voice as he picked it up.

"You don't want to know her, trust me. She's a psycho," Mike said.

I gritted my teeth. Great. People think I belong in an insane asylum.

"She is not," May's voice defended. "She's one of the nicest people I know."

"What about me?" Adam asked.

"See you guys later," Christian told them.

Having great hearing has its perks, but there were times I wished I were deaf.

Christian returned to my table and sat down. "Adam's my cousin," he said as he carefully unwrapped his chicken sandwich.

I swallowed the bite in my mouth. "Huh?"

"You asked me how I knew Adam. He's my cousin on my mother's side. We used to hang out a lot before his family moved here four years ago."

"Oh."

"What about you? Do you have family around?"

Yikes. Personal questions. Definitely not a direction I wanted to go. I shrugged. "Not sure. So May tells me you're going to be the new quarterback?"

He shrugged. "I guess. I told coach I'd play whatever position, but he wouldn't hear of it. Alex is pretty mad."

"He'll get over it. Why did you move here?" A fly buzzed near my face. I flicked my wrist at it.

"My dad's work."

"What does he do?" I swiped at the fly again when it landed on my arm.

"He buys businesses that are in trouble and then makes them profitable again. Something like that. I'm not real sure."

"What about your mom?"

His eyes fell; the color changed to a melancholy blue, the shade of great sadness. I recognized it because I'd seen the same color in my own eyes.

"She died when I was three. Cancer. My dad never remarried."

I stopped a french fry moving to my mouth. Suddenly I wasn't hungry any more. "I'm sorry. That must've been hard."

"At times." He took a bite of his sandwich and chewed quietly. From across the room May's high-pitched, chipmunk-like giggle broke the silence.

"That's some laugh," Christian said, smiling again. His eyes returned to normal, the sadness pushed back to wherever he kept it hidden. But sadness like that never leaves you.

I nodded. "It's contagious."

"So what about you? What does your dad do?"

The fly returned. I frowned as it completed an aerial swoop toward my half-eaten burger. Suddenly Christian's hand shot through the air like a missile. He caught the fly between his thumb and forefinger.

I gasped. "That was fast!"

He wrapped the fly in a napkin with as much delicacy as he had unwrapped his chicken sandwich. "Not really. My dad is faster."

"Do you two catch flies often?" I mused.

"When the fish aren't biting. Whoever catches the most wins a prize."

"Have you ever won?"

"Not once, but I'm getting close."

"What's the prize?"

"I'm lucky if it's a bag of chips."

"Your life sucks."

He laughed, nodding. "I know, right?"

We continued talking. I could tell he was trying to get to know me, but little did he realize that I'd practically written the rules of the dodging-personal-questions game. Every time he asked one, I countered back, sending the conversation into a different direction.

I was really racking up the points, until he asked, again, "So where did you grow up? I don't think you answered me."

I reacted quickly. "Yes, I did. Remember? The sky?"

"Wait, what?" He looked totally confused. "You grew up in the sky?"

I laughed. "No, you were talking about your trip to Mexico over the summer and how a bad storm ruined it. Did you guys have to come home early?"

"Yeah, we got stuck at the airport."

I leaned back in my seat and smiled as Christian told me all about his nightmare at the airport.

"You two seem to be having fun," May said, approaching our table with Adam in tow. "You about done?" she asked me.

I picked up my water and took a long sip. "I'm done."

From the door, Mike called, "When you're done with freak-girl, I'll be outside."

Christian's eyes moved to mine. "Sorry. He's a jerk."

"I don't care." I gathered our garbage with Christian's help. My breath caught when his hand brushed mine.

"Still, he didn't have to be rude. I'll say something to him," he said.

I stood up, holding the tray. "Please don't. I really don't care." I moved to empty the garbage, but Christian took the tray from me.

"I'll get that," he said.

"Let's go, Llona," May called from the door. "I have to stop by the library before next period."

"I'm coming." I glanced one more time at Christian. With one clean jerk of his arm, all the garbage fell into the trash bin. He was different from the other students. But good different or bad different? And did I really want to find out?

Outside, we moved to our separate cars.

"See you around," he called. He flashed me the kind of smile that probably made most girls swoon. For me, however, it did nothing but make my stomach flutter once. But that was more than I'd ever experienced with anyone else.

FOUR

WHEN THE DAY FINALLY ENDED I COULDN'T WAIT TO GET HOME, but when I walked through the front door of our house, I almost turned back. Everything was a wreck—the same as it had been that morning. I marched back to Jake's bedroom and cracked open the door. Jake was asleep, lying diagonal across the bed wearing the same clothes he'd had on yesterday and maybe even the day before.

White static from the television projected ghostly images into the cluttered room. Jake's clothes carpeted the floor, and I wondered if he had anything clean to wear. I closed the door hard and walked back to my bedroom.

Jake's spirit died the day we buried my dad. In a way, my dad, his older brother by ten years, had been like a father to him. From what I'd been told, their mother (and my grandmother, whom I'd never met) worked as a waitress in a Vegas casino. She worked hard but played hard too. She played men as often as she played slot machines. My dad and Jake didn't share the same father, but you'd never know, as close as they were.

My father and mother married when they were both twenty, and they had me shortly after. I was five when Jake moved in with us on his fourteenth birthday. To me, Jake had always been an older brother, not an uncle.

When my mother died shortly after, it was Jake who was there for me. He practically raised me while my father was off trying to avenge her death. So when my dad died it only seemed right to choose Jake to be my guardian.

The only other option was my aunt Sophie, my mom's sister. She had offered, but she also wanted me to move to New York to attend Lucent Academy, where she served on the board. I wasn't ready for that. Attending Lucent would've been like an announcement to the world, and maybe myself, that I was different. No, I chose to stay with Jake. Jake was safe—depressed—but still safe.

I closed my bedroom door and cranked the music. Because I hadn't heard a thing in math class, I opened my book and began to read over the lesson, which looked like it was written in hieroglyphics. I hated math, but I had to get a good grade. I'd been left with plenty of money, but I didn't want to spend a dime of it on college. I figured if there were people out there who'd give me money for an education, then I was going to try and get it.

I rolled onto my stomach thinking a different position would help me retain more information. My gaze moved to the inexplicably rising hair on my arm. Weird. Then my heart began to pound. I tried to swallow, but it got stuck in my throat as if I was trying to jam an orange down my trachea.

Instinctively, I looked toward my window. I couldn't see anything beyond the darkness, but all my Auran senses told me I was being watched. Stop it! I closed my eyes and shook my head. No one is out there. But to be sure, I stood up and looked outside.

There was just enough light from the half-moon that I could see the previous owner's metal swing set. One of the three swings was swaying back and forth as if someone had just jumped from it. You're being paranoid, I told myself.

I shook my head and walked to the kitchen to get a drink but couldn't find any clean glasses. They were all piled up in the sink along with the rest of our dirty dishes. This is getting ridiculous. I turned on the faucet and waited for the water to get hot while I unloaded the dishwasher. By the time I was almost done loading, Jake finally woke up.

"Could you be a little louder?" he said half-intelligibly through a yawn. His worn Levi's had a big grease stain on the thigh and his wrinkly red shirt looked like crepe paper. He moved to the refrigerator and pulled out a gallon of milk, drinking it straight from the plastic jug.

"Can you not do that?" I asked.

He lowered the jug. "There's no cups."

"You could wash one."

He looked at me and blinked. "What did you do today?" His shaggy brown hair, which hadn't been cut in months, looked like road kill.

"I went to school." I poured dish detergent into the dishwasher and closed the door.

"So how's your senior year going?"

"It's going." I opened the pantry and pulled out a Twinkie.

"Can I have one?" he asked.

I grabbed a second Twinkie and tossed it to him. "Isn't this like breakfast for you?"

He chuckled. "I guess. So tell me about your classes?"

"Regular school classes."

"Meet any friends?"

"No."

"Any boys?"

"Double no."

He frowned. "You really need to get a social life. This is your senior year. You should have some fun."

"*You're* telling me to get a life?" I walked past him into the living room and sat down on the couch. The television came to life.

"What's that supposed to mean?"

Without turning to him, I said, "Last time I checked, twenty-six-year-old men are supposed to have jobs."

He let out a long, drawn-out sigh. "I was going to apply this week."

"That's what you've been saying for months."

"It's not like I was sitting around. I had school."

"You took one online class about making websites. That's not the same as being in school."

He scratched his head. "Why are you being so grumpy? Did you have a bad day?"

I groaned and flipped through the channels, trying to find something to distract me from the fight I felt brewing.

"So, you're not talking to me now?" he said through a mouthful of Twinkie.

"Go back to your video games," I mumbled.

He waited a minute before walking back to his room.

I should feel bad, but I didn't. I'd put up with his crap for so long it was only a matter of time before I really blew up.

*   *   *   *   *

It was a sunny Tuesday morning. I hated Tuesdays. As far as I was concerned, Tuesdays could be removed from the days of the week and no one would ever notice. I swung my feet over the bed and slipped them into matted blue slippers to avoid the cold, wood floor. After getting dressed in record time, I left my room feeling invincible. Must be a full moon tonight.

On the way to the kitchen, I peeked in on Jake. He still slept, covers pulled high over his head. The room smelled like sour milk and old pizza. On the TV, a chef skewered a halved banana. The comic potential drew me into the room, but the rank smell stopped me. I sighed and closed the door. Ever since our fight, I'd done my best to avoid him. This made the past few weeks endurable, but lonely.

I picked up my backpack from the hall closet and flung it over my shoulder, barely feeling the weight of the four thick textbooks it contained, and then grabbed an apple. My body pulsated with so much energy that I decided to run to school. It was hard to control my body with my muscles firing away, and only extreme exercise helped relieve the prickly sensation.

I laced up my tennis shoes and stepped outside into the cool, morning air. The sun was just beginning to touch the tops of the golden trees; a few birds chirped its arrival. I didn't bother stretching. My leg muscles knew what was coming, and they hummed beneath my skin.

Across the street, my overweight neighbor suddenly opened his door. His tattered robe gaped open, revealing saggy man boobs that fell nearly to his navy blue boxers. As he bent over to grab a newspaper, the two flaps of skin hung from his chest like slabs of beef. I couldn't help but stare. Distracted, I took my first step, but when my foot came down it pressed upon something other than flat concrete. My ankle twisted, and I fell to the ground.

Lying on the porch, only a foot from my front door, was a woman's shoe. And not one I recognized. It was far too nice to belong to me. It was red with at least three-inch heels, and extremely narrow. It definitely wasn't my shoe. Even if I bound my feet in Chinese foot wrappings for months, permanently deforming them, my brick-like stubs wouldn't ever fit into such a shoe.

I placed the dainty high heel to the side of the porch, wondering where it had come from. I knew it didn't belong to any lady friend of Jake's—as if he had any. No woman would tolerate a man who woke up at noon and played video games all day, breaking only for food and the bathroom.

I stood up and brushed dirt from the back of my sweats. Maybe it would be gone when I returned later. I hoped so. I didn't know what to do with the thing. I felt guilty throwing away such an expensive shoe.

My legs jumped. "All right. I'm going," I said to no one.

After pulling my jacket hood over my head, I took off in a sprint, not stopping for anything. It felt exhilarating running at full speed, and not getting the least bit winded. I leapt over fences, slid over parked cars, sidestepped traffic. At one point, to turn a corner sharply, I ran up the side of a brick wall and then twirled in the air, completing a perfect 360. I felt like a freerunner.

The people up this early, the dog walkers, joggers, or other kids on their way to school, stared in awe as if I weren't human. I didn't stop to think how I was drawing attention to myself until I heard a little boy cry, "Look, Mommy—Supergirl!"

I stopped in my tracks, suddenly frightened by my behavior. What was I thinking?

After collecting myself, I forced my somewhat relaxed body back onto the sidewalk. My muscles received the burst of energy they required, but I knew it was only a matter of hours, if not minutes, before they'd need it again. I removed my hood and smoothed my hair into a neat ponytail. Casually, I proceeded down the street as if I was nothing more than an average seventeen-year-old girl on her way to high school.

At Highland High the halls were beginning to fill. The first bell wouldn't ring for another fifteen minutes. I'd arrived too early. Now what was I going to do?

I was about to close my locker and head to the library when all of a sudden Christian appeared. Why? Why? Why? I closed my eyes and wished him away. When I opened them back up, he was still there, wearing a blue shirt and black suit jacket. I wanted to pretend I hadn't seen him, but that would've been very difficult to do seeing how he was standing directly in front of me.

"Hey, Llona."

"Hey." I looked past him down the hall. Maybe if I appeared like I was waiting for someone, he'd leave me alone. His sudden interest in me the last few weeks made me nervous.

Accidentally, my eyes passed over his. A lone speck of brown in his right, blue eye stood out like my uncle Jake at a Celine Dion concert. Inwardly, I groaned. Why did I have to see that speck?

"So basketball tryouts are today, right?" he asked.

"That's what I hear." Act casual.

"Weren't you on the team last year?"

"Much to everyone's dismay."

"What does that mean?"

"Oh, I'll make it all right, but give it two weeks and the coach will wish I hadn't."

"Why's that?"

Why am I saying so much? More answers lead to more questions. Trying not to appear too frantic, I glanced around for a way out of this conversation mess. I wasn't on my game today.

My savior came in the form of a three hundred pound linebacker who looked like he'd just eaten a dozen powdered doughnuts. White dust sprinkled the corners of his mouth. Wow. I thought guys like him only existed on the Disney Channel.

"Hey C. Where were you last night?"

Christian turned around. This is my chance. I quickly dove in line with other students on their way to first hour.

I moved fast, maneuvering my way in and out of them like an Indy race car driver. My muscles screamed for more of a release, but I refrained from pulling any stunts like I had earlier. I didn't stop walking until I reached my government class.

I was the first student in the room, even beating Mr. Allen. A television high up in the corner of the room was quietly tuned to the local morning news. I ignored it and opened my book. I pretended to read, but stopped when my exceptional hearing heard the chipper news lady say, "Her body was found at approximately 5:00 a.m."—the reporter pointed to the side of a country road—"by a man on his morning run. According to the man, the woman's throat had been cut, but authorities have not yet confirmed cause of death. Because the woman had no identification, the police have asked us to notify our viewers of her description in hopes someone may come forward to identify her. The deceased woman is described as 5'7", 130 pounds, midthirties, with red hair and blue eyes. She was found wearing a short black cocktail dress, black nylons, and one red high-heeled shoe."

FIVE

THE REPORTER CONTINUED TALKING, BUT ALL I COULD HEAR was a sudden buzzing in my ears. I found a shoe. A red shoe. On my front porch.

The humming continued, causing an instant headache. I breathed deeply and waited for the pain to pass. Over the high pitch ringing, the muffled sounds of students filled my head as they filed into the room, but I could no longer distinguish one sound from another. The walls around me shifted and my eyes lost focus. Then, as the teacher stood to take his place in front of the class, I bolted. I'd never freaked out before, but if these were the beginning signs of a major freakapalooza, I'd prefer to do it without any witnesses.

Walking quickly, yet cautiously, my hand against the wall, I headed for the double doors at the end of the hallway. My vision failed, making everything around me look like a scene from Pink Floyd's "The Wall."

"It's just a shoe!" I yelled at myself. "A freaking shoe! Calm down!"

A garbage can sprung at me from nowhere, and I stumbled. Behind me, a gentle touch pressed against my back.

"Are you all right?" I heard a male voice ask, the sound slightly distorted. Please, heaven, let it be a teacher. I turned around slowly, my eyes searching for clarity. I couldn't see distinct features, but by the way his hair fell to the side of his head, I knew it was Christian.

"I'm fine," I said.

"You don't look fine." He kept his hand on my back.

"I just have a headache. I'm going home."

"You can't drive in your condition. You can barely walk."

"I can walk fine." And it was true. My muscles could've ran a marathon with the way they were feeling, but it was my vision and hearing that made the rest of my body behave like a theme ride massacre.

"You just ran into a trash can. Let me take you home. I won't take no for an answer."

Against my better judgment I agreed, and even let him hold my hand all the way to his car—for stabilization purposes only, of course. During the mile drive to my house, I kept the conversation light (mainly because I couldn't understand half of what he was saying), but when we reached my house, I turned him away despite his protests. I didn't need to be babysat. I just needed to be alone.

To clear my mind, I dropped to the couch and turned on the TV while my vision began to return. Judge Judy was in the middle of chewing out an overweight lady in a black tube top and a red miniskirt.

Jake appeared from the hallway rubbing his eyes. "Aren't you supposed to be at school?"

"Aren't you supposed to be in bed?" I snapped back. I wasn't in the mood to be lectured by someone whose vocabulary consisted of short video game phrases. If I had to hear, "You failed us, Nightwing!" one more time . . .

"What's your problem?"

"Forget it, Jake. I didn't mean to wake you."

He stepped in front of me, blocking the angry judge.

"All right. Let's have it."

I leaned to the side to see around him. "Have what?"

He shut off the TV. "You've been mad at me for weeks, and I want to know why."

"No, you don't."

"Yes, I do. We used to be close, Tink, but now all you do is glare at me."

"Why do you think that is?"

He sat down and rubbed the scruff on his neck. "I know I don't have a job, or do anything else for that matter, but things have been rough. I just can't shake it."

"It's been five years, Jake. Get over it!"

He looked at me, eyes full of the same sadness I used to see in my own. "He was my brother, Llona. I can't just get over it. He was all I had."

I stood up, suddenly furious, the raging bull released. "Boo-freaking hoo! He was my father. I've lost both my parents, remember? And instead of grieving, I had to take care of a depressed uncle. For years I've had to be the strong one while you cried your heart out to Mario and Luigi. Who was there for me, Jake?"

His shoulders slumped and his head lowered, but I didn't stop. "Every day I go to school alone—I come home alone—I am in this house alone. I keep everyone at a distance, because I'm afraid that just by knowing me they could end up dead." My fingernails dug into my palms. "All I want to do is live. I want to make it until I'm a hunched over ninety-year-old with arthritis and varicose veins. When's the last time you heard of an Aura living that long? It doesn't happen! So on top of losing my parents and taking care of you, I have to worry about dying young." I took a step toward him, my insides trembling. "Don't ever tell me again how things are rough for you."

His eyes met mine and his mouth opened, but no words

came out. I stormed to my room and slammed the door. Like a caged tiger, I paced, opening and closing my hands. Fevered light raced through my veins, igniting my body as if it were on fire. I had to expel the extra energy, and fast. Already, I felt my body temperature rising.

I threw open the window and shoved the screen out. My feet hit the ground running.

I'd specifically chosen this house because of the backyard, which wasn't a yard at all but more of a steep hill. The old home had been built against the Wasatch Mountains; they loomed over the house like a sleeping giant.

I raced up the giant, anxious to get as far away as possible. The steep grade proved no problem for my energized muscles. I dodged in and out of the trees like a ferocious wind until I reached the top. I'd never pushed myself this hard before, but then again, I'd never been this mad before, either. With the clear blue sky laid out before me, I realized it wasn't just anger that had spurred me on, but also fear, and something else.

I couldn't find the words to express how I felt. I was frightened and angry, but also felt something I thought I'd buried long ago, thanks to Christian. These feelings turned my body into an emotional blender, and the only way to sort through them was to run them right out of me.

After a few hours, I had calmed down and decided to head back. Basketball tryouts were soon, and I didn't want to miss them.

I was no longer angry at Jake, but more at myself. I should never have acted the way I did. I didn't regret what I'd said, but the way I had said it. As for the shoe on my porch, I wasn't afraid any more. It was unlikely the shoe was tied to the murder, but just in case, I decided to call the police later and tell them about it. I did consider myself a good citizen, after all.

Finally there was Christian. I simply vowed to not think

about him any more. Problem solved. How hard could that be?

I crawled back through the window and opened my bedroom door. Immediately, I knew Jake was gone. The house was void of the familiar gaming sounds that were about as constant as a ticking clock. His absence made me feel even worse.

I drove to the school parking lot and, while I waited for the bell to ring, called the police to tell them about the shoe I'd found. By the tone of the lady's voice on the other end, she wasn't taking me seriously. Whatever. I did my civic duty.

I turned off my phone just as the bell rang. Students poured from the high school, but I pushed my way through, dodging in and out of the teenagers.

May found me at my locker. "Do you mind if I watch tryouts?" she asked as she swept dark hair behind her ear. It was styled perfectly, wavy and smooth, and by her preppy outfit, she must've been hanging with the cheerleaders today.

"I don't care. It'll probably be boring though."

"Not the way you play, especially on your good days. Is today a good today?"

I couldn't help but smile. "Incredible."

When we entered the gym, a couple of girls were already practicing. I resisted the urge to turn back. I hated the social aspect of belonging to a team, but I loved the exercise. It gave me a break from my constant running. I also secretly loved the competition.

I don't think my mother would've approved of me playing sports. Auras were supposed to be gentle, loving, and kind. But most of all, because of our Light, we were supposed to be humble. According to my aunt Sophie (and probably my mother too, but I was too young to ask) sports were prideful. Sophie thought they were a form of fighting—man pitted against man to see who was better. A few years ago I'd mentioned to her that I was trying out for soccer, and she'd completely flipped out. I tried to explain that I only wanted to join because it made my body feel better, especially around the full moon, but she'd thought that was just an excuse. "Go running for five hours instead," she'd told me. I didn't bring up sports ever again.

I quickly dressed in the locker room and then rushed to join the others.

"Let's get started!" Ms. Lindsey, the basketball coach, yelled from across the court.

I sat down on the bleachers while Ms. Lindsey handed out a schedule. She was a tall, barrel-chested woman with short, blonde hair. Her shoulders were much larger than the rest of her body, making her look like an anime character.

"It's great to see so many of you today. I see the usual group and some new faces. That's good. It means we will have a much better chance of creating a winning team," she said.

I glanced behind me. There were about twenty-five girls. Most of them I recognized.

She continued, "Now I know you girls are mature enough to realize I'll only keep the top ten and maybe a few alternates. Just the hardest-working players will make the team, is that understood?"

We nodded.

"All right. Let's get started. Laps first. Everybody on the court."

The girls stood up looking a little nervous, except for me—I jumped up. Ms. Lindsey was known for trying to break those who wanted to be on the team. Behind her back, the girls called her "The Hammer," and I couldn't wait to feel The Hammer's pain.

Ms. Lindsey focused on me. "You seem awfully anxious, Llona. Why don't you get started first? The rest of you follow. I'll tell you when to stop."

After fifteen minutes of circling the gym floor, the whistle blew again. "Line up beneath the basket," Ms. Lindsey barked.

I jogged over to the edge of the basketball court. The others weren't so quick.

"Ladders next, girls. You know the routine. For those of you who don't, follow the girl in front of you. Go until I say stop."

I took off running, moving back and forth between the lines on the court. I thought I was focused on the task until my eyes caught movement in the doorway of the gym. *Christian.* My legs suddenly became like strings of licorice. The effect was ruthless.

I fell flat on my face and slid a short distance from him. The sound of flesh tearing on polished gym floor screeched as loudly as Ms. Lindsey's whistle. The other girls, thinking they'd heard just that, stopped. Several of them began to laugh when they saw me sprawled on the floor.

Christian knelt in front of me. "Are you okay?"

I jumped up. "I'm fine," I said and forced a smile, even though my legs felt like they'd slid through a meat grinder.

He shook his head. "No way. It sounded like your skin peeled off."

We looked down at the same time. Sure enough, the top layer of skin on both my knees and part of my shins was gone.

"You all right, Llona?" Ms. Lindsey called.

"I'll be fine," I said.

"She could use some bandages, Coach," Christian told her.

I looked back at him sharply. He shrugged.

"You know where the stuff is. Can you take care of it?" Ms. Lindsey asked him.

"Sure. I've got this." He grinned as I cringed.

"Who told you to stop?" Ms. Lindsey snapped at the other girls.

A few audible sighs lifted into the air, but they did as they were told.

"Let's go, speed racer." Christian nodded his head toward the locker rooms. I reluctantly followed.

"You know," he said, once we were out of earshot from the other girls. "I can't keep taking care of you." He held his mouth tight to keep from smiling.

"It was your fault I fell," I accused.

"Hardly! I was twenty feet away."

"Well, you're hard to miss."

He looked at me. "Really?" There was no sarcasm in his voice.

I visibly jerked. "I didn't mean—I was just surprised to see someone standing there." I thought I saw disappointment flash in his eyes, but couldn't be sure.

"The first aid kit's in here," he said.

"In the men's locker room?"

"There's probably one in the girl's, but I don't know where. Come on. No one's in here."

I followed him through the blue-tiled doorway. Inside was a typical locker room with wooden benches in the middle of each aisle. "It stinks," I blurted, covering my nose and mouth.

"We can't all smell like roses."

"Roses? I'd settle for day-old meatloaf. It smells like wet cat bum in here."

He laughed. "It's not that bad."

I followed him into the coach's office where he removed a first aid kit from the wall.

"Sit down," he ordered.

"I can put a Band-Aid on myself."

"Not while I'm around." He opened the kit and pulled out bandages and antiseptic wipes. "I'm surprised to see you here, after the way you were this morning. What happened?"

"Bad headache is all. I'm fine now." I flinched when he pressed an alcohol wipe to my leg.

"Sorry," he said.

"No, it didn't hurt. I'm just not used to—" I stopped, startled I was just about to admit that I wasn't used to being touched.

"Getting hurt?" he suggested.

"Something like that."

After a minute, he said, "You're really fast out there."

"Today I am."

"Do you run track too?"

I nodded. "How come Ms. Lindsey seems to know you so well? Aren't you supposed to be new?" I asked.

"She sits in at a lot of our football practices. Sometimes I think she wishes she were coaching."

"That makes sense." On top of being pushy and competitive, Ms. Lindsey was also a control freak.

I looked down as Christian attached the final strip of tape to a bandage on my shin. He kept his warm palm on the back of my calf, sending chills through my whole body.

"Are you cold?" he asked.

"No." I stood up and backed away. "Thanks for helping me, but I better get back."

"Are you sure you feel up to it with those wounds?"

"You have no idea."

He looked at my questioningly, but I turned around, took a deep breath, held it, and then moved quickly through the reeking men's locker room. Christian caught up to me in the gym just as I exhaled.

"Do you mind if I stick around?" he asked.

"Why?" I kept walking.

"It's fun."

"You so need a life."

"Then you don't mind?"

I shrugged and jogged onto the court to continue running ladders. I had to get my mind off Christian and his touch that still lingered on my skin. I felt it more than I did the pain from my legs.

After ladders, Ms. Lindsey rounded us up for other drills. Shooting was my favorite. I only missed a couple of shots—and those had been on purpose. I didn't want to seem too good, because I knew it was only a matter of weeks before I'd really stink it up.

Ms. Lindsey blew her whistle. "Have a seat, girls." She waited for us to sit before continuing, "Tomorrow I'll post a sheet on my office door of the girls who made first cut. If your name is on it, return tomorrow at this same time. You all did a great job, but remember, I can't keep all of you. Have a great night."

Everyone stood and began gathering their belongings.

"Llona, can I have a word with you?" Ms. Lindsey asked.

I cringed, knowing what she was going to say. Last year she'd been furious at me for the way I'd played in some of the games. At first she'd tried to be all nice and understanding, thinking maybe I was sick, but when I couldn't give her a satisfactory answer as to why I was suddenly playing like Shaq on crack, she'd blown up. At one point I'd thought she was going to slap me, but luckily the gym had been crowded.

"Yes, Coach?" I asked, staying out of arm's reach just in case.

"You probably know what I'm going to say."

"Yes, ma'am."

"Don't call me that."

"Yes, Coach."

"Did you come to play this year?"

"Yes, Coach. I want to be on the team."

She shifted her considerable weight. "That's not what I meant. Are you going to give it your all, each and every game?"

"Absolutely. I will never quit."

"Like you did last year?"

"I didn't quit."

She snorted. "You could barely run down the court half the time. I can't have you playing like that this year. I need you a hundred percent during all practices and games. Can you do that?"

"I promise to give it a hundred."

She squinted. "Why do I get the feeling that we're going to have the same problem?"

My shoulders slumped. "Look, Coach, I promise to do my best, but I can't promise that it will always be what you want. I understand you have to do what's best for the team, I really do. I won't have any hard feelings one way or the other."

She rubbed her chin, like a man does when feeling his scruff. "Fair enough. I'll be watching you, Llona." Her gaze moved behind me. "Can I help you?" she asked.

"We're looking for Llona Reese," a deep voice said.

I turned around. Two policemen stood side-by-side. "I'm Llona," I said.

The larger one spoke, "I'm Officer Pieut and this is Officer Bryant. May we have a word with you?"

"Um, sure." I turned to Ms. Lindsey. "See you tomorrow."

She nodded. Her eyes darted back and forth between the officers and me, and then she walked away.

Officer Pieut looked down at a small notebook in his hand. His bulbous nose protruded into his thick mustache. "You called us earlier today about a shoe."

I swallowed. "Yes. Did you find it?"

Officer Pieut looked at Officer Bryant. "We did. And we have some questions for you. What time did you find it?"

"About seven this morning. I was leaving my house to go running when I tripped on it."

"Where did you find it, again?" he asked.

"On my front porch."

The officer's looked at each other again.

"Did you hear or see anything strange last night?" Officer Bryant asked.

"No. Why?"

Officer Pieut scribbled on his notebook. "Thank you for your time. We'll contact you if we have any further questions." They turned away.

"Wait!" I said.

They stopped and turned back toward me.

"Did the shoe belong to that woman?"

Officer Pieut glanced around and then focused his gaze on me. "It looks that way. But don't worry. A dog probably dragged it onto your porch," he said, and then walked away with his partner.

I wanted to believe him, but I'd seen the shoe. There hadn't been a scratch on it—no teeth marks, nothing. I looked up and waved to May and Christian. It's nothing. Strange coincidence is all. I had to believe that—for the alternative terrified me.

Six

"What was that all about?" Christian asked, once he reached the bottom of the bleachers. His eyes followed the officers out of the gym.

"Nothing, really. They just wanted to know about a shoe I found."

"A shoe?" May asked.

"You know that lady who was killed?"

"The one who had her throat slit?" May said, swallowing hard.

"Yeah. Her shoe showed up at my house."

"No way!" May said. "How?"

"The police think a dog ran off with it and left it on my porch. Weird, huh?"

Christian touched my arm. "Are you all right?"

"Of course." Think of something else. "You guys want to get out of here, go do something?"

"Aren't you tired?" May asked.

I shook my head.

"I'm in," Christian said.

"Good." I heaved my bag over my shoulder and started outside.

"Let me get that for you," Christian said.

I scowled and darted away. "I can handle it."

"I know you can, but you don't have to. You can let someone help." He opened the gym doors.

It was a strange thing to say. It was something my father would've said.

"So what do you guys want to do?" May asked, once we were all sitting in the car. "Do you want to get something to eat?"

"How about it, Llona?" Christian asked.

"Sure. I can eat." And pretend the incident with the shoe never happened. I took a deep breath to clear my mind.

"Where to?" May asked.

"Wherever you want," I told her, tapping my fingers against the side of the door.

"Let's go to Johny's then. I'm craving a burger," she said.

Johny's was a 1950s-style burger joint, and a popular hangout for high school kids. It wouldn't have been my choice because it was always packed, but it fit May's personality.

"It looks crowded," I said to May when we pulled into the parking lot.

"Is that okay? Do you want to go somewhere else?"

"Um, no. This is fine."

"Look! There's Adam," May said. As soon as she parked the car, she jumped out and rushed over to say hello.

When I opened the door to Johny's, the smell of grease and vanilla punched me in the gut. I hadn't realized how hungry I was until now. Surprisingly, there were still a few tables unoccupied. Fifties paraphernalia littered the walls, and Elvis Presley bellowed "Heartbreak Hotel" from a lit-up juke box in the corner.

"How many?" a waitress dressed in a poodle skirt and pink top asked. Her hair was pulled into a tight ponytail; stray strands from a long day's work fell to the sides of her flushed face. She looked like one of those single moms who worked hard for every dollar she earned.

"Three," Christian answered.

"Right this way," the tired woman said.

I tried to think of something to say that might lighten her burden, but I wasn't used to reaching out.

"We'll tip her good," Christian said once we sat down.

"Huh?"

"Let's leave a good tip for the waitress. She looks burned out."

"You noticed?"

"Sure. She's probably a single mom or something. I can't imagine how hard that would be." He opened his menu and scanned over its contents.

Once again, I stared at him. Who was this guy?

May bounded up with Adam next to her. She was in the middle of telling him about basketball practice. Adam pulled out a chair and sat next to Christian, while May sat next to me. Just then the front door opened, and in walked Mike. I shuddered.

"Hey, Adam! I thought I recognized your car, you big putz," Mike called from across the diner. He waved the waitress out of his face and moved toward us.

"What are you losers doing?" he joked, even though, to me, he sounded serious. He stole a chair from a nearby table and sat at the end next to May and Adam.

"We just ran into each other," May said.

"Don't you guys have anything better to do?" he sneered.

"Don't you?" I shot back.

He glared at me. "What are you doing here? I didn't think you had any friends."

"We just came from Llona's basketball practice," Christian said. He sat up straighter in his seat.

"Did she fall on her face?" Mike asked. He motioned the waitress over.

"Actually, she was amazing."

"Whatever. Girls can't play sports."

"We can too," May blurted. "In fact, I bet Llona could waste you at basketball."

"Yeah, right. I saw her play last year. My one-eyed dog could've played better," Mike said, looking disgusted.

"If you played her tonight," Christian said, "she'd murder you."

"What can I get you?" the waitress asked from behind me.

"Get me a double burger with extra cheese. And a large Coke," Mike said, his lips wet with spit. The waitress turned to Adam, but Mike interrupted her. "And by the way, make sure the cook doesn't drown the burger in ketchup. Last time I got one, I felt like I was drinking the soggy thing."

The waitress nodded, looking even more miserable. She moved around the table, taking our orders, and when she got to me, I noticed her eyes were glistening with tears. Her suffering tore at my heart. Instinctively, I reached out and touched her arm, wishing I could help. All of a sudden Light's energy passed through me and warmed the skin beneath my palm. "Everything will be okay," I said.

The woman visibly relaxed as if I'd injected her with melatonin and, for a reason she probably didn't understand, she smiled. "Thanks. It's just been one of those days." I returned the smile and gave her my order. When she turned to May, my eyebrows rose, and I mouthed the word "wow" to no one. I couldn't believe I just did that. It had come naturally, like learning to walk. I never knew what my mother had meant when she said she could comfort others—now I did.

"I'll be right back," Mike said, after the waitress left. He stood and walked over to a girl whose name I thought was Amanda.

"Why does he have to be such a jerk all of the time?" May asked the guys.

"That's just Mike. He's been like that for as long as I've known him. Everyone just ignores him," Adam said in a lame attempt to justify Mike's behavior.

"Well, I think he needs his butt kicked," May said. "The other day in Mr. Steele's class"—my head snapped up— "Mike made a girl cry. It was horrible."

"What did Mr. Steele do?" I asked.

"Gave him detention. He is the nicest teacher," May said, her eyes drifting toward the heavens.

Christian and Adam laughed. "I don't think the girls like him because he's nice."

"He can't help it if he's hot," May said.

"What do you think, Llona? Do you think Mr. Steele is hot?" Christian asked.

May answered for me, "Are you kidding? Llona's got it the worst. She's in a complete daze every time she walks out of his class." She turned to me. "Speaking of which, what's your math grade like?"

I shook my head. "Horrible. I don't know what my problem is."

"I could tutor you if you'd like. I do okay in math," Christian said. "And since I'm not as hot as Mr. Steele, maybe you'll be able to learn something."

"I think you're hot," Adam said. He leaned in for a pretend kiss. Christian shoved him away.

Ten minutes later our food arrived, bringing Mike back to our table. We dove in, especially me. It was hard to consume enough calories to make up for all the energy I burned.

Through a mouthful, Mike said, "Did you guys see that girl I was talking to?"

"Amanda?" May asked.

"Yeah, I guess that's her name. Anyway, she's going out with me tomorrow."

"You asked her out without even finding out her name?" Christian asked.

"She's hot," he replied.

"Your'e terrible!" May cried.

Mike shrugged. "I'm a player. That's what I do."

"Are you serious?" I asked.

Mike leaned forward. "Yeah, so? What's your problem?"

"You're my problem. You like to play games? Let's play horse. I'll be the front end and you be yourself."

Adam dropped his head, shaking it back and forth. May looked pleased and Mike looked mad—no—furious. He barely opened his mouth as he hissed, "Why don't you pull that halo down and choke yourself with it, you self-righteous little—"

Before Mike could finish his sentence, Christian lunged himself across the table and punched Mike in the mouth.

SEVEN

MIKE FELL BACKWARD OUT OF HIS CHAIR WITH CHRISTIAN on top. He attempted to wiggle free, but Christian pinned his shoulder to the ground. With his free hand, Christian continued to punch Mike's face despite Adam's attempts to pull him back.

"Get off him, man!" Adam yelled.

Just then an enormous fry cook bounded out of the kitchen. He too tried to pry Christian off, but was unsuccessful. May burst into tears.

Finally, I found my voice. "Christian!" I thought I yelled it, but his name barely squeaked out.

As if he'd heard me, Christian stood, breathing heavily, fists clenched tight.

"Get out of here!" the cook barked at Christian. Grease dripped from a spatula in his hand.

I wasn't sure if Christian heard or not, because all he did was turn to me and stare in shock—no, horror is more like it. He walked around the table, stepped over spilled food, and took me by the arms. "Are you okay?" he asked, as if I'd been the one fighting.

"I'm fine. Let's go." I pulled him toward the front door, but he stopped briefly, reached inside his pocket, and pulled out a fifty-dollar bill. He dropped the money on the table and then followed me out.

Mike's voice echoed behind us, "Watch your back, Knight!"

May caught up to us outside. "Are you all right, Christian?" she said, face streaked with tears.

He looked at her as if he wasn't sure what she was talking about. "Why wouldn't I be?"

"Can we just get out of here?" I asked. I didn't want to admit it, but the fight had frightened me. I stuffed my hands into my pockets to keep them from shaking.

Christian's eyes never left mine. "May, will you take us to my car? I'll save you a trip and take Llona home."

No one said a word the short ride back to the school and only when May parked the car did she turn and say, "I know Mike had it coming, but I hate fights."

"Sorry," Christian said.

It bothered me to see May so distraught. Like I'd done with the waitress, I reached over and placed my hand on her arm. Almost like saying a prayer, I summoned Light. When it warmed my palm, I willed it to May and in less than a second her rigid body and face muscles relaxed. "Go home and get some rest," I said.

She smiled and nodded, looking almost dreamy. That was easy. Too bad I couldn't use it on myself.

I stood next to Christian, arms folded, as May's car drove away. The extreme energy I'd felt before now felt scattered, like metal balls fired inside a pinball machine.

"I'm so sorry," Christian said again.

"Huh?"

"I should never have fought in front of you."

I shook my head. "It's me who should apologize. I'm the one with the big mouth."

"No. You spoke the truth, but I didn't have to fight."

"It's not a big deal. Don't worry about it."

"Not a big deal?" He pulled my arm from my chest and held my hand. "You're shaking."

I pulled it back, embarrassed. "I just overdid it today."

"It's more than that, and you know it."

"Can we just go? I'm really tired."

Christian eyed me thoughtfully. "Sure. If that's what you want."

He opened the SUV door and waited until I was inside before closing it. I looked around. The upholstery was all leather and the car had been equipped with GPS, DVD player, the works. "This is a nice," I said as we drove out of the parking lot.

"Thanks. My dad split the cost with me. I worked three summers saving up for it."

"Doing what?"

"Private lessons."

"What kind of lessons?"

"Um, fighting and stuff."

"Fighting? Like karate?"

"Something like that." Christian glanced in the rearview mirror after rounding a corner.

"So you're a professional fighter?"

He laughed. "I wouldn't say that. I've just had enough years of experience that I can teach."

"But you've been teaching for three years."

He shifted in the seat and cleared his throat. "It's nothing really."

I couldn't tell if he was being modest or if he was avoiding my questions. I decided not to press the issue. I looked out the passenger window and toward the full moon.

"You like the moon, don't you?" Christian asked.

"Yeah, I guess."

"It is beautiful, especially when it's full." He checked the rearview mirror again, and I thought I noticed his grip tighten on the steering wheel.

I casually glanced behind us, but didn't see anything. "Why do you keep checking the mirror?"

"What?"

"The rearview mirror. What are you looking at?"

"Nothing. Just trying to be a good driver."

The remaining way to my house, he tried to be more casual, but I still noticed his obsession with the mirror. And he didn't look happy.

"Is your uncle home?" Christian asked when we pulled into my driveway.

"Yeah." Even though the garage door was shut, concealing his car, I knew Jake was there. Where else would he be?

"How can you tell? The house is dark."

"He's always home." I opened my door. Christian jumped out and ran around to my side.

"I can get myself out," I said, wondering why he was acting like we were on a date or something.

"I know you can. I just want to walk you to the door."

That's what he said, but as we walked toward my house, he continued to shift his eyes the way a babysitter does when she feel she's not alone in the house.

And then she's murdered.

I pushed back my paranoid thoughts and turned to him at the door. "I never said thank you."

"For what?"

"For standing up for me. No one's ever done that before."

Christian sighed and shook his head. "If Mike had any idea how special you are, he wouldn't have said what he did."

My eyes met his. "What?"

He spoke quickly. "I just mean you are an incredible person.

You're great at sports, you're kind, you're not afraid—"

"All right, that's enough."

"No, it's not, but I'll let you off the hook." He smiled.

When I reached for the doorknob, he said, "Before you go, promise me something."

I waited for him to continue before I agreed to anything.

"Promise me you won't go running tonight."

"Why would I do that?" Actually I was planning on going out later. It was only eight o'clock.

"You just seem to have this crazy energy. Will you promise?"

"Can I ask why?"

"With the murder that happened up Ian Road, I think it'd be safer if you stayed inside."

Right, the murder. The red shoe. That seemed like years ago. "Sure. I'll stay inside."

"Good. See you tomorrow?"

I nodded.

"Sleep well." He reached out and lightly squeezed my hand. A thousand butterflies bloomed in my stomach at once.

I waited for his car to disappear before I went inside. All the lights were off and the house was unusually quiet. With a single thought, I mentally turned on the kitchen light and almost died from shock. The kitchen was spotless. I turned around. So was the living room.

I walked to Jake's room and peeked in. "Jake?" When I didn't hear a reply, I turned on the light. His bedroom had also been cleaned and his empty bed was made. A note on his dresser read:

Tink,

I'm sorry about earlier. You were right about everything. I promise things will be better. Don't wait up for me, I'll be home late.

—Jake

P.S. I hope tryouts went well!

I carried the note to my room, reading it several more times. Jake had never done anything like this before. Maybe things would be different.

*   *   *   *   *

My eyelids snapped open sometime in the middle of the night. It was dark—coffin dark. I felt my way to the window and peered into the black sky. Storm clouds must be hiding the moon. I placed my palms on the glass and summoned Light to my hands; a soft bluish glow shined into the dark. Suddenly the wind blew and shook the windowpane beneath my hands. I stumbled back, surprised

I was about to return to bed when I heard what I thought was a cat howling outside my window. It wailed and moaned, sounding like a creature from a horror movie. Once again I called on Light's power. Squinting, I tried to locate the tortured feline. Without warning, a shadow, blacker than night, bolted past my window.

Eight

I FINALLY THREW THE COVERS OFF AT 6:00 A.M. WHEN THE morning sun warmed my room. I mentally turned on the lights and dressed quickly, anxious to get out of the house and away from the memories of such a horrible night's sleep. After whatever had bolted past my window, I'd ran back to bed and buried myself in the covers. The shadow had moved so quickly I couldn't be sure if the form had been human or animal. I didn't fall asleep until I'd convinced myself that it had been a deer. I'd seen plenty of them in our backyard, so I logically figured that's all it probably was.

I peeked in on Jake, who was sleeping peacefully without the television on. I quickly scribbled a note, telling him I was going running and then placed it on his dresser. I stepped out our back door, stretched a little, and then raced up the mountain, toward the sun, and over to my favorite trail. When I returned an hour-and-a-half later, Jake was gone. A short note told me he had some errands to run and would be home before I returned from school.

While I showered and got ready for school, I wondered what Jake was up to. As far as I knew, he didn't know anybody in Utah.

Once again, I ran to school. The moon would be full for

at least another day, and I couldn't be more pleased with the timing. If basketball tryouts had been one week later, there'd be no way I'd make the team.

I headed straight for first hour instead of going to my locker. The last thing I wanted was to run into Christian. As much as I wanted to be near him, he was merely a high school distraction and one that would only cause me pain in the end. Eye on the prize, I reminded myself as I sat down.

By the end of second period, I had to go running again. The tapping of my foot had bothered everyone around me, including the teacher. While no one was looking, I quickly darted outside and headed toward the track. I ran as hard and fast as I could to expend the most amount of energy (although I barely broke a sweat). I hoped that might help me pay attention in my next class, math. I was really starting to fall behind, and for the first time in my academic life, I was worried.

By the end of Mr. Steele's class, however, I realized the running had been wasted. I left his classroom feeling like I hadn't learned a thing. I learned more math from watching late night talk shows than I did from Mr. Steele. What was my problem?

At lunch I avoided May and ate in the lunch room, knowing she would never go in there. I really liked May, but I needed things to return to the way they were.

Matt sat a few tables over. Apparently he'd found others to join his book club. Two girls sat next to him hanging on his every word. No surprises there. A guy as cute as him and who could actually understand Shakespeare could have his pick. Maybe down the road I could join a club and be part of social gatherings like this. College perhaps.

After lunch, Christian finally caught up to me in the hallway. "How's it going?"

"Good. You?" I kept my face forward.

"Good. Do you mind if I come to tryouts again today?"

"Actually, I'd prefer it if you didn't."

"Really? Um, okay. Can I see you afterward?"

I opened my locker. "I think my uncle has something planned."

He didn't say anything while I switched out my books, but when I closed my locker, he asked, "Did you go running last night?"

"No, which turned out to be good because of the storm and all."

"What storm?"

"Last night. The sky was pitch black and the wind was going crazy. It was kind of scary."

"There wasn't a storm last night. What time?" His body tensed.

"Not sure. I woke up to the sound of a cat howling like it was in heat or something. It was really weird."

"And you didn't go outside?"

"No."

"Don't go out tonight either, okay?"

"Why?"

"Just don't, please?"

I sighed. "Look, I appreciate the concern, but if I want to go running in the dark, I will. I'm a big girl."

Suddenly he grabbed me by the arms, a little too rough in my opinion. "You can't go outside."

I shrugged him off. "Let go. What's your deal?" I hurried away, surprised by his sudden aggressive behavior.

The second day of basketball tryouts went as expected. I completely wowed Ms. Lindsey and gained the respect of all my potential teammates, for the time being anyway.

After tryouts, I raced home, anxious to see Jake.

"Did you make the team?" Jake asked, the moment I walked

through the doorway. He was standing in the kitchen wearing an apron, and I noticed he'd shaved and gotten a haircut.

"What are you doing?" I asked.

"Making cookies." He turned on the oven light and peeked in.

"Since when do you bake?" I tossed my backpack onto the couch.

"I used to make them all the time, don't you remember?"

"Vaguely. But why are you making them now?"

"To celebrate. Did you make the team?" Jake poured me a glass of milk.

"I won't know until tomorrow. I guess we'll have to save them until then."

"Actually," Jake paused. "They're for my celebration."

"Does this have anything to do with where you've been yesterday and today?"

"Yes, but before I tell you any more, I need to apologize again."

"No, Jake. I need to apologize."

"Would you stop? You were right about everything. Ever since Mark, I mean your dad, died, I've been living in a fortress of solitude. Your dad, well, he was special, more so than even you know. After your mom died, we went through some crazy stuff together, and I think that kind of messed me up too. I thought I could be like him, but I'm not."

"What are you talking about?"

He shook his head. "I promised your dad I'd take care of you, but how can I do that? I'm not him."

"Jake, I couldn't ask for a better second dad." I placed my hand over his and mentally transferred Light to him. I hated seeing him like this.

He jerked his hand away. "When did you start doing that?" he asked, almost as if he were appalled.

"Huh?"

"You're transferring Light to me. When did you learn to do that?"

I shrugged. "Just the other day, I guess. Why? What's wrong?"

"Your mother. She used to do the same thing whenever I felt bad. I can't believe you can do it too."

"But can't all Aura's at a certain age?"

"Maybe. I don't know. I only know what your mother did. What else can you do?"

"Just manipulate light and stuff, nothing big. And mostly when the moon is out."

He nodded.

"Is there anything else I should expect?" I asked.

"I'm the wrong person to be asking. You should call your aunt."

"No way. She'll try and make me go to that stupid school again."

"What's wrong with Lucent? Your mother went there."

"A lot of good it did her. I think I'm a lot safer out here than in there. All they do is fill your head with illusions of grandeur."

He laughed. "I doubt that. Maybe we can check it out together?"

I grunted at the same time the oven buzzer went off. "So you haven't even told me—what are we celebrating?"

Jake removed the cookies and placed them on the counter. "Well, after our little argument, I called a few people who I haven't spoken to in years. They were more your dad's friends than mine, but they did remember me. Anyway, one of them just happens to be living right here in Bountiful. He offered me a job. Last night I was over at his house discussing the details."

"No way! That's great, Jake. What's the job?"

"It's working in one of the petroleum plants at the Point of the Mountain."

"It sounds awesome."

"I hope so. I was there this morning checking it out."

"So when do you start?"

"Well," he frowned.

"What?"

"I haven't officially accepted yet."

"Why?" I cried.

"Because. I'll only take it on one condition."

"What's that?"

He looked directly into my eyes. "I will take this job, completely change my life, but only if you promise to do the same."

I leaned back into the chair. "What?"

"I know how you are, Tink. You keep everyone at arm's length and other than sports, you don't do anything. You have no life to speak of, and I think that needs to change."

"You don't know what you're talking about."

"Yes, I do. This is your last year of school and you should be enjoying it, not hanging out here, plotting out every move of your future. Life is not meant to be scripted. Your mother and father would want you to be happy."

"I am happy," I mumbled.

"You're about as happy as a dill pickle. You're not being who you were meant to be."

"I like pickles."

"Seriously, Llona, let's do this together. What do you say?"

"Can I think about it?" I asked.

"No! No more thinking. Take a chance and say yes. Come on. You can do it, right here, right now. Say yes, and you can have one of my famous cookies."

I wasn't sure if it was Jake's pep talk or the Light within me that made me say it, but all of a sudden I heard the word "yes" roll from my lips. Before I could take it back, Jake had his arms around me, jumping up and down.

"This is going to be great," he cried.

I tried not to laugh along with him, but I couldn't help it. I would have fun this year, I resolved. All the things I hadn't allowed myself to do before, I would do now. The possibilities flashed before me, especially with Christian. I laughed even louder at this new thought and danced with Jake around the room.

Things were finally looking up.

Nine

THE NEXT MORNING I COULDN'T WAIT TO GO TO SCHOOL AND find Christian. I would've called him the night before, but Jake insisted we go out to dinner and a movie, and I couldn't turn him down.

It was both strange and liberating to walk down the hallways with my head up. I was no longer afraid to be noticed. I said "hi" to several people. Some of them said "hello" back out of habit, but I saw their surprise when they realized whom they were talking to.

I made it to Christian's locker just as he was placing his bag inside. He seemed shocked to see me.

"Llona. Hey, about yesterday—"

"Forget it. I was wondering if you wanted to go out tonight? Maybe go running together or something?"

His eyebrows lifted. "Of course. I have football practice until seven, but I'm free after that."

"Great. It's a date then." I turned away, but he stopped me.

"Hey, congratulations!"

"For what?"

"You made the team. Haven't you checked yet?"

"I was on my way."

He frowned. "I hope I didn't ruin it for you."

"No way. I'd way rather have heard it from you."

He smiled, but his eyes narrowed as if he didn't believe me.

"See you," I called over my shoulder.

I headed to May's locker and found her talking to a bunch of people who I thought were in band. I walked right up to her and squeezed my way into their circle. "How's it going, guys?"

They stared.

"Are you working Friday?" I asked May.

Her eyes widened and she stopped chewing her gum. "Yeah."

"Shoot. I wanted to hang out. How about Saturday? We could go to Lagoon. I hear their Frightmare rides for Halloween are pretty cool." Lagoon was a theme park nearby. I'd always wanted to go but could never bring myself to do it.

"Awesome. I'm in."

I looked around at the others. "Anyone else can come too, of course."

A couple of them smiled, but the others were still in a state of shock.

"See you at lunch, May."

I walked away feeling great. Was this what it felt like to be normal?

In science class I felt like sitting in the front, so I did. I even answered one of the teacher's questions about mitosis. He couldn't have looked happier.

I deliberately arrived early to English class and waited for Matt outside the door. He moved obliviously down the hall as if he were strolling through a park instead of a school.

"Matt?"

"Hey," he said and nodded. He tried to get by me into class, but I blocked him.

"I was wondering if I could still join your book club?"

His nose wrinkled. "Why?"

"It sounds fun."

"Really? Huh. Well, we're meeting Monday at 7:00."

"Where at?"

"The city library."

"Perfect. What book are you guys reading?"

"*Asher Lev.*"

I nodded. "Cool. I'll see you then."

So far this social thing was really working out.

And so my senior year at Highland High officially began. And I was happy. The only problem with being happy was my slippery grip on time. There never seemed to be enough, but this was a consequence I could live with.

May and I became even better friends, and at least a few times a week we hung out after school when I didn't have basketball practice and she didn't work. I learned a lot about her. She'd been adopted from Italy when she was two and her adoptive mother was an artist, and quite a good one. The only problem with that was they often fluctuated between very rich and very poor. They'd moved to Bountiful four years ago so her mother could teach art classes at the community college.

As for May's adoptive father, she hadn't seen him in years. Her parents had separated when she was six. Last she heard he was living in California, working as a building contractor. Every once in a while she'd receive a letter from him, and I could tell that she resented his absence.

Because of our sudden closeness, I almost asked her about the lab fire incident, but whenever I tried to bring it up, she quickly changed the subject. I figured when she was ready she'd tell me, and when that time came, I'd have to tell her why my hair never changed.

The thought of sharing my secret with someone was both exciting and liberating. Exciting because my aunt had told me it was strictly forbidden and for some reason I just didn't feel like obeying her, and liberating because it sucked keeping this secret. I could talk to Jake about it, but he was a man and barely understood me as it was.

My new social skills turned out to be a major help on the basketball team. I thought my weakened state would make my teammates beg the coach to kick me off the team, but because I was reaching out, they actually defended me to the coach.

Leah had said, "Come on, Coach. Look at her. You can tell she's not feeling well. At least she's trying."

The coach gave some sort of snort/grunt meaning I could keep playing. It was amazing how just being open and friendly to others endeared you to them. It made life so much easier.

Then there was the book club. I thought nothing would ever compare to my love for sports, but I was wrong. Book club had turned out to be more than I expected. Not only was I gaining new friends, but I was learning a lot about the world through the books we were reading. There were six of us that went to book club. In addition to Matt, there was Tracey, Anna, Stephanie, and Ryan. Each was unique and I loved figuring out what made them tick. It was like being a mind explorer, uncovering both their weaknesses and strengths.

Of all the new changes that had occurred, Christian was the one I couldn't do without. He had become like my favorite pair of jeans. I didn't mind wearing other pants, but whenever I wore them, I always found myself wishing I was wearing my perfect-in-every-way jeans. This was my Christian. We had become inseparable and even though we hadn't officially declared ourselves a couple, I thought we were.

The moon was barely a sliver, looking more like an old lady's painted-on eyebrow. I shouldn't be out here, I thought. My body still felt weak. I hated feeling vulnerable and it didn't help that I was out in the woods in the middle of the night. But Christian had asked me to meet him, saying it was extremely important. Even if it wasn't important, I still would've come simply because he asked.

I leapt to a fallen log and spun around slowly on one foot, completing an almost perfect pirouette. Any minute now and I'd see his handsome face and his kind, gentle eyes, and his wonderful mouth that was always turned up into an amused grin, showing his one, seemingly endless, dimple.

I tried to distract myself from checking the time by seeing how far I could see into the dark—it wasn't very far. I loved this place in the daytime, but with little light it was about as great as walking in my backyard.

I peered up the dirt path hoping to see where it disappeared into the woods, but the darkness hid the opening from me. No matter. I spun again and hopped to the ground. I knew I had only to follow the path up a small hill to be back at my favorite bench, tucked between two oak trees. The bench overlooked a windy, babbling brook. I'd always loved the words "babbling brook." The phrase made the water sound alive with a personality. That's why I frequented the place. Babbling Brook had heard more than her fair share of my problems over the year. She was the perfect friend. I was lucky the only words she knew were "gurgle," "spray," and the occasional "glurp." If I would've been able to translate into English, "glurp" was probably a curse word.

I lifted my arm and touched the silver knob on the side of my wristwatch. The yellow face with a black Batman symbol lit up. Five minutes past midnight. Christian was late.

I imagined his crooked smile and bashful blue eye's gazing at me when he finally arrived, apologizing. I would easily forgive him and if I felt courageous enough, despite it not being a full moon, I'd throw my arms around him and plant a big, fat—

I saw movement out of the corner of my eye and turned my head sharply to the left. "Christian?"

Silence echoed back.

I stared into the dark, wondering if I'd imagined the movement. I took a step forward and again saw something bolt past into a tree not far away. I squinted my eyes, trying to make sense of what I was looking at it. The dark form was partially concealed by a tree branch. Every few seconds it would shift its weight. Whatever it was, it was large. An owl?

I watched quietly, short breaths barely escaping my lungs. My uneasiness grew when I realized the forest had suddenly become deathly still—even the crickets had lost their voice. Resisting the urge to run, I bravely yelled, "Shoo! Fly away, bird!"

The shadow remained still.

Watching me.

I'll take care of this. I bent down and scooped up a small pebble. Moving my arm back in a pitching stance, I tossed the rock in the direction of the dark form. Instead of the shadow flying away like I hoped, an arm snapped out and caught the rock midair.

Ten

I BOLTED, RUNNING AS FAST AS I COULD, BUT BECAUSE MY muscles weren't a hundred percent yet, I kept stumbling. The dark didn't help either. Glancing at my watch, I used my powers to illuminate its face until a brilliant light shined onto the path before me. This helped me find my way back down the trail and to my house without being stabbed by a branch or mauled by a Twilight Zone creature. I was so frightened I didn't take a breath until I closed my bedroom door behind me.

This was exactly the kind of thing that would get me killed. I'd kept myself safe for years, but faster than I could say "love sick" I'd purposely put myself in a dangerous situation—alone in the woods with someone—or something—I didn't recognize. The realization of how far I'd let my guard down frightened me. Christian was just a boy after all and, apparently, I'm just a silly girl.

I ignored the sick feeling in my gut as I decided it was time for Jake and me to move again. Too many strange things had happened. I'd made this decision many times before, but this time it hurt the most.

The next morning I prepared to say the words I'd practiced all night. "Jake," I would say, "I know things are going good for us here, but certain events have made me feel uncomfortable and not safe. We need to move." Straightforward and simple, like all the other times. And like all the other times, he would agree.

Then why was I so nervous?

"Jake," I began as I sat across from him at the breakfast table. "I need to tell you something." I looked up, my eyes meeting his. For not being an early person, he sure did have a huge grin on his face. "What?" I asked.

"There's something I need to tell you too." He was actually squirming in his seat.

"Um, okay, but me first." I squared up my shoulders and took a deep breath. "I know things are going good—"

Jake waved his hands, still with that silly grin. "I'm sorry, but I can't stand it anymore. I have to go first. You'll never guess what happened to me."

"You won the lottery?"

"Better. And Utah doesn't have a lottery. I met a girl. No, not a girl, a woman. Her name is Heidi. But get this, she was flirting with me! I haven't had a girl flirt with me in over five years."

"That's because you never left the house or showered."

"But it's not just the flirting. Heidi, she's . . . different. She's not like other whiny women who complain about everything and get into cat fights."

"I thought guys liked that."

"She's tough, yet kind. And she's funny like your dad was." He sighed. "I didn't think I'd ever have a chance, but last night she told me she likes me. Can you believe it? She's actually into me."

"Why wouldn't a girl like you? You're a great catch when you don't have a game controller in your hand."

He smiled, still in a daze. "I haven't been this happy in a

long time. Thanks for moving us here and for kicking my butt into gear."

I shrugged like it was no big deal.

"Now, what did you want to tell me?"

Did I dare tell him after he just found love? He hadn't been this happy in years. "I'm failing math," I blurted. I'd have to figure something else out. Maybe I'd overreacted. I guess it could've been a mountain lion. With an arm. I shook my head to dismiss the image.

"Is that it?" Jake said. "That's not a big deal. I failed lots of classes."

"You're supposed to tell me to do better or else."

"Really? All right, do better or you're grounded."

"Thanks, Jake." I stood up. "Congratulations on finding a girl who will talk to you." I forced a smile.

"Are you going out with Christian tonight? Maybe we could double?"

I shuddered. "I'll pass. Later." I left the house quickly to the sound of Jake laughing.

Instead of driving to school, I decided to walk. I needed time to think. So Jake had a girlfriend. I wanted to be happy for him, really I did, but all I could think about was how I was going to end things with Christian. And I did have to end it. I needed to get focused on me again. On my survival.

Just the thought of not seeing Christian anymore made me sick. I placed my hand against a tree to keep myself upright. My stomach was suddenly killing me. I waited for the pain to pass before I started walking again.

I couldn't push Christian's face from my mind: his bright blue eyes, the lone brown speck, his crooked smile, the dimple. My stomach tightened again, this time forcing me to sit down. Why did Jake have to find a stupid girl-friend? This would be so much easier if I could just move away. I doubled over, gritting my teeth.

Before I realized what was happening, huge tears welled in my eyes. I was crying! I never cried. And the thought of not being around Christian made it impossible to stop.

I cried for several minutes, completely unaware of my surroundings, until a shadow blocked the sun. I looked up through my hair.

In front of me was Christian. I groaned and flopped my head back down to my knees.

"Llona?" His voice was gentle and kind.

Too kind, I thought. This guy can't be for real.

"What are you doing here, Christian?" I said in anguish.

"I came to give you a ride to school."

"Why?" He'd never done that before.

"I don't know. Maybe I sensed that you needed me."

I stopped breathing. Me, needy? Not in this lifetime, not ever. I looked up at him, the tears already drying on my cheek. "Well, I don't. I'm fine." I stood up.

He ignored my curtness. "What's upset you?"

"Nothing I can't deal with." I started walking down the street. I can do this. Keep moving. Don't look back.

"Hey, wait up!" He jogged to catch up to me. "What happened last night?"

I stopped. "What do you mean? I waited, but you never came." And then I had the crap scared out of me.

He looked down. "I did, but I was late, but only by fifteen minutes. I'm really sorry. Is that why you were crying?"

"I wasn't crying. I have allergies." The pain in my gut returned.

"Nice try. What's wrong?"

"Nothing. I'm late for school. And if it's all right with you, I'd rather be alone."

"Can I walk next to you if I'm really quiet?"

"Isn't your car back there?"

"Do you want a ride?"

"No."

He stopped, but I kept walking.

"I'll see you at school," he finally called.

Once I sat down in class and had a chance to clear my head, I relaxed. It was going to be hard to stay away from Christian, but it was the right thing to do, especially after what he'd said. How could he have known that I needed him? Thinking about it, I realized that he often said strange things. It's like he knew me, *really* knew me, and that terrified me.

At lunch I went straight to the cafeteria to eat in the corner. It was weird to eat by myself again, but at least I felt more in control of my life. I still talked to people in my classes, but had lost my previous enthusiasm. It felt forced, and those around me seemed to sense it too. Eventually, I gave up. After a week of isolating myself and avoiding Christian at every turn, May finally cornered me.

"What's with you lately?" She was dressed super preppy with stylish jeans and a black top. She had straightened her hair and had it flipped back just so. She looked like she could've been a model, and I couldn't pin the crowd she belonged to today.

"I'm fine."

"No, you're not. You're totally avoiding people again."

I suddenly got angry. Who was May to tell me how to live my life? "I'm only doing what you do, but instead of having a million friends, all of whom you keep at a distance, I choose to have none. We both have our ways of protecting ourselves. This is mine."

May's eyes moved past me, and she nodded slowly. "Right. See you then." She walked off without looking back.

My shoulders sagged. I felt horrible the rest of the day.

* * * * *

At about 7:30 that night, the doorbell rang. I pushed my chair back from the dining table and my math homework, which I was still failing, and opened the front door.

Christian stood in the doorway with a bouquet of yellow roses. "Hi, I hope this is a good time."

"Um, it's fine. What's up?" I kept one arm on the door, only letting it open so far.

"These are for you." He thrust the flowers toward me.

My stomach began to ache again, and I almost couldn't bear it. "They're beautiful, thank you. But why?"

"I feel bad we haven't hung out, and I can't help feeling like I did something wrong."

I shook my head. "You didn't do anything wrong, seriously."

"Can I come in and talk?"

While I hesitated, the infamous angel and devil duo appeared on each of my shoulders.

"Let him in," the angel said. "He brought you flowers."

The little devil snorted, "Flowers. Ha! He abandoned you. You can't count on anyone but yourself."

"Ah, come on. The guy said he was sorry," the angel retorted.

"Llona?" Christian asked.

The angel and devil disappeared.

I sighed and opened the door. "Come on in." Somewhere in the distance, I heard my imaginary devil curse.

"Thanks," Christian said.

"Have a seat."

He dropped onto the sofa. "I'm not sure what happened or what I did, but I want you to know I'm sorry. Maybe you felt we were getting too serious or something, and maybe we were, I don't know. But what I do know is I miss you. I want to be friends. Can we at least be that?"

"I don't make a good friend."

"Let me be the judge of that."

"I like to be alone."

Christian laughed. "Not someone like you. You were born to make people happy."

There he goes again. "You don't know what I was born to do. Don't act like you know me."

He was silent for a moment. "Fine. Can we just hang out once in awhile?"

"Why, Christian? I've completely blown you off. Why would you still want to hang out with me?"

He stared straight into my eyes with an intensity I could feel and said, "You're like no one I've ever met before."

"That could be a bad thing."

"In your case, it's not. Friends?"

I shrugged, too emotionally exhausted to care anymore.

We talked a little longer before he finally left. I felt much better about me and Christian (we could be friends, right?), but I still didn't feel good about what I'd said to May. Before I went to bed, I dialed her number.

"What?" she said.

I took a deep breath. "Sorry about what I said earlier. I didn't mean it. I've just been trying to figure out where I belong. Does that even make sense?"

She paused before saying, "Of course it does, but just try to remember who your real friends are. People like us need to stick together."

This jolted me. This was the first time she'd hinted at what we knew about each other. "Right. Sure. Anyway, I really am sorry."

"No problem. I have my bad days too. Just let me know when you want to hang out."

"Will do. Thanks and have a good night." I hung up.

Now I felt better.

*   *   *   *   *

The next day at lunch, I sat by myself eating a barely warm slice of pizza.

"You missed book club last night."

I looked up. Matt stood over me, holding a tray of food.

"I know, I'm sorry. I'll try to come next time."

"Can I eat with you?"

"I guess."

He slid in next to me and pulled out a book from his backpack. "We're reading this for next month."

I looked down at a book titled *1984* by George Orwell. "I've been wanting to read that," I said.

"It's good. I'm almost done."

And that was the gist of our conversation. He said nothing else until the bell rang and then said good-bye. It was nice being around Matt. He didn't seem to have a care in the world, and he didn't feel the need to find out more about me. It was refreshing.

The next day Matt appeared again at lunch. This time he didn't ask if he could sit by me, he just did. Our conversation once again consisted of a few syllables while we both ate and read.

On the third day, Christian found us. He said to Matt, "I'm Christian. I don't think we've met."

"I'm Matt." They shook hands.

"We're in a book club together," I volunteered.

"Oh yeah? What book are you reading?"

"I doubt you'd know it," Matt said, closing his book.

"I might."

"*1984*."

Christian took it from him and examined it. "George Orwell. It's an interesting book. I love the way it shows how easily humans can be controlled by fear from an obviously psycho government. I hope I never become that weak."

Matt's eyebrows raised. "Very true. Maybe you should join our book club?"

Christian's eyes moved to mine. "No. I better be going. Just wanted to say hi." He stood up. "I'll call you later, Llona."

I nodded.

After he left, Matt said. "He's different."

"Because he's read *1984*?"

"No, but it does show football isn't everything to him. Not only that, but most guys would have hung around, throwing insults at me because they think I'm hitting on you or something. He was very cool about it."

I set my book down. "How come you are so different from everyone else?"

"How do you mean?"

"You come to high school, but you don't seem to care about any of it. It's not like you act above us or anything, you just act like we don't exist, but in a sophisticated way, know what I mean?" I suddenly felt very stupid.

Matt laughed. "I'm not sure I do, but see all this?" He waved his fork around the room. "None of this means anything in the real world. All high school is, is an exaggerated adult world, like a reality TV show. It's as if everyone's lost their ability to reason. Every event, whether good or bad, is emotionally intensified. For example," he pointed across the room to a group of girls. "See that girl over there? The one with the red shirt?"

I nodded.

"Last week I heard her crying to her friends about how a stylist had cut her hair too short. She almost didn't come to school because she was so traumatized by the event. Now give this girl fifteen years and three kids, a butchered hair cut would be the least of her worries." Matt shoved a bite of food into his mouth. "Unless of course she becomes like one of those people who don't ever let go of their high school glory days. Take my aunt for example. She still shops in the junior clothing section and thinks it's a bad day if she hasn't heard a juicy piece of gossip. She hates anyone who's overweight, when secretly I think she's bulimic. So you see, for the majority of people, high school is just a training ground for real life. Some of us learn from it and take the best with us, while others of us of get trapped, thinking there will never be anything better."

I stared at him, mouth open. "How old are you?"

He laughed. "I know I sound like an eighty-year-old—the curse of having two parents who are college professors. They've helped me see the world in a different light."

"High school's not all that bad," I said.

"No, of course not. High school life is necessary."

"You make it sound so boring. There is fun to be had in high school: sport games, parties, hanging out."

"I can't see what I would learn from those things so I just don't go."

"But it's not about learning anything. It's just about having a good time." It seemed weird that me of all people was giving someone else a pep talk on being social. I'm such a hypocrite.

He shoved a french fry into his mouth as he pondered my words. "Maybe you're right. Isn't there a football game Friday night?"

"Yes," I answered, thinking immediately of Christian.

"Why don't we go?"

"Okay, deal." One little game wouldn't hurt.

When Friday came, I almost cancelled with Matt. There was no moon, and I was feeling extremely weak and exhausted, but when I found out Jake wanted me to go out to dinner with Heidi and him, I decided to keep my plans. The last thing I wanted was to be around a lovey-dovey couple.

I met Matt at the game and as we sat down on the bleachers, I snuck a peek at him. Like always, he was very cute, wearing baggy Levis and a plain red T-shirt. I wondered why I wasn't attracted to him that way. Maybe it was because he didn't seem to be attracted to me. We were just two friends hanging out, no motives.

I knew immediately why I wasn't attracted to Matt as soon as we started watching the game. The moment I saw Christian, my heart leapt within my chest. I loved to watch him play. His movements were quick and his passes flawless. When our team scored, I stood up to cheer with everyone else, but after only a few seconds I had to sit back down.

"What's up?" Matt asked me.

"Nothing, just feeling a little light-headed."

"Do you want me to take you home?"

"No," I said, a little too quickly. I wanted to watch Christian as much as possible. A couple of times during the game, I noticed Christian look our way. I smiled but wasn't sure if he saw me because he didn't smile back.

When the game was almost over, Matt leaned over and asked, "Are you ready for Mr. Steele's midterm on Monday?"

"Midterm?" I didn't mean to stare, but I honestly had no idea what he was talking about.

"Yeah, his big test. If you don't get a passing grade, he'll fail you for the whole semester."

I shook my head. "I'm dead."

"I can't believe you didn't know. All we did in class today was review for it. At least that's what we did in ours. Maybe you did something different."

"I wouldn't know," I mumbled.

"What?"

I stood up. "I'll be right back. I have to go get my math book so I can study this weekend."

"Do you want me to come with you?"

"No, watch the game. I'll hurry." I carefully stepped down the bleachers. Of course if I did fall, maybe I'd break my leg and could miss the test.

I moved deathly slow across the lawn toward the school. I hated walking in the dark when the moon wasn't out. Gratefully, the stadium provided just enough light for me to see my next step, preventing me from falling on face.

I entered the front doors and, as quickly as possible, maneuvered my way around the half-lit school until I found my locker. I retrieved my math book and was about to close the door when I heard laughter. I held still and focused my hearing, but jumped when something smashed against what sounded like lockers.

More laughter.

I moved to where I could peer around the corner to see what was going on. On the other end of the hall three guys walked in my direction. And one of them was carrying a bat.

ELEVEN

I PRESSED MY BACK AGAINST THE WALL. GREAT, JUST WHAT I need. I moved back down the short hallway to the doors. Very quietly, I pushed on the bar that normally opened, but what I suspected turned out to be true. The door was locked. I would have to go back out the main entrance, past the wanna-be gangsters.

"If we can't beat them on the field," I heard one of the boys say, "We'll at least make sure they remember us." Another crashing sound. My nerves jumped as if I'd been hit instead of the metal lockers.

Their voices were getting closer. I frantically looked around for a place to hide, but schools weren't designed to have hiding places. I decided my best option was to act like I'd heard or seen nothing. I turned the corner and began to walk quickly.

"Hey!" one of them shouted.

I kept moving, gripping my math book tightly.

"Wait up," a deeper voice called.

I quickened my pace when I heard footsteps pounding the hard floor behind me.

A hand on my shoulder stopped me dead and spun me around. A tall boy stood in front of me with a crazy grin and dilated pupils. His face was littered with pimples, and if I wasn't so frightened, I might've been tempted to connect the dots.

"Where you going in such a hurry?" he asked. His buddies moved behind him like a pack of wolves.

"She sure is pretty," said a frumpy-looking boy. He held an open can in his hand, and I was pretty sure it wasn't soda.

"I was just going back to the game," I said and turned to leave.

Pimple-face put his hand on my shoulder again. This time he didn't remove it.

"So you're a student here at Lame-land?" he snickered. The other boys joined him. "Why don't you hang out with us? You can help us decorate your own school."

"I really have to be going." I shrugged my shoulder hard enough to make him loose his grip.

"Whoa! Not so fast." This time he grabbed both my shoulders. My math book crashed to the floor. "I bet you're a cheerleader here, aren't you? Looks like it's our lucky day." His friends laughed.

"Let go of me," I growled. I would've given anything for it to be a full moon. I could've annihilated all of them. But Light was no good to me right now. I was on my own.

"Let's decorate her," one of the other boys suggested.

"That's a great idea, Tek. What do you think, Blondie? You wanna show some school spirit?"

I brought my knee up as hard as I could, connecting it with his little man gems. He doubled over with an agonizing grunt.

I bolted toward the doors but was too slow. A boy tackled me from behind, and I fell to the floor, splitting my lip.

"I've got her!" Tek yelled. "What should we do with her, Jared?"

"Give me a sec, moron," he moaned.

Tek rolled me over while pinning me down. Above me, the fatter kid who's name I had yet to learn, stared as if he'd never seen a girl before.

"I've never seen a chick this hot before," he said.

"That's cause you only hang out with dorks," Tek spat. A string of spit fell from his mouth to my face.

"Please, just let me go. Please?" It was useless to struggle. The last of my energy had drained, and I could taste blood in my mouth.

Jared stumbled toward us, still hunched over. "Who has the paint?"

Big-kid reached inside his jacket and pulled out a can of black spray paint.

Jared tore it from his hand. "How 'bout that school spirit, pretty?" He bent over and began to spray paint my forehead. I turned my head to the side.

"Don't get her hair!" Big-kid cried.

"Quit being such a jack—" but Jared didn't finish his statement. His body flew over me, stopping only when it crashed into a wall.

Tek looked behind him just in time to get punched in the face. He toppled to my side, gasping for air.

"Get out of here before I call the police," a familiar accent said.

This is the point where things became fuzzy. My eyes fell upon an angry Mr. Steele; his face blurred with the ones around me. I remember hearing footsteps running away and the crashing of a door, but the sounds were muffled, as if they were being filtered through a foam pad.

Mr. Steele leaned over me. "Are you all right? Do you need help?"

I mumbled something incoherent, but felt my head shake no.

"You don't look well. Let me help you up."

His arm slipped behind my shoulders, and as if I were a

piece of cotton, he lifted me to a standing position. I couldn't help but take a big whiff, my head only inches from his chest.

"Why don't you come to my office and I'll call your parents?" he suggested.

When I began to lean precariously to the right, he took me by the waist and guided me down the hall.

"By the way, don't worry about those creeps," he said. "I have their picture and will make sure they are severely punished."

I followed him blindly. If only I could find my voice. I'd tell him I was okay; I just needed to get back to—was someone waiting for me?

"Llona?" My name sounded distant. Mr. Steele stopped and turned around.

"Llona, what happened?" Rushing toward us was Christian wearing his football uniform—a perfect combination of red, black, and white. For a second I thought he was going to tackle me.

"I was taking her to my office so she could call her parents," Mr. Steele told him.

Christian didn't seem to hear him. "What happened?" He reached up with his hand and carefully touched my lip. I flinched.

"Some boys from the other school were too rough in their celebration."

"Did you call the police?" Christian asked.

"I took care of it," Mr. Steele said, but it sounded almost like a sneer. I couldn't be sure though because I wasn't good at deciphering someone's emotions when they had an accent. He could've sounded happy and I wouldn't have known the difference.

"I'll take her," Christian told him. "I know where she lives. I'll drive her straight home."

Mr. Steele seemed reluctant. His grip tightened on my waist

to the point where it almost hurt. And then just as quickly his grip relaxed. "Go ahead, Christian, but I'll be calling to check up." He released me. "Is that okay with you, Llona?"

I nodded.

"Fine." Christian took me by the arm and led me away. Once outside, I inhaled deeply and let my mind clear.

"Are you all right?" Christian asked again.

"Uh-huh." I moved my neck around. It felt like I had whiplash.

"Why didn't you talk to me back there?" he asked.

I shrugged. "I guess I was more upset than I realized."

"What happened?"

"I went into the school to get my math book but ran into some boys. They tried to decorate me is all."

"Mr. Steele should've called the police."

"I'm glad he didn't," I said. The only times I'd ever spoken to police is when someone had died—my mother, my father, the red shoe lady—Cops made me ill.

Christian looked over my shoulder. "What did they look like?"

"Oh please, I'm fine. I need to get back to Matt. He's probably wondering where I am." Already cars were leaving the parking lot.

"That's what you're worried about? This could have been a lot more serious."

"But it wasn't."

He let out a sigh through his nose and then pursed his lips together as if he wanted to say something. I guess he decided to go for it because he asked, "What were you doing in there alone anyway?"

"It's a school. Why would I ever think I couldn't go into one alone?"

"That's not what I meant. You're weak. You shouldn't be by yourself."

My heart stopped, and I stepped away from him. "What did you say?"

"I mean you look sick," he said, a little too quickly.

"Get away from me, Christian." I took another step back.

"Llona, please. That's not what I meant." When he moved toward me, I began to run.

"Llona, stop!" he called.

Gratefully, he didn't follow. I made it all the way to the bleachers before I finally stopped, a surprising feat considering I could barely breathe. I ducked around the corner from the exit and waited for the crowds to die down. I could only imagine what I looked like.

After everyone left, I stepped out from my hiding spot and found Matt staring toward the school. His eyes widened when he saw me. "What happened to you?"

I shook my head. "Do you mind taking me home? I'll come back for my car tomorrow." I was too shaken to drive.

"Sure." He quickly walked to his car and opened the passenger door. Once we were out of the parking lot, Matt asked again, "What happened?"

I took a deep breath and relaxed into the seat. "A couple of kids from the opposing team ambushed me, but Mr. Steele chased them away."

"Wow! I'm so sorry. I should've gone with you."

"How could you've known? It's not a big deal."

"Are you for real? Most girls would be bawling their faces off."

I shrugged. "There's nothing I can do about it now. Besides they were just stupid boys."

"Yeah, but what if Mr. Steele hadn't come by?"

"But he did. I'm not going to get upset over a 'what if.'" I probably should've been upset, but all I could think about was what Christian had said.

"You're a different girl, Llona. You know that?"

"I know."

"That's a good thing. You're one of the few who will actually make it far in life. Not just survive but really succeed."

I stared at him. "Do you really mean that?"

"Of course."

"I think that's the nicest thing anyone has ever said to me."

He smiled.

"Did we score again while I was gone?" I asked.

Matt proceeded to give me a play-by-play of the last few minutes of the game. "I must admit, I had more fun than I expected. Thanks for inviting me."

"I'm glad you came."

Matt nodded. He tapped his palm on the steering wheel to music just barely playing through the speakers. "By the way, did you get your math book?" he asked.

I moaned. "I did, but it got knocked from my hands. What am I going to do?"

"You can borrow mine. I'll bring it by tomorrow."

"Don't you need it?"

"No. I get math. You can borrow it."

We were almost to my house when I noticed a car in our driveway: Jake's girlfriend. I thought they were going out. "Can you drop me off at Mueller Park? It's just a few blocks away."

"Why?"

"My uncle has a date over and I don't want to bother him quite yet."

"So what are you going to do?"

"There's a trail that practically leads to my backyard. I'll sneak in my window." I wanted to wash the paint off my face before Jake saw it and freaked out.

"Do you want me to join you?"

I looked out the window to the darkened trees beyond,

wondering what my chances were of meeting tree-creature again. It was only ten o'clock, I told myself, as if that mattered. "No. That's okay."

Matt parked his car next to the entrance to the canyon. "I feel funny dropping you off here, especially after what just happened."

"You saw how close it is to my home. I'll be fine. Thanks for going with me tonight." I jumped out before he could protest any further.

I walked up the trail until the light from Matt's car disappeared. I hadn't realized how dark it was until his headlights were gone. I felt for my watch, hoping I could use it for light, but then I remembered I'd left it at home.

I remained still, listening to the night's gentle symphony: crickets chirped, water babbled, leaves rustled, and the wind sighed through the tops of the trees. Its melody soothed my nerves and for the first time in a long while I felt at peace.

Because I couldn't see as well as I'd hoped, I considered cutting over to a trail that ran parallel to the road. It was in the opposite direction from my house, but it was close enough that light from the street lamps should make it easier to walk. Once the trail ended, I figured I could just walk on the road back to my house. It also happened to cross over a thin finger-like appendage of Mueller Park Lake. During the day it was a pretty cool place to visit, but I'd never seen it at night. Now's a good as time as any. And hopefully by the time I returned, Heidi would be gone.

I cut through the trees, pushing my way through heavy vegetation. Normally, this wouldn't have bothered me as I was used to being outdoors, even at nighttime, but for some reason my heart began to pound and sweat pooled in my pits. Maybe it was the fact that I couldn't hear the crickets anymore, or maybe it was the wind that had suddenly stopped blowing.

Whatever it was, I was really starting to freak out.

I picked up my pace, shoving one branch after another out of my way. The night grew inexplicably cold, chilling my skin. A sound, like claws on bark, pierced the silence of the night. I froze.

A twig snapped to my left.

And then another.

"Hello?" I said.

"Hello?" A mocking voice echoed.

Move! I screamed in my head. My body responded sluggishly, moving up and around a thick bush. Behind me I could still hear the snapping of twigs picking up its pace in response to my own hurried movements.

"Llona," the voice, a high-pitched, almost whining sound called.

I couldn't tell which direction it was coming from. It seemed to be floating around me, teasing me as if we were playing hide-and-seek. And I was terrible at hiding, but "it" was doing a great job of seeking.

A sharp branch tore through my sleeve, and I stifled a cry when it cut into my skin. Finally, I broke free from the dense forest and ran toward the bridge. If I could just get there, then at least I'd have some options of escaping whoever was stalking me. The old railroad bridge was about thirty feet above the appendage to the lake. I'd jumped from it a few times before, landing safely in the water, but that was when I had Light's full strength to back me up. I didn't feel like jumping from it now, but if it would save my life and help me get away, I'd do it.

I was almost to the bridge when I heard, "Llona!"

This voice was different. This voice was familiar. I stopped and turned around. Jogging on the trail, coming out of the woods, was Christian. I backed away from him. Could it have been Christian messing with me in the forest?

"What are you doing out here?" he said.

"How did you find me?" I took another step backward, my feet finally on the bridge.

"Why don't you tell me what you're doing out here first?" He moved toward me.

"Why are you doing this Christian?"

"Doing what?"

"Messing with me. It's not funny!"

"What are you talking about?"

I ventured, "You know what I'm talking about. Back in the woods. You were trying to scare me to death."

I couldn't see his expression, but when he spoke his voice was stern. "I wasn't in the woods, and I wasn't messing with you. I wouldn't do that."

"Oh yeah? Then how did you find me if you didn't follow me?"

He spoke slowly. "I ran into Matt at the gas station. He said he dropped you off here and that you were going to walk the rest of the way home."

"But this isn't the way to my house."

"I know. I just had a feeling you went this way." He took another step.

"Nice try. Now leave me alone."

"No. I'm not leaving you out here, especially after what happened to you tonight. There's no way."

"And I'm not going to let you mess with my head." I took another step toward the side of the bridge. I had to get away, and fast. I knew I wouldn't be able to outrun him, but I hoped if I jumped, he wouldn't follow and then I could swim to the other side.

"What happened in the woods, Llona?" He was moving forward but very slowly, probably hoping I wouldn't notice.

"You should know. You were there."

"It wasn't me."

"So you're saying it wasn't you calling my name and— hunting me?"

Christian froze. "Why did you use that word?"

"What word?"

"Hunted."

"Because that's what it felt like."

He began moving quickly toward me. "We have to get out of here now. It's not safe." His rushed movements caught me off guard, and before I could stop to think, I made a mad leap from the bridge. I thought I'd cleared the wood railing until my hand caught on something. My body dangled in the darkness like a fish on a hook. I could see nothing but a bottomless black world. I looked up to see what had stopped me.

Christian was leaning over the ledge on his stomach, holding my hand. I couldn't believe he had gotten to me so fast.

"Give me your other hand," he grunted.

I felt my hand slipping but did nothing to stop it.

He stared directly into my eyes. "Trust me, Llona. Please."

I couldn't trust anyone but myself. Completely calm, I said, "I can't."

And then I let go.

TWELVE

I FELL THROUGH THE NIGHT LIKE A SHOOTING STAR, EXCEPT I wasn't a star. I was a complete idiot. What was I thinking falling from this distance in my condition? Before I could come up with an answer, I smashed into the cold water. I kicked my legs hard, but they may as well have been taped together. I simply had no strength to fight my way to the surface.

Before I had the chance to panic, an arm came around my waist and pulled me upwards. I gasped for air the second my head broke the surface. Of course the person saving me was the same person I'd just accused of wanting to hurt me. I relaxed against Christian's chest, too exhausted to offer any assistance.

I dreaded the conversation we were going to have once we reached the shore. Jumping from the bridge had been a bad decision, and I was sure he was going to tell me that. When my feet touched the murky bottom, I stumbled with him until we both collapsed to the ground, waves lapping at our legs.

I rolled onto my back and stared into the sky, which was blacker than ever. The stillness of the night was broken up only by our labored breathing, and that's when I realized how dangerous my foolish decision had been. I could've hurt not only myself, but him too.

I opened my mouth to speak, but closed it again. What

could I possibly say? I guess something was better than nothing. "Christian," I began, "I'm so sorry."

He rolled towards me. Propping his head up with his hand, elbow on ground, he smiled. "You still don't get it, do you?" He pushed wet, stray hairs away from my face. "I would never let anything happen to you."

"In the woods, it really wasn't you, was it?"

His smile disappeared. "No. We need to get out of here." He stood up and offered his hand. This time I accepted it without question.

"Do you know who it could be?" I asked as I wrapped my arms around my shivering body.

He shook his head, seemingly oblivious to the cold. "A couple of weeks ago, I came running up here. I thought I was being followed too."

"Do you come here often?"

"Sometimes." He guided me back to the trail. I could tell he wanted to move faster, but he didn't rush me. He kept his head on a swivel, alert and ready. When we heard a branch snap, his hand tightened on mine, and he pulled me close. "Keep moving. It's probably nothing, an animal maybe," he said.

We made it to his SUV alive, no thanks to me. He opened the passenger door.

"I don't want to get your seats wet," I said.

"That's the last thing I care about. Get in."

After helping me in and handing me a blanket, he moved to the rear of the car and opened the hatch. A second later he jumped in next to me holding a duffle bag and a towel. He removed his shirt and dried off. "Let me see your arm," he said.

"Why?" I asked suddenly suspicious.

His eyebrows lifted. "Serious?"

"Sorry, bad habit." I moved my arm out from under the blanket. I wasn't used to trusting others, but I was ready to start with Christian. What else did the poor guy have to do?

Christian rolled up my sleeve revealing the cut I'd gotten earlier. "That's bad."

"I've seen worse."

"I'm sure you have." He pulled out several butterfly bandages. "I don't think you need stitches, but you might want to have your uncle look at it. Speaking of Jake, how are you going to explain the paint and these injuries?"

"Could we go to your place so I can wash it off?"

He hesitated.

"Never mind. I'll just sneak in the back," I said. "I was going to do that anyway."

"Why don't you want your uncle to know?"

I shrugged. "I don't want him to worry."

Christian looked out the window. "You can come to my place." He started the car and turned up the heat. Halfway there, Christian took my hand and pulled me next to him.

"Are you getting warm?" he asked.

"Mmm," I moaned. I was so warm I began to fall asleep.

"Llona?"

I sighed deeply.

"Llona, wake up. We're here."

I opened my eyes, but still didn't move because I was shocked to find myself in my current position. My head was lying on Christian's bare chest with his arm wrapped around me. "How long have I been out?"

"About twenty minutes."

I sat up. "Sorry. I didn't mean to fall asleep."

He grinned. "And I didn't mean to enjoy it."

My face reddened, and I turned away. In front of us was a huge white house with tall pillars leading from the roof to the ground. Two wings spanned out from a thick center, and on each side of the front double doors, two lions perched regally.

The house looked more like a hotel than a home. "Is this were you live?"

Christian didn't look up; he was rummaging through a bag. "Yup."

"I had no idea you lived on top of the hill." It was one of the richest places to live in Bountiful, and the further up people built, the richer they were. I didn't think we could get any higher.

"It's too big for me, but my father loves being the center of attention." He pulled out a T-shirt.

"Remind me again, what does he do?"

"Buys other people's companies." He smelled the shirt, and I assumed he found it acceptable because he pulled it over his head.

"He must have great business sense," I said, still in awe of the house.

"That he does, but that's where his good qualities end." Christian jumped out of the car.

When he opened my door, I asked, "Is it okay I'm here?"

He paused and darted his eyes to the house and then back to me. "Yeah. It should be fine. My dad can be kind of weird sometimes, so just ignore him if he is. Come on."

His sudden nervousness made me feel guilty, and I instantly regretted coming. It had been a strange enough night without having to meet a weird adult.

Christian opened the door to a grand entryway. I could practically see my reflection in the polished floor. In the center of the massive entrance was a marble staircase that swept up to a second floor. It reminded me of Daddy Warbuck's home in the movie *Annie*.

"You have got to be kidding," I whispered, afraid the sound of my voice might break the crystal chandelier above us.

"You can talk normal." He moved up the staircase. I walked

as closely behind him as possible.

"I feel like I'm in an episode of *Cribs*," I told him, my voice still low.

"And that's why I never have people over. I mean, seriously, who can feel comfortable in this?"

Christian turned left at the top of the stairway. We were about halfway down a wide hall when a male voice said, "Christian? Is that you?"

"Yeah, Dad."

"Who's with you?" he called from behind slightly parted double doors.

Christian moved toward the doors and opened them. Inside was an office or a library, or I guess both. The walls were lined with dark wood shelves and there were at least four love seats in the room and several tall Queen Anne chairs. A man that I assumed to be Christian's dad sat behind a long, mahogany desk with a laptop in front of him. He was thin with a full head of blond hair and a narrow face. His eyes were the same almond shape as Christian's, but they were dark blue instead of Christian's electric blue. He had very few lines on his face, unless they were hidden behind his five o'clock shadow. He reminded me of James Bond, the modern version.

"Who's your guest?" he asked Christian, but he kept his eyes on me.

Christian hesitated, as if embarrassed. "This is . . . Llona."

He may as well have said, "This is the devil" because all of a sudden his dad stood up and the lines that I thought were missing from his face suddenly appeared in angry creases across his forehead.

"What are you doing with her?" he demanded.

It was the way he said it that made me step closer to Christian. It wasn't a generalization, like "what are you doing with a girl," it was directed entirely at me.

"Calm down, Dad. As you can see, she ran into some trouble. I brought her here to clean up, that's all."

The lines in his forehead disappeared, but he still didn't sit. "What happened?" he asked me.

"She ran into some—"

"I was speaking to her. Can't she speak for herself?"

I searched frantically for my voice. "Some students got a little too exited in their celebration," I croaked. "I got caught in the crossfire."

He looked at Christian. "You can't afford to be careless."

"I wasn't, and none of this was her fault, Dad."

He shrugged and sat back down. "It never is. Show her to the guest bathroom and get her some clothes in the closet."

Christian led me out with an expression that was anything but friendly. "Sorry about my dad," he said, once we were out of ear shot.

"What did he mean by *It never is my fault*?" I asked.

"Who knows? My father is pretty bitter toward all women, so it was probably some kind of derogatory comment."

"Why doesn't he like women?"

"He just thinks they're the cause of all his problems."

"It doesn't look like he has many problems to me," I mumbled, glancing around at all the fancy artwork.

"Looks can be deceiving." Christian opened a door and showed me into a room. "This is the guest bedroom. There's a bathroom over there and in the closet is a bunch of girl clothes. You should find something that fits you."

"Why do you have a bunch of girl clothes if your dad doesn't like women?"

"Oh, he loves women when the mood fits him, which is entirely too often in my opinion. I'll be waiting for you downstairs."

After the door closed, I quickly ducked into the bathroom.

The last thing I wanted was to stay in this house any longer than I had to. I had a distinct impression Christian's father highly disapproved of me, and not just because I was a woman.

It took me longer than I thought to scrub the streak of spray paint off of my face, and by the time I was done, my face sported a big red welt. I frowned. It was a slight improvement from the paint.

After showering, I opened the bedroom closet and gasped. It was bigger than my room at home. I moved among the designer clothing trying not to touch anything unless I thought it looked my size.

A few minutes later I found the least dressy outfit: a blue empire style shirt with a black satin sash that tied below my breasts. I also found a pair of black slacks that were a little too big. A skinny belt hanging from a hook made it possible to keep the paints around my waist. I combed my hair and then searched the bathroom for a rubber band but came up empty. You'd think a room dedicated to women would contain a rubber band, a hair clip, or something.

Because my shoes were still wet, and no other shoes fit, I left the room barefoot. I didn't make a sound as my bare feet padded across the carpeted floor. Up ahead, raised voices echoed from the office. I was about to let my sensitive hearing eavesdrop on their conversation, but jumped when I heard a loud thumping sound from inside, along with Christian's dad saying, "That is enough!"

Suddenly the door opened. I darted back into the bedroom before whoever was coming out saw me. Just as I shut the door, I heard Christian say, "Just because you did things a certain way doesn't make it the right way." I heard a door slam.

I waited several minutes before I dared venture out again. When I peered back into the hallway, everything was quiet. I moved quietly, careful to avoid the closed office doors, but

I inadvertently ran into a picture that was jutting out further than I had anticipated. It made a scraping sound against the wall.

"Christian?" The door opened.

"Hello, sir," I said, avoiding direct eye contact.

He stared at me for a moment before he said, "Christian's probably downstairs."

"Um, thank you." I hurried past him, but he stopped me.

"Tell your uncle hello," he said.

I turned around. "My uncle, sir?"

He frowned. "Yes. Didn't you know he works for me? At Primatech."

"No, I didn't."

"He's a good worker. It's hard to find men like him. Mark taught him well."

I visibly jerked at the sound of my father's name. "You knew my father?

Christian's dad stepped into the hallway. I noticed he was limping on his left leg. "I did, a long time ago."

"How did you know him?"

"We went to school together."

"In Vegas?"

"No. It was a private school in Washington."

Now I was really surprised. "I didn't know my dad lived there."

He rubbed the back of his neck, looking suddenly tired. "We had our differences, your father and I, but I always respected him. I was real sorry to hear about his death. I always told him he was too careless."

"Careless? He was killed by a drunk driver."

He stared at me for what seemed like a long time. "You have a nice night, Llona." He turned around and walked back into his office, closing the door behind him.

That's it? Who says something like that and then walks away? I had half a notion to storm in there and give him a piece of my mind.

"Llona?"

Christian stood at the top of the stairs. There was a sadness in his eyes that I didn't understand. "You okay?" I asked.

He nodded. "It's getting late. I should probably take you home."

I followed him down the stairs. "My car's back at the high school. Can you drop me off there?"

"Sure." He opened the front door for me. "And sorry about my dad. Sometimes he talks too much."

I turned around, surprising Christian, who practically ran into me. Only inches a part, I looked at him. "I don't care how your dad is. It's you I want to hang out with, not your father."

"Are you saying you trust me now?"

I took his hand and smiled. "With my life."

On the way back to school, I said, "You never told me Jake works for your dad." I watched his reaction.

"Really? I didn't know." He seemed genuinely surprised.

"You really didn't know?"

"Why would I? He owns so many different companies, he probably employs half of Utah's population." He pulled up next to my car, on the passenger side.

"Thanks again. For everything," I said.

"Of course. I'm always here if you need me."

I nodded and slid out of the car. Hopefully I wouldn't need him anytime soon. I waved good-bye and then rounded the back of his car toward my own.

I stopped suddenly.

A cool autumn breeze blew through the loose knit of my sweater; its breath gave me pause. Not because it chilled me, but because it was laced with an odd smell. The odor reminded me of a leaky, rusty pipe in an old basement.

Instinctively, I glanced down. My tail pipe looked normal, but what was sprayed beneath it wasn't. Someone must have broken a bottle of Merlot, I thought. My foot partially rested on the crimson splatter. As I moved forward, my foot sticking slightly, I came in view of the carnage scattered along side my car.

I didn't immediately process what I saw, or didn't want to, and instead found myself staring into the night sky. The dull stars seemed to be swimming in a sea of black. Lost. Disoriented. I stepped back and took a deep breath.

Convinced I'd imagined the grisly scene, I lowered my eyes. The side of my car was no longer white—it was red. Shattered glass lay scattered on the pavement, stuck in the same scarlet fluid. But this wasn't what made me collapse to the ground, darkness overtaking my mind. It was the mass of blonde hair and bloodied flesh clinging to the broken glass poking through my driver's side window.

Thirteen

When my eyes opened, Christian was staring down at me. Behind him stood Officer Pieut.

"Llona. Llona! Can you hear me?" Christian said.

I moaned and tried to sit up.

"Lay still," the officer said. "Help is on the way."

"No. I'm fine. I just want to go home." I stood up, but my legs gave out when I saw the blood again. Christian caught me.

"Why don't you take her home?" Officer Pieut said. "We can get her statement later."

"Thanks, Officer." Christian kept his arm around my waist as he guided me to his car. "It's okay. I'll get you out of here."

I let him help me into the passenger seat. I even allowed him to buckle my seatbelt. All I wanted to do was pretend I was dreaming. Any minute I'd wake up. The blood, the torn scalp never existed. Death wasn't following me. But when I opened my eyes, I couldn't fool myself.

We were almost to my house before I finally spoke. "What happened?"

Christian took hold of my hand. "There was another murder."

"But there wasn't a body."

"The police found it across town. It appears the murderer

attacked a woman in the school parking lot and then dumped her body at the park."

"Did we know her?"

He squeezed my hand. "No. It was the mom of a kid from another school. The team we were playing against."

I turned to him, my heart suddenly racing. "Was she the mom of one of the kids who attacked me?"

"Why would you think that?"

I shook my head, unable to answer, but my stomach replied, twisting and turning in knots.

"I told the police what happened," Christian said. "I'm sure we'll find out later who it was."

I leaned back in the seat, feeling even more sick. "Why my car?"

Christian pulled into the driveway and shut off the car. He turned to me. "You need to know that this had nothing to do with you. It was just a coincidence, nothing more."

"And the shoe?"

His eyes met mine. "There's nothing to worry about. I promise. You trust me, right?"

I nodded.

"Good. Let's go inside and get you to bed. I'll explain everything to your uncle."

I nodded again. It was nice having someone else take control for once. I let my mind shut down. Christian did the rest.

I slept in the next morning. When I stretched my arms they felt better, stronger. But my mind felt like it had been battered by horror films all night.

Jake accosted me the moment I stepped out of my room. "How are you feeling?"

"Better."

He hugged me. "I was worried about you."

I shrugged and walked into the kitchen. "So what happened after I went to bed last night?" I asked, pulling a mug out of the cupboard.

Jake took it from my hand and poured orange juice into it. "Christian stayed for awhile, filling me in. I'm so sorry you had to go through that."

I shrugged again and turned on the oven. German pancakes sounded really good right now. "What should we do about my car?" I asked, taking out eggs and milk from the fridge.

Jake pushed me aside and began to crack the eggs.

"Just two," I said.

"The police will have your car for awhile. They said we'd get it back in a couple of weeks. Are you going to be okay with that?"

"Totally." I'd be happy if I never saw the thing again. I measured a cup of flour, but Jake took it from me. "Would you stop already?" I said. "I'm fine!"

"I'm sure you are. How much milk?"

I gave in and just let him do it. "One cup."

Jake stirred for a minute. "The police stopped by this morning."

"They did?"

"Yeah. They want your statement. I told them you'd go by the station later today."

"Okay."

"Do you want me to come with you?" he asked.

"No. I can do it."

"Are you sure you're okay?"

I let out a long sigh. "I think so. No. But I will be."

"I'm here for you. If you ever need to talk."

"I know. Thanks."

"Oh, I almost forgot. Christian called and asked if he could come over tonight. I told him it was fine," Jake said.

"Okay. Thanks."

After we finished eating, I said, "I met Mr. Knight."

"You did? Where?" Jake asked.

"I was at Christian's house last night. How come you never told me you work for his dad?"

"I didn't think it mattered. What were you doing there?"

"Washing off paint. I was only there for a little while." Before he could question me further, I asked, "How come I never knew my dad went to a private school?"

Jake stiffened. "Who told you that?"

"Mr. Knight."

Jake waited a moment before he answered. "Yeah. He went to one for a little while. It's where he met your mother."

"I thought he met my mother in Vegas."

Jake looked sideways at me. "Yeah, sort of."

"So which is it?"

He threw up his hands. "I don't know. I only heard about it. I don't remember the details."

"Then what about my dad's accident?"

"What do you mean?"

"Mr. Knight said my dad was being careless. Why would he say that?"

Jake clenched his fists. "It's none of his business."

"But why would he say that? Is there something I don't know about my father's death?"

"I'm not having this conversation." He stood up. "I'll be in my room."

"Jake—"

"Another time, Tink." He disappeared before I could say another word.

The doorbell rang at noon. I quickly pulled a beanie over

my messy hair and opened the door.

"Hi, Matt, Tracey," I said. "What are you guys doing?" Tracey looked like she was attending a movie premiere. She always did look her best around Matt. I suspected she had a major crush on him, but he was oblivious.

"We were at the library. Here's my math book." He handed it to me.

"Right. Thanks. Come on in."

"I like your house," Tracey said, her cheeks puffed when she breathed. With her short brown hair and brown eyes, she reminded me of a chipmunk. "I bet it's fun to have a mountain in your backyard."

"I like it. Have a seat."

"How're you feeling?" Matt asked.

"I'm good, much better."

"You make it home okay last night?"

"In one piece."

"I felt bad leaving you like that, especially after Christian tore into me."

"What did he say?"

"He asked if I dropped you off at home. When I said you wanted me to take you to the park, he completely freaked out. I thought he was going to punch me, but he didn't. Did he ever find you?"

"Yeah."

"Were you okay?"

I wondered how much to tell him. I didn't want him to feel bad. "I was fine. He didn't need to worry."

"Good. Do you want any help studying?"

"No, I got it, but thanks."

"Do your parents work on Saturday?" Tracey asked.

"I live with my uncle. Are you guys doing anything fun today?" I quickly changed the subject before she could inquire further. I hated explaining why I didn't live with my parents.

Tracey looked at Matt expectantly. Matt didn't notice. "Um, no. I have to go home and help my dad. We're remodeling our basement."

"That sounds fun. What about you, Tracey?"

"No plans. My parents are out of town, so it's just me. Are you doing anything?"

"No. Just hanging out."

"Do you want to go shopping?"

I hesitated. My expression must have been awfully grim, because Tracey said, "That's okay. We can do it another time."

"No. That's not it at all. It's just that—well, I have to go to the police station."

"Why?" Tracey and Matt said together.

I took a deep breath and told them what had happened.

"Wow," Matt said. "That sucks."

"I heard on the news they found another body. I can't believe you're involved," Tracey said.

"Hoping to be uninvolved by this afternoon."

Tracey stood up. "Why don't I go with you? Then, if you feel like it, we could go shopping afterwards."

"Yeah. Sure. Why not?" At least it would take my mind off the blood-soaked hair.

I gave the police my statement, which wasn't very long since I didn't know anything to begin with, and then Tracey and I drove to the mall. I never did like shopping—of course I always did it alone so the whole experience never lasted long. "In-and-out" that was my motto, but being with a friend suddenly made the whole experience new and exciting.

We shopped for a little while and then decided to take a break and eat. We sat down at a table in front of a restaurant kiosk that served just about every kind of food you could think of on a stick. I was leery at first, but quickly found that for some reason food did taste better on a stick.

Tracey took a long sip from her soda. "What are you doing tonight?" she asked.

"Christian's coming over."

"Are you two dating?"

"Not sure."

"Then you are. You just need to make it official. Maybe that's what tonight's about. You should—" Tracey grabbed my arm suddenly, eyes wide. "You'll never believe who's walking toward us."

I turned around, but regretted it a second later because all of a sudden I went weak. Strolling toward us, as if a super spy in a preview for a blockbuster thriller, was Mr. Steele. At any moment I waited for him to pull a shiny revolver from behind his back and arrest the skinny wiener man behind the counter for being a terrorist.

"Hello, girls," Mr. Steele said.

"Hello, Mr. Steele," Tracey chimed back.

"I didn't know you two were friends." He smiled.

Tracey winked at me. "Best," she said.

"That's wonderful. It's good to see two kids from different groups become friends." He touched my shoulder. "I want you to know, Llona, that those boys were punished."

I think I nodded.

"Did you get home all right?"

I mumbled something. It must have been an acceptable answer, because Mr. Steele said, "Good. You girls have fun and stay out of trouble."

"We will," Tracey called after him. She turned to me. "He has got to be the hottest man I know. Don't you think?"

My senses returned. "For a teacher, yes."

"So what boys was he talking about?" she asked.

I chewed the last of the cheese off the stick. "Just some rowdy guys from the game last night."

By the time we were done shopping, I ended up with two new pairs of jeans and several tops that I would never have had the courage to pick out on my own. I chose one of these pieces, a black punk-style T-shirt with a black blazer and a pair of jeans, to wear on my date with Christian—if it was a date.

Jake returned with Heidi shortly before Christian arrived. It was good to finally meet the woman who occupied his thoughts. Heidi was very pretty, like Jake said. She had black spiky hair and dressed skater—exactly the type Jake would go for. After we finished talking, she even agreed to play old school Nintendo with Jake. She was definitely a keeper.

I finished my hair, which I actually curled and left down (but I still put a hat on) and then waited for Christian in the living room. Five minutes before he was to arrive, the doorbell rang.

"You're early," I said to Christian, who stood in my doorway looking exceptionally good. It wasn't that he was wearing anything special, but his jeans and blue T-shirt fit his muscular frame like a glove.

"I wanted to make sure I wasn't late. I remember how mad you got last time. Are you doing better today?"

"Much, and I wasn't mad at you. I was mad at myself."

"For what?"

"For letting myself become distracted. I've always done things a certain way and since I met you, I've been doing things differently."

"Is that good?"

I nodded. "I think so. I guess I just got scared, but after what you did for me last night, I don't see how I can't trust you. And others for that matter. It's time I let go of my fears." I squared my shoulders.

His arms came around me. "You are the bravest person I know." His tone was mocking, but his expression was serious.

I lifted an eyebrow. "That's nice of you to say, but you don't know me."

"I know you better than you think I do."

"What does that mean?"

He smiled. "I've got something special planned tonight."

I eyed him suspiciously. "Okay."

"But before we go, I need to give you some bad news." I opened my mouth to speak, but he interrupted me. "And then afterward, I want you to forget it. It means nothing. It was just a coincidence."

I swallowed and waited for him to continue.

"The woman they found last night. She was the mother of one of the boys who attacked you."

My knees went weak, and I sat down on the nearest chair. "Why didn't the police say anything?"

"I asked them not to. I wanted to be the one to tell you. They had my statement and Mr. Steele's. If they needed more information, they said they'd talk to you after a few days."

I looked up at him. "What does this mean?"

"Nothing. Like I said, a coincidence."

"Who do they think did it?"

He shook his head. "They didn't say, but they know it's the same person who killed that other woman. And she had nothing to do with you. So don't worry."

But the last murder did have something to do with me. Her shoe anyway. I inhaled deeply, trying to remain calm. Christian was right. I needed to forget about this. Shove it as far down as I could.

"You've had a rough time, but tonight I want to give you something else to think about, okay?"

I barely nodded.

"Good." He took my hand and led me outside toward his SUV.

I stopped him halfway. "By the way, why were you late that night you asked me to meet you in the woods?"

He looked down. "I had something very important to do."

"At midnight?"

He looked me in the eyes. "I promise I'll tell you, but not now. Is that all right?"

I guess it didn't matter. I had worse things to stress about. "Don't worry about it. It's not a big deal."

"No, it is. And I promise to tell you when the time is right."

I nodded. "Come on, let's go." I was so ready to think about something else.

We didn't stay in town. Instead, Christian drove up a canyon toward Park City. The light from the setting sun blanketed the valley, changing the autumn leaves into golden ribbons of yellows, reds, and oranges.

"This is amazing. I've never seen anything like it," I said.

"I thought you'd enjoy it. I love coming up here this time of day. It's so peaceful—just what you need."

"Can we pull over?" I had a crazy urge to touch the golden leaves to see if they were real.

He nodded. "That's exactly what we're going to do. There's a pull-off just up ahead."

I was expecting it to be more of a rest stop, but it was exactly as he said. There was barely enough room for his car to park alongside the shoulder. When I stepped out of the car, I practically tripped over a concrete barrier. On the other side, the ground dropped off sharply and at the bottom was a small creek. It reminded me of my babbling brook.

Christian rounded the car and joined me. "Get on my back. I'll carry you down."

"That's okay. I can make it," I lied as I imagined myself

rolling end-over-end until I belly flopped into the water. Even though I felt better, I didn't feel steep-hill good.

"Whatever. Get on my back." He turned around.

Reluctantly, I put my arms around his neck and jumped up; my legs wrapped around his waist. He groaned.

"Am I hurting you?" I cried. I tried to get off, but he clung to my legs, laughing.

"I'm just kidding. I can barely feel you."

I stared down the steep incline. "You sure you can do this?"

"Have you ever seen *The Man from Snowy River*?"

"No."

"Huh. Well, this is going to seem a lot less impressive then. Hang on!" He leapt over the concrete barrier and practically ran down. With every step his foot slid, and I thought for sure we were going to eat it, but somehow he maintained his balance. I placed my chin on his shoulder to keep my head from bouncing all over. My cheeks flushed when I felt the heat from his neck warm my skin. Before I knew it, we were at the bottom. He let go of my legs, dropping me to the ground.

"You're like a freaking Sherpa," I said and grinned.

He laughed. "Come on. I want to show you something."

I followed behind him alongside the creek. The further upstream we walked, the brighter the light became and the more magnificent the colors. After a short distance he stopped at a rock wall where a miniature waterfall spilled from a rocky ledge, spraying the trees around it. The sun on the wet leaves transformed them into thousands of jewels: rubies, topaz, and garnets. The only word I could come up with to describe the luminescent trees was "celestial." I stared, mouth open.

"It's amazing, isn't it?" Christian whispered.

I simply nodded.

And then something strange happened.

Light jumped inside me, giving me a huge adrenalin rush.

It seemed to push away the anxiety still lingering from the previous night. I gasped for air and staggered to the side. Christian caught me.

"What's wrong?" he asked.

"I, I don't know," I stuttered. My insides vibrated like a tuning fork. I took several deep breaths until, very slowly, I felt Light retreat back to wherever it went when the moon was small.

"Do you need to sit down?"

I shook my head. "I think I'm okay now. That was weird."

"Maybe I shouldn't have brought you here," Christian mumbled.

"What? No. I'm so glad you did." I turned to him. "Thank you."

He smiled and reached for my hat. Instinctively, I moved away.

"Do you mind?"

I didn't say yes or no, but I didn't move away either. Christian took off my beanie and ran his fingers through my hair.

"I don't know why you cover this up. It's so beautiful."

I looked down. "How much longer do you think the trees will look like this?"

"Turn around."

I turned back around. The sun had already shifted positions; its light no longer transformed the leaves.

"It's only like this for a few minutes," he said.

"Thank you for showing it to me. It was awesome."

"You act like this is the end of our date."

"Isn't it?"

He shook his head. "Not quite. Hop on. We've got a long drive ahead of us."

Back at the car, Christian stopped me just as I was about to get into the passenger seat. "There's one rule. You have to wear this." From behind his back he produced a black bandana.

"What? Why?"

"It's a surprise. I don't want you to see where we're going."

"Can't I just keep my eyes closed?"

"No, you'll be tempted to peek. Now turn around so I can put this on you."

I eyed him suspiciously, but then smiled and did what he asked. He tied the bandana around my eyes and helped me into the car. After I heard the driver's-side door close, I expected to hear the sound of the cars engine, but after a minute of silence, I finally said, "Christian? What are you doing?"

"Right. Sorry. I just can't get over how beautiful you are."

I laughed, remembering the last time a guy had said something about my looks. "Whatever. Let's go."

"I'm serious."

"Uh-huh. I know I look like the bride of Frankenstein or something. You don't have to say things like that."

"What are you talking about? Your exotic look only makes you that much more beautiful." I felt his hand move across my knee and give it a gentle squeeze.

I grew quiet. "Can we just go?" I was not prepared for this. I thought this was going to be a "friend" date, but the way he was acting, maybe this was more? Dare I hope?

He waited a second before finally starting the car. We drove in silence, and I hoped that I hadn't made him mad, but not long after, he began to whistle and took hold of my hand. His warm palm felt good since mine was inexplicably cold. I slid over next to him and rested my head on his shoulder.

A short time later Christian turned onto what felt like a dirt road. I could tell by the way we bounced around as if we were riding in a horse-drawn carriage. "Where are we?" I asked.

"In the mountains. It's not far now."

Several minutes later he stopped the car. "We'll have to hike the rest of the way."

I cringed. "How far?"

"Not far. Don't worry. I'll help you if you need it."

I know he said he'd help me, but he probably wasn't counting on me being so clumsy. He practically had to carry me the entire way as I kept tripping over the smallest things. Without my eyesight, I was ten times worse. I wished it was a full moon, or even a half moon. He probably thought I was the weakest girl he'd ever met.

Christian stopped and let go of me. A moment later I heard a zipping sound. "Duck your head and step up," he told me.

"I'll try." I did what he said, but still tripped and fell onto canvas-like material.

"You can take the blindfold off now," Christian said.

I ripped off the bandana and about fainted when I saw what he'd done.

Fourteen

We were inside a tent that looked like it was meant for eight people. It had been filled with pillows on one side and on the opposite end was a big screen TV. A pizza box and a six pack of root beer lay in the middle.

"This is awesome. How did you get electricity out here?" I asked.

He flashed me a you'll-never-know smile. "Hungry?"

"Starving."

"Help yourself. I'll start the movie."

I moved to the other side of the tent, still in shock that he was able to pull something like this off. But I was also incredibly flattered. No one had ever done anything this thoughtful for me before.

After we ate, we propped ourselves up with pillows behind our backs. He continued to hold my hand, even caressing it sometimes. I tried to pay attention to the movie, which was one of my favorites, but I couldn't stop thinking about Christian and all the effort he had put into our "date." I kept glancing over at him, and I noticed he was doing the same back.

Finally I couldn't stand it anymore. Before I could reason my next move, I sat up and stared directly in his eyes. And then, as if he were thinking the same thing, we moved together, our lips ready.

I'd love to say we shared a passionate kiss, a kiss to end all other kisses, but as far as first kisses go, this one was a complete dud. Two fishes bumping into each other would've had more passion. It's not that I wasn't attracted to him and hopefully vice versa; it's just that when our lips met, Christian suddenly froze. His lips stayed unnaturally still for a few seconds until he finally moved away. I stared at him, lips still puckered.

"I'm sorry. I shouldn't have—I don't know what I was thinking." He dropped his head into his hands.

I glanced to my left, hoping someone would be offstage. Line? But no one was around to tell me what to say during such an awkward moment.

Eventually he looked up at me. "I like you. Really I do, but I can't get serious."

"It was just a kiss. I didn't know we were getting serious."

"That's what kisses lead to."

"Wow, okay. So just to clarify, since we were about to get serious and all, you can't get serious with anyone or just me?"

His eyes grew big like a deer in headlights. "Anyone of course. I can't let anything distract me from college, you know. And sports. I have to do good in sports. A girlfriend would really complicate that." He continued to rattle on for several minutes, one excuse after another. Half of them didn't even make sense. I finally stopped him.

"Look, I get it. You don't want a girlfriend. Fine. No big deal."

"Really?"

I shrugged. "We can continue to be friends, but only on one condition."

"Name it."

"No more of this." I waved my arms around. "No more holding my hand, hugging me, or even touching me. You're sending all the wrong signals for someone who doesn't want a girlfriend."

He hesitated and then glanced around as if seeing it for the first time. "You're right. I never realized what I was doing. It just felt right."

If it feels right then why do you want to stop? I said to myself.

"Will you forgive me?" he asked.

I sighed and forced a smile. "What are friends for?"

"You are such an amazing girl."

Hooray for me. Bloody fantastic. Let's hear it for the girl. This sucks. "I know the movie's not over yet, but do you mind taking me home? I'm kind of tired."

His eyes grew big again. His stupid, perfect blue eyes. I couldn't stand to look at them any longer.

"I made you mad, didn't I?"

"No, I really am tired, and it just feels weird being out here so secluded."

He smiled.

"What?"

"We're not that secluded. Look." He unzipped the tent and helped me out. Not more than fifty feet away was a huge cabin. And not far from it were several other cabins, most of which had lights on.

I turned to him. "You mean we've been this close to civilization the whole time?"

He nodded.

"And here I thought you were a magician."

"I'm really disappointing you tonight, aren't I?" His smile disappeared.

"No big deal. I'm used to it." I forced a smile so he'd think I was kidding, but as soon as I turned around, my smile was replaced by utter disappointment, masked by the cover of darkness. At least Christian had achieved his goal. He'd said he wanted to give me something else to think about.

"Ready to go?" he asked.

"Yup."

I didn't cry that night even though I wanted to. So he had rejected me as a girlfriend, whoopty-stinkin'-doo. I still had him as a friend and that should be enough. Then why did I feel so crappy? I flopped into bed, clothes and all.

When morning came, I felt better—invigorated actually. And not because the moon was stronger, but because I knew exactly what I was going to do.

I quickly showered and dressed in one of my new outfits; one that was much brighter and tighter than the clothes I normally wore. I left my hair down and styled it. No hat today. I even upped the makeup. When I looked in the mirror, I almost jumped at the girl before me. I looked . . . dare I say it? Normal.

I couldn't wait to get to school and show Christian my new look. Oh, I know what I was doing was so 90210, but I wanted Christian to realize what he was missing.

I waited until I heard Jake leave for work before I left my room. Gratefully, Heidi had picked him up for work so I could borrow his car. I grabbed a granola bar in the kitchen and then headed to the garage for Jake's Toyota.

I arrived at school several minutes early and parked in the back next to a storage shed. I hid in my car until I saw Christian's SUV. When he got out, my heart began to ache. His sandy blond hair looked messy; uneven bangs flopped to the side of his face. He was dressed nicer than usual in tan slacks and a black shirt. Must be a game tonight. He walked toward the school with a confidence I rarely saw in other boys.

I sighed and leaned my forehead against the cool glass. Why couldn't he like me? I let my pity party last only a minute before I straightened up, inhaled deeply, and glanced in the mirror one more time. The mini-me devil appeared on my shoulder. "You are smoking hot," it said, and blew me a kiss. The tag-along angel appeared on the opposite shoulder, frowning. "I don't even know who you are."

"Are you blind?" the devil sneered. "This is what she was meant to look like."

The angel shook its head. "No, it's too hard. It takes away Light's innocence."

"Who cares about Light? Isn't she allowed any 'me' time?"

"Be careful with your definition of 'me' time. This isn't me time; this is her trying to get even."

"You're so lame," the devil said.

"That's enough," I finally cried. "I'm going in."

I quickly opened the car door and jumped out. Who invented a conscience anyway?

When I walked into the school, I kept my eyes forward and moved straight toward Christian's locker. I was vaguely aware of people staring and whispering in my direction. I even managed an occasional whistle, but I blocked it all, afraid any disruption in my concentration would cause me to chicken out.

I turned the corner, my strides long and confident. In the back of my mind the *Rocky III* theme began to play: "Rising up, back on the street, Did my time, took my chances . . ." I felt like I was on my way to save the world. This was for all the girls who'd been rejected. Vengeance was mine!

"Llona?"

I came to a screeching halt at the sound of Christian's voice. I took a deep breath and turned to face Christian who had somehow managed to get behind me.

"Hello, Christian," I said and flashed the most brilliant smile I could come up with.

He stared at me with a strange expression—not the expression I'd been expecting. It was several seconds before he said, "You look incredible."

I tried not to grin. "Thanks."

"But why the sudden change?" He tilted his head and looked at me as if a scientist studying a bug.

"I just felt like shedding my cocoon."

He shook his head. "Not buying it, not you." Then his eyebrows raised, and I wouldn't have been surprised to hear him say "Eureka!", but instead, he said, "You're getting back at me, aren't you?"

I heard the countdown of a bomb in my head. "What? No way."

Three.

Two.

I looked around frantically for an escape route.

"Llona, I'm so sorry. I thought you said everything was cool. I didn't mean to hurt you."

One.

The bomb exploded. "You didn't hurt me. I got to go." I turned around and hurried off before he could stop me. He called after me several times, but I ducked into the nearest bathroom, which of course happened to be the men's room. One boy, a freshman who was relieving himself into a filthy urinal, shrieked like a girl while two other boys with dilated pupils whistled. I managed to squeak out a "sorry" before I speedily exited.

Once I was safely inside the girl's bathroom and behind a locked stall, I slumped upon the toilet, head in hands. What a morning. I went from bad to stupidly worse. I should've known Christian would see right through my scheme. Argh!

"What are you doing?" a voice from above asked.

I looked up. Peering over the bathroom stall was May. She was grinning from ear to ear.

"Just having a bad morning," I grumbled.

"I noticed. But at least you look hot."

I rolled my eyes.

"You really do look good, but this isn't you. Has your body been invaded by an alien?"

"I wish. You think that's what I can tell people?"

"I know a few who would believe you. Serious, why the sudden change?"

I shrugged. "Thought I'd try something new. I know. It was a stupid idea."

I heard May step off the toilet next to me. "You want to come out?" she asked.

I sighed and unlocked the door.

"It wasn't stupid. You really do look amazing. Your hair makes your eyes look white. No, not white. More like the color of water in a white sink. There's a hint of blue."

"So you're saying I look like a watery ghost?"

"Not at all."

"Whatever. I'm going home at lunch to get out of this drag. I'll catch up with you later."

I headed straight to first hour, head down, and dropped into a desk at the back of the room. I hoped to go unnoticed, but a boy whom I'd never talked to, leaned over and asked me, "Are you new?"

I stared at him. Really?

A girl sitting in front of me turned around. "She's not new. That's Llona. She just looks different."

"Llona?" he said. "Oh! You're on the girl's basketball team, right?"

I nodded. "That's me."

"Huh. I didn't recognize you with your hair down."

I kept waiting for him to turn around, but he continued to stare.

"Anything else?" I asked.

He blinked. "What? No."

When he finally faced forward, I slumped my head into my hands. How in the world did my mother do this? I hated the attention.

The rest of the morning was much of the same with me causing a commotion. It wouldn't have been a big deal if I could've embraced my new look instead of being such a spaz about it, but I didn't know how to act. I felt like an ant in a beehive.

By the time the lunch bell rang, I was more than ready to go home. I headed straight for my car, clenching my keys tightly. I was vaguely aware of someone approaching me from the right. Keep moving, I told myself. I didn't want anything or anyone stopping me from changing out of my 90210 outfit. I was through with drama.

"Wait up, Llona," a male voice called.

I kept walking but glanced over. Mike caught up to me.

"What do you want?" I snapped.

Neither of us had spoken to each other since the encounter at Johny's, and I was just fine with never speaking to him ever again. I kept walking.

"I never had a chance to apologize for what I said to you."

I grunted. He was as transparent as a jelly fish.

"I mean it. I was very rude."

When I reached my car, I turned to face him. "What do you want, Mike?"

He folded his arms to his chest, forcing his biceps up. "I want to make it up to you. Can I take you to dinner tonight?"

"Just because I look different doesn't mean my personality has changed." I put the key into the lock.

He smiled. "I don't care about your personality. You're hot."

"Well, I do. We will never hang out for any reason, do you understand?"

His arms dropped to his side, and his large beefy hands balled up. "Any girl here would die to date me."

"Then go find them and leave me alone." I opened my door, but he shoved it closed, whirled me around, and pressed himself against me. Immediately, I brought my knee up hard enough to make him childless for life. He doubled over and stumbled to the ground.

"Is there a problem?" Christian called. He was jogging toward us.

"Not anymore." I opened the car door again and hopped in. Christian knocked on my window just as I brought the car's engine to life. Reluctantly, I rolled it down.

"What happened?" he said.

"Go ask weenis over there." I nodded my head toward Mike who had managed to get back on his feet and was hobbling across the parking lot.

"Did he hurt you?"

"Do I look like I'm the one who's hurt?"

Christian leaned his head against the top of my car and closed his eyes. I felt like reaching up and touching his face. He doesn't like you, I reminded myself. I remained face forward.

He took a deep breath before he said, "Llona, I really am sorry. It was mean of me to lead you on like that. I guess I let myself get caught up in the excitement and didn't stop to think what it could mean for the future."

"Not to be rude," I interrupted, "But I need to go."

"You really do look beautiful, but I thought that before the dramatic change." He moved away from the car.

I wanted to speed off in blaze of glory, but I didn't. I was done playing games. I turned to Christian. "Thanks. And don't worry about anything. We're friends. I'm just being insecure."

"You don't need to be."

I shrugged. "See you later, okay?"

"Um," Christian paused. He looked back toward the school and then back to me. "You mind if I come with you?"

"Yes."

He nodded. "Right. See you when you get back then."

I drove home, changed into practical clothing, and tied my hair back, but I couldn't bring myself to go back to school. After the way my day had gone, I felt I deserved a break.

I made lunch and then sat on my bed, eating and listening to music. My eyes wandered around the room, looking at nothing particular until I saw a yellow daisy painted onto an old shoebox sitting on a shelf in my closet. It had been months since I'd looked at it.

I pulled it off the shelf and set it on my bed. Everything I had left of my mother was in it and in a way it made me sad. She'd had such a huge personality, so to have her whole life confined to an old shoebox was depressing.

I took off the lid and thumbed through several pictures and letters my mother had written to my father. There was only one letter written to me. Very carefully, I unfolded it and remembered the day I'd found it.

It was the day of my mother's funeral. I remembered it clearly because it was the first letter I had ever received. I discovered it resting in the arms of my stuffed teddy bear, which usually sat at the foot of my bed, but that day the bear had oddly been sitting on top of my pillow. The over-stuffed animal normally held a red heart pillow in its paws, but the heart was gone and in its place was the letter. I never stopped to think about the missing heart; I only wanted to know what the letter said.

Secretly, I hoped the envelope was left by my mother. Maybe she knew she was going to die and had written me a farewell note, but even as I tore into the perfectly sealed envelope, I knew my hopes were in vain. My mother never thought of the future. She lived every day to the fullest, enjoying life as if it were a rollercoaster—except her ride never came down. But it had come down—crashing down—destroying herself and all those around her.

As I read the words, a new (foolish) hope entered my head. The fancy calligraphy words read:

Little one,
You are so lovely, despite your fitful sleep as if the weight of the world is on your shoulders. But all this is about to change. I wish I could take you now, but you are too young and the time is not yet ripe. But I promise, I will come back and you will fear no longer!
Forever,
Your Angel

At first I thought the letter was from my mother who loved anything dramatic. I'd convinced myself that this was just the sort of thing she'd do: fake her own death only to follow it up with the biggest surprise she could ever give. I tried to logically, as logical as my little brain could reason, think of a way my mother could still be alive despite the fact I'd seen her dead body only hours before. Perhaps it was her evil identical twin we'd buried. Or maybe my mother had pretended to be dead in the polished, wood casket and the strange way her head looked as if it had been pieced together had only been a really good makeup job. My mother did have the most interesting friends. They could've fixed anything with makeup.

But even the best Hollywood makeup job couldn't have fooled my father. No, my mother had died, and no matter how many fantastic stories I came up with, none of them seriously convinced me that she had survived.

So if my mother hadn't written the letter, then who? I never once thought it could be my father. It just didn't make sense. He was still alive and taking care of me. There was no reason for him to say he would come for me when he already had me.

I never showed him the letter. He had enough to worry about, but as I grew older, I wondered if that had been a mistake. Regardless, it was too late now. My father was dead too, no doubt spending an eternity with my mother in some heavenly tropical paradise.

When my father died, I had pulled out the letter again and read it several more times, even though I already had it memorized. I then slipped it into my wallet where it remained up until a few months ago. It had become so worn that I wasn't able to read a few of the faded words. Afraid it would get damaged even more, I'd returned the letter to the shoebox with the rest of my mother's things. It was one of my most cherished belongings as it gave me hope. For I knew one day someone was going to come for me, and I'd never be frightened again.

FIFTEEN

MAY FOUND ME EATING LUNCH WITH MATT AND TRACEY IN the cafeteria. "Tonight a bunch of us are going to a corn maze. Do you guys want to go?" she asked.

"What's a corn maze?" I still wasn't accustomed to "western" talk and activities. Like when I'd first moved here last winter, everyone kept talking about how well they could "spin dough-nuts" in the parking lot. I had the funniest image in my mind of what they were doing until I learned that spinning doughnuts was the same as spinning cookies on ice with your car.

"A corn maze is just what it says it is. Some guy has taken a tractor to a corn field and made a maze. People go through it," May explained.

"Really? Sounds kind of fun." I finished the last of my milk.

"It does sound interesting," Matt said.

"Isn't this beneath you, Matt?" Tracey asked.

May and I stifled a laugh.

Matt narrowed his eyes. "No."

"Good. We're meeting there at eight. It's the one in Centerville."

"I know where it's at," Tracey said. "Do you want me to pick you up, Llona?"

"Why don't you pick us all up?" May suggested. "That way we can go together."

"I'll actually drive separately. I live a ways out, but I'll meet you there," Matt told us.

A few minutes after eight, we pulled up next to Matt's car. He jumped out to join us.

"Anyone else coming?" I asked May.

"Um, Adam, Christian, and whoever else they invited," she said, averting her eyes.

"Oh." I thought it strange Christian hadn't said anything.

We walked toward the entrance and as soon as we rounded the small, wood pay booth, I realized why Christian hadn't said anything. He was standing next to a girl I didn't recognize, but was later introduced as Haley. Adam stood on the other side of him with a date of his own.

"How's it going, guys?" May asked. She looked over at me nervously.

They all began to talk and laugh, about what I couldn't be sure. My main goal was to appear like nothing was wrong. I could feel my beauty queen perma-grin as if it were painted on my face and every once in awhile I felt my head nod. I avoided looking at Christian as much as possible. As long as I did that, I could possibly endure the rest of the night.

I had no right to be upset. Christian had been very clear about not wanting anything serious. My subconscious heard someone say, "Should we do this in teams?"

I snapped back to the conversation. "Teams are a great idea. Let's do boys against girls," I told the group. This would be easier if I didn't have to see Christian with Haley the whole night.

May agreed. "Good idea, seeing how we're not evenly numbered."

I still had yet to look at Christian, even though I could feel his eyes burrowing into me.

Tracey began to hand out blue cards. "First team to get their card stamped at all stations wins. Meet back here when you're done."

I looked down at my card, trying to figure out exactly what it was we had to do. Apparently, we had to find our way through the maze to various stations like "Demons Alley" and "Witches Way." With it being a full moon and me feeling as great as I did, this should be a breeze. Already, if I concentrated hard enough, I could sense the first station, as I could hear kids talking at it.

"You ready, ladies?" I asked.

The two girls who were with Adam and Christian looked at each other hesitantly. "You're not going to let them beat us, are you?" I asked.

They shook their heads and smirked at the boys. "No way."

"I didn't think so. Let's go," I said.

We were each handed a flashlight and, after parting ways with the boys, who spoke very confidently about their abilities, we were off.

The cornstalks towered well over our heads, and the second we entered the maze we realized how important our flashlights were going to be. It was very dark, despite the full moon. The tall cornstalks cast shadows in every direction.

I turned to the girls the moment we entered the maze. "How do you guys feel about running? I think we can win if we do, just follow me."

"How do you know where you're going?" Tracey asked.

"Let's just say I have a sixth sense about mazes."

"Lead the way," May said.

I quickly took off to the left in a fast jog, and made sure I adjusted my pace when I felt the girls fall behind. We took a few lefts, a couple of rights, and in a matter of minutes we were already at the first station.

"You weren't kidding about mazes, were you?" Haley asked, out of breath.

I shrugged. "Ready for the next one?"

They all halfheartedly agreed. I took off again and in less than ten minutes we had four more stamps.

"How about we walk to the next one?" Tracey suggested, panting heavily.

Though I would've loved to run, I agreed. From the back of the group, I heard May call, "Hey, Llona. Wait up! My flashlight isn't working."

"You guys go ahead. Take your next two rights."

I walked back to where May was standing. She was shaking her flashlight.

"It just stopped working," she said. "Stupid plastic piece of crap."

"Let me see it for a sec," I said.

She handed me the flashlight, and I pretended to examine it while I secretly transferred my Light into it. After a few seconds it lit up as if the batteries were brand new.

"What did you do?" May asked, surprised.

"My secret touch." I grinned.

We continued to walk. Up ahead I could hear the other girls laughing. Occasionally I'd shout out an order for them to turn a certain way.

"So what's up with those girls Adam and Christian brought? Do you think they're serious?" she asked.

"I doubt it. I've never seen them hang out before."

"That's because they don't go to our school. They go to a school in Layton."

"How do you know?" I said.

"I asked one of them when we first starting playing."

"I'm sure they're just friends." I couldn't bear to think of them as more than that.

"May!" I heard Tracey's voice call. "Come up here. Haley thinks she knows your cousin."

"I'll be right back," May said.

As she jogged off, I called, "Tell them to take the next left, and then the next two rights."

"You got it."

As soon as May disappeared around a bend, I turned off my flashlight and let the light of the moon guide me. There was something calming about walking by myself in the dark, especially under a full moon. It made me feel more connected to nature than any other time, and I hadn't realized until now, that I hadn't done it in months. Mostly because I'd promised Christian I would stay indoors at night.

All of a sudden, I became aware of movement from within the cornstalks. A dog? I stopped and strained my ears. No. Definitely human footsteps.

I was about to quicken my pace when without warning my head began to spin, not like I was dizzy, but like I was falling asleep after a long day of swimming. My eyelids became heavy, but my body still moved forward—and I was walking in the wrong direction.

Echoing, as if far away, I heard May call my name. I wanted to stop and call out to her, but I felt like I'd been hypnotized. I shuffled forward toward an unknown destination, no longer in control of my limbs.

Abruptly, my body turned sharply into the cornfield. The cool stalks brushed my face and arms, but I didn't bother pushing them away. I just continued to follow . . . follow what? What was I doing and where was I going? Wherever I was headed, the pull became stronger, stopping my ability to think clearly. And then everything went black.

It took me a moment to realize where I was. I was still in the cornfield, but was now standing directly inside a clearing no more than ten feet in diameter. There were no paths leading to it, and I wasn't sure how I'd gotten there. In the distance, I could still hear May calling for me. I was about to call out when my eyes focused on the only other object within the circle.

I stared at it for what seemed like an eternity, trying to determine exactly what was lying in a crumpled heap at my feet. Hands shaking, I turned on my flashlight and screamed.

Sixteen

I COULDN'T STOP THE SCREAMS THAT TORE FROM MY LUNGS. They just kept coming in great waves of pure horror and absolute fear. Never before had I seen anything so cruel and sadistic.

My screams finally stopped when May swung me around. "Llona! What's wrong?" she cried.

I still couldn't believe what I'd seen and had to look one more time. Very slowly I turned around and shined the light. Lying in a pool of blood was a dead, white dog. Its throat had been slit, and carved into its side was my name written in blood.

"Who would do this?" May gasped. "It's horrible!"

"Llona!" Christian's voice called. I clearly detected a hint of panic. He was nearby and moving fast.

I grabbed May by the arms. "Please! I don't want him to see this." I don't know why I was begging her to do something about the dead dog. I just knew she could.

"Please, May," I begged again.

Her eyes flashed to the dog and then back to me. I could see the conflict in her eyes.

Finally, when I heard footsteps rushing though the stalks toward us, May lifted her hand and with the flick of her wrist, the dog caught on fire, completely erasing my name.

Christian burst into the clearing. "Are you okay?" He

looked at me and then at the fire, which looked like it was burning nothing more than a pile of rags.

"What happened?" he asked.

"A stupid prank," May answered for me. "Llona saw the fire through the corn and came to inspect it."

Christian turned to me. "Why were you screaming?"

I crossed my arms to my chest to stop them from shaking. I didn't want to lie to him, but I couldn't tell him the truth either. He seemed to have this obsessive need to protect me. I wanted him to want to be with me, and not because he thought I needed him.

"She fell," May blurted. I looked at her gratefully.

Christian was about to say something more, but the others joined us.

"What is that?" Tracey asked. She circled the now dying fire.

"Someone started a fire," May answered.

Matt walked over to me. "Why were you screaming?"

"Someone scared me," I whispered as if I were alone.

"I thought you fell," Christian said, his eyes narrowing.

"I scared her and she fell," May corrected.

I have to get out of here, I thought. I wasn't thinking clearly and was going to end up saying something I'd regret.

"So who won?" I said, changing the subject.

Adam pulled out his card. "We've got nine stamps. How many do you guys have?"

"We've got eleven," Tracey cheered.

Christian stared at me. "Let me see your card, Llona."

Without thinking (of course) I moved to give it to him, but my hand shook so badly the card dropped to the ground.

"I'm taking you home," Christian said. He reached to take my arm, but I stepped away.

"No. I'm fine. You guys owe us a dinner." I tried to make

my voice sound as steady as possible, but it still cracked.

"Don't try and get out of this, Christian," May said, elbowing him. "Let's go. I'm starving." May turned into the cornstalks, and I quickly followed. Everyone else followed too, except for Christian. I wondered what was taking him so long. When he finally appeared, he looked angry.

"Can I ride with you, Matt?" I asked Matt suddenly.

"Sure. Where we going?"

"Let's go to that new restaurant on fifth," Tracey said. "I hear it's really good."

"Cool. We'll meet you there," Adam agreed. "Let's go, Chris."

I hurried and jumped into Matt's car before Christian could say anything. Only when Matt started driving away did I see Christian get in the car with Adam and the other girls. Because I was still shaken up over what happened, I knew I didn't want to continue the night socializing or be around a now angry Christian. So on the way to the restaurant I asked Matt to take me home.

"What's wrong?" he asked.

"It's not a big deal. I just don't feel very good."

"You mean you don't feel like socializing," he said.

I shrugged. "Maybe."

He looked over at me. "You were the one that told me I need to socialize more, remember?"

I smiled.

"But I know how it is," he continued. "It's nice to have a break every once in awhile. I'll take you home."

"Thanks, Matt."

After a few moments of silence, he asked. "So what's the deal with you and Christian?"

"What do you mean?"

"He always gets weird around you. Not like he's madly in

love or anything"—my heart sank— "but he acts like he's your dad or big brother, know what I mean?"

"Yeah," I mumbled. I know what you mean.

"He shouldn't be. From what I've seen, you're the toughest girl I know."

I stared at him. "Thank you. That means a lot."

"Well, it's true."

"I don't know about that, but it's nice to hear."

Matt pulled into my driveway. "Do you want me to come in?"

"That's okay. My uncle's here."

"I'll see you on Monday then." I jumped out of the car and waved good-bye, wondering why I couldn't like him.

As soon as Matt's car was out of view, fear reclaimed me. I dashed inside, my eyes scanning the darkness as if it were a cobra ready to strike.

"You're back early," Jake said, surprising me. I expected him and Heidi to be gone somewhere as they rarely hung out here, but there was Heidi sitting next to him with a big smile. It quickly disappeared the moment she saw my face.

Jake must've noticed too. "What's wrong?" he asked. He stood up and walked over to me.

"Huh? Nothing. Why?" I darted into the kitchen and pretended to be looking for something to eat.

"You look scared."

With my head in the fridge, I made my face as calm as possible. I turned around. "I'm fine. We had a lot of fun. Those corn mazes are really cool. Have you ever been, Heidi?"

Heidi and Jake began to reminisce together about their childhood, and I could tell it wasn't going to be a short conversation. The two were so obviously in love, it made me sick. One of them could've said they had rabies and the other would've thought that was the most adorable thing in the world.

With the two distracted by the sparkles in each others eyes,

I easily snuck back to my bedroom and shut the door. Finally I could think without having to put on a "brave" face. What I'd seen tonight had been terrifying. Who could have done it and why, were the only questions that raced through my mind. I was so consumed with the question that I didn't even notice Light's energy. My worry and fright were enough to expel it.

Faster than any brain should work, images of everyone I knew flashed through my mind as potential suspects. I started with those who were there that night. I'd been alone much of the night, either ahead of the group or toward the end, walking behind with May. I crossed off the girls from my list first. I just couldn't see a girl slitting a dog's throat and then carving my name into it. I also didn't think they would've had enough time to get it done and then still be able to find us in the maze.

That left the boys. There was just Adam, Christian, and Matt. No matter how hard I tried, I couldn't see any of them doing something so horrible. Besides, what would be their motive? I thought of other people I knew. There were several others I could think of that didn't like me, but enough to do something like this?

I sat up in bed. There was one person I thought could be ruthless enough and definitely would feel I deserved it: Mike. The more I thought about him, the more I convinced myself that it was him. He could've easily found out where we were going from Adam and then planned the whole thing ahead of time.

My suspicions made sense except for one thing: the strange feeling that had came over me and led me to the dog. Maybe I'd sensed the dead animal. I still wasn't sure how Light worked exactly and maybe because it was a full moon, I was more sensitive to death. I liked this theory best as it was much easier to accept than what the back of my mind kept trying to tell me.

I shook my head, dismissing the ugly thought again. It just wasn't possible. A Vyken wouldn't mess with me like that. He would just kill me and be done with it. That's what I convinced myself, but the truth was I didn't know what a Vyken would do. My mother and father never told me, and if my aunt said anything, I hadn't been listening.

I made a mental note to call my aunt and ask her about it later. I dreaded the call, but better to be safe than sorry.

I stayed home from school the next couple of days, partly because of what had happened, but also because the moon had disappeared again.

I was in bed when Jake knocked on my door that night. "Llona? You still awake?"

I mumbled something incoherent.

"May's here to see you. Should I send her back?"

"What time is it?"

"Ten."

I sat up and turned the light on. "Send her back. Thanks, Jake." My room was a mess and I looked like a train wreck, but I was so tired that I didn't care. I tried to smooth my hair back with little success.

"Hey, Llona. How's it going?" May asked as she moved into my room.

"Fine. It's just been one of those weeks."

She nodded as if she understood. She cleared off my desk chair.

"Sorry about the mess," I said.

She sat down and for the first time I noticed how uncomfortable she looked.

"Is something wrong?" I asked.

May bit her bottom lip and looked away. "I was wondering if we could talk."

"Sure." I lay back down and prepared to listen to guy trouble. "What do you want to talk about?"

She looked at me. "About what happened. In the corn maze."

I wasn't expecting this. I thought for sure we could just pretend like nothing had happened. "What do you mean?" I thought playing dumb was my best option.

May scowled. "Come on. You saw what I did."

I sat up. "We don't have to talk about it."

"But I want to. I have no one else, and for some reason I trust you. Probably because I know you're different too."

I looked away.

"Can we please just be honest with each other?"

I sighed. "Listen, May, I don't care what you can do. So you're different. We're different, but I think it's better if we don't talk about it."

"Why?"

"To keep us safe."

"But what about what happened out there? Someone's messing with you, and I think it's because of what you can do."

"You think someone's messing with me because I can't cut my hair?"

May laughed, halfheartedly. "Do you really think I'm that dumb? There's a lot more to you than just invincible hair."

"I don't know what you mean."

She let out an exaggerated sigh. "Really? So you're saying you can't manipulate light?"

I stared at her. "What makes you think that?"

"I wasn't sure at first." She leaned back. "I mean I definitely had my suspicions. Lights do crazy things when you're around, like the blackout at the school assembly and the way you acted afterward. There were other signs too, but after the corn maze I knew for sure."

"What happened at the corn maze?"

"I took the batteries out of the flashlight, yet you still made it work."

"Maybe you thought you took them out."

"We're both different, Llona, and the sooner you admit it, the sooner I can feel a whole lot better about myself."

"How's that?"

"My whole life I've felt out of place. And because of my freakiness, I've never allowed myself to get close to anyone. I was afraid they'd see what a psycho I was, but now that we're friends, I finally feel like I'm not so different. Because if there's you and me, then there's got to be others too."

"When did you first find out about your ability?"

May looked down. "A few years ago. It was really scary at first because I couldn't control it. Little fires would appear out of nowhere. I could just be looking at a wall and all of a sudden it would burst into flames. For the longest time I didn't believe it was me doing it."

"What did your mom say?"

"She thought I was a pyromaniac. For almost a year she had me going to a shrink. It was horrible. Finally, I was able to get it under control, mostly anyway, and just in time too. She almost sent me to an institution."

"Where does it come from?"

She shrugged. "I have no idea and I have no one to ask. I almost wonder if it came from my real parents, but I have no way of finding them to ask. Maybe when I'm older . . ." her voice trailed off.

"I'm really sorry. I can't imagine not knowing where it came from. What a trip."

"So what about you?"

I swallowed hard. I couldn't believe I was about to tell someone my secret. "I know this is going to sound crazy—"

"Highly unlikely."

"—but I can only explain it by starting with a story because that's how it was told to me." I tried to think of a way to tell my tale without it sounding weirder than it was.

"Apparently, thousands of years ago, Light used to be an actual personage, sort of like us. The world was a good place then. There was no evil and everyone was happy. But then some Prince killed his brother and the forbidden darkness entered his heart, changing him. He spread his dark poison to others and soon they were hunting Light. They became known as Vykens. To protect themselves, Light hid within the female DNA. We call ourselves Auras. As for the freaky hair, I think it's just a weird side effect or something."

May's eyes were big. "What about the Vykens?"

"They're still out there somewhere. The real crappy part of it is they've figured out that if they drink the blood of an Aura then they are no longer confined to the night."

"Wait a minute. So Vykens are like vampires?"

"No vampires are like Vykens. The myth came from them."

"Can they do the same things as vampires?" she asked.

I shrugged. "I know they're strong, and incredibly fast, but they don't drink just anyone's blood. I guess they could, but it would be pointless. Only an Aura's blood gives them power."

"Don't they need blood to survive?"

I shook my head. "From what I understand, they don't even need to eat."

"So they're like a demon in a human shell," May whispered.

We both shivered.

May shook her hands as if to rid herself of the blanket of creepiness that had just spread across the room. "Okay, I am totally freaked out now."

"So you believe me?"

"Of course. I wish I knew were my ability came from. I'm probably possessed or something."

I laughed.

"I guess that explains why you isolate yourself so much."

May stood up and sat down next to me. "This may be too personal, but can I ask how your mother died? Was it a Vyken?"

I nodded.

"What about your father?"

"After my mother died, he became obsessed with trying to find who killed her. He barely ate or slept. One night while he was away, he was hit by a drunk driver and killed." Tears filled my eyes. I'd never spoken of this to anyone. "The thing that really sucked was, the night before he left, I never told him good-bye. I was mad at him for leaving again so I threw a dumb temper tantrum. I've never forgiven myself for being so stupid."

May's arm came around me. "There's no way you could've known."

I wiped at my eyes, suddenly feeling very silly for crying in front of May. "It's not a big deal."

"Stop that. It is a big deal. You don't need to hold everything in all of the time."

I gave her a weak smile. "So my secret's out."

"Mine too."

"You can't tell anyone, May."

"And you can't tell anyone either."

"Deal." I held out my hand.

"Deal."

After shaking hands, May asked, "You coming to school tomorrow?"

"I don't know." I walked to the window and stared up into the sky. "I'm still pretty tired."

"Why do you get like that?"

"It's the moon. When it's gone, I can't feel Light anymore. All my energy is zapped. You don't know how embarrassing it can be to fall asleep in the middle of class."

"Well, I hope you come. I feel better when you're there."

I turned around. "I'll try."

After May left, I felt better than I had in a long time. Not physically but emotionally. I had no idea sharing my secret with someone could feel so good. It even helped take my mind off whoever had killed the dog. That is until I returned to school.

I kept my eyes open for anyone acting strange, especially Mike. I'd convinced myself that it had been him who had tried to scare me, but he was his obnoxious normal self, throwing out insults whenever we crossed paths. He didn't act like he had done anything as sadistic as killing a dog.

Christian, however, was acting strange. I would catch him lurking behind corners and staring at me from a distance. He didn't try talking to me and I didn't try talking to him. I would've been fine with this arrangement if it hadn't have been for all his stalker-like movements. I thought I was exaggerating until both May and Tracey commented on his actions in the lunch room. I tried not to notice until, finally, I didn't. As long as I wasn't looking for him or thinking about him, I was fine. It was as if I'd never liked him to begin with—almost.

SEVENTEEN

I WAS STUDYING MATH IN THE KITCHEN WHILE JAKE WATCHED TV in the living room, when the phone rang. Jake reached to the end table and answered it. By the tone of his voice, it sounded like he was talking to someone from work. His answers were short and formal.

I returned to solving a complex calculus problem, but then I heard Jake say, "Sure, she's right here. One sec."

I looked up, confused.

Jake covered the telephone's receiver and whispered, "It's your aunt. She wants to talk to you."

I suddenly remembered the note I'd written to remind myself to call her. So much for that. Jake handed me the phone.

"Hi, Aunt Sophie. How are you?"

There was a slight pause. "I'm good, Llona. How—"

"It's Lona."

"Huh?" she asked.

"I go by *Lona*." I could tell by the silent seconds ticking by that she didn't aprove of the mispronounciation, but I didn't care.

Finally, Sophie said, "Okay, Lona. How are you?"

I mostly told the truth. "Great. This has been one of my best years. I really like it here."

"That's nice."

"How's Lucent Academy?" I asked.

"We've added more classes that I think you'd really like. Maybe you could join us when you graduate?"

I groaned internally. Not this conversation again. Sophie had been trying to get me to go to her clannish school since I was a freshman. The idea of being in a school with others like me sounded about as fun as walking on hot coals. "Probably not. I want to go to college out here somewhere."

"Oh really? And what do you want to major in?"

"I haven't gotten that far, but I was thinking maybe education; a P.E. teacher or something."

Another pause. "I'm not sure that would be appropriate, Llona."

"And why's that?"

"Because you would be teaching kids to be competitive."

"So?"

"You're teaching kids to be better than others. We are all equal, Llona. Light does not divide."

"You think we're all equal? When is the last time you lived in the real world, Sophie? The only way we are all equal is we are all human. Other than that we are very different. Some of us are lazy, others hard working. Some of us are good at sports, while others of us are really smart. Some are loud, some quiet, some fast, some slow. We are very different, and I want to help kids discover their unique abilities." I took a breath.

"That's very noble of you, but that's not your job."

"Then what is my job?"

I heard a deep sigh on the other end of the phone. "I didn't call to argue, Llona."

"Then why did you call?"

"I want to come see you for Thanksgiving. Jake said I had to ask you."

It was my turn to pause. This is not what I had expected. Sophie had only come to visit me once since my mother's death and that had been when my father died.

"Why?"

"I think we have a lot to talk about. I'm sure you've experienced some strange things since you've moved into your teenage years. I want to help you better understand what's going on."

I wanted to eagerly agree, but I was still mad. "Do you really think that's necessary?"

"Yes, I do."

"Fine then."

"Wonderful. I'll be there in a couple of weeks. I'll see you soon." She hung up, leaving me staring into the receiver.

"What did she say?" Jake asked.

"She's coming for Thanksgiving."

Jake sat up. "You said yes?"

I shrugged.

"Just great. Just what I need," Jake complained.

He was still mumbling under his breath even after I left the room. Apparently, he felt the same way about her as I did. It wasn't that she was deliberately mean or anything; she just had this super ability to make you feel like you couldn't do anything right. She had Light in her too, so you'd think she'd make you feel all warm and fuzzy like my mother, but not her. She used Light to tell the truth exactly how she saw it. She had no desire to try and understand how Light could comfort others. Light was truth and should only be used for that, she'd always said. This is where she and my mother always disagreed.

*   *   *   *   *

It was the day before Thanksgiving. Both Jake and I sat in

153

the living room watching TV, but it was turned down too low to hear. Neither of us noticed because we were too busy watching the clock. In one hour we were supposed to pick up my aunt at the airport.

The last couple of weeks had flown by no matter how hard I tried to slow them down. I dreaded the day of my aunt's arrival more than the time I had to give a speech in front of the school board last year for missing too many school days.

"You ready for this?" Jake asked, breaking the silence.

"About as ready as a cow is before it's branded."

He nodded. "I know the feeling."

"How's Heidi?" I asked.

"I talked to her last night. She's having fun visiting her family."

"So she likes California?"

"Yup."

And then we were silent again. Jake bounced his knee up and down. He stood up.

"I can't just wait here. Let's get something to eat."

"Right behind you."

I was putting my coat on when Jake opened the front door and made a choking sound, almost like a gasp, but more like the sound a chicken might make right before its head is cut off.

"Surprise!" I heard a women's voice say.

I didn't want to do it, but I couldn't help myself. Very slowly I peeked onto our porch. Walking up the stairs, in what looked liked a hundred pounds of flowing material, was my Aunt Sophie.

"I thought we were picking you up at the airport," Jake stuttered.

"You were, but I love to surprise people." She brushed by Jake and moved into the living room.

"Llona! Look how you've grown."

I looked down at myself.

She threw her arms around me. "You are the spitting image of your mother, with your father's nose, of course."

I frowned, unsure if that was a good or bad thing. Very lightly, I returned the hug. She was almost the same as I remembered except older. Her long, wavy brown hair smelled of cinnamon and nutmeg, and her face was still covered in way too much white powder.

Sophie was my mother's older sister by twelve years. There was such an age difference that they had very little in common. Where my mother was sensitive, full of life, and always willing to help others, Sophie tended to be blunt, reserved, and highly suspicious of others to the point where she seemed paranoid.

"It's good to see you, Aunt Sophie," I said.

"Please, call me Sophie." She tossed her bag onto the couch, removed her coat and took a deep breath while looking around the house, her mouth turned down.

Jake closed the door.

"So this is where you've chosen to live?" It wasn't really a question but more of a statement. Her bright red lips tightened to match the lines on her white forehead.

"Llona picked it out," Jake was quick to say.

I glared at him.

"Is that true, Llona?"

I shrugged. "Yeah. I like this place. It's right next to a mountain."

"But with all the money your parents left you, couldn't you have found a nicer place?"

"I don't want a nicer place."

Sophie leaned toward me and said in a low voice. "Has Jake been spending your money?"

"I can hear you," Jake said, as he walked into the kitchen.

"Sophie," I emphasized her name, "I like this place. I don't need anything big or fancy. Simple and plain is what I like."

She straightened up. "Odd for a daughter of my sister. She never liked to keep Light hidden."

At the mention of Light, Jake said, "I have to go to the store. I'll leave you two alone."

"No," I blurted. "Stay. She just got here."

Sophie placed her bony hand on my arm. "Actually, I think that's a good idea. It will give us some time to talk about things he wouldn't understand." Sophie gracefully set herself on the couch. It took several seconds for all the rainbow-colored material to settle against her thin frame. There was so much of it that I couldn't tell if she was wearing a dress, or some sort of blouse/skirt combo.

Jake grabbed the car keys off the counter. "You girls have fun then. See you, Tink." He shrugged his shoulders as if to say, "She's your problem now."

With Jake gone, I felt exposed. I could feel Sophie's eyes examining me up and down. I tried to think of something to say, but my mind was blank.

"You look so much like your mother," Sophie said again.

"That's what I hear."

"You're a little thin though. Are you eating enough?"

"Put food in front of me and I'll eat." I glanced up at the clock. This was going to be a long day.

"Do you have friends at school?"

"Yes."

"Really?"

"Yes. Why wouldn't I?"

Sophie shrugged. "I just know you didn't have any friends last year or any other year for that matter."

"How would you know?"

"I make it a point to check up on you."

I clenched my fist beneath a pillow on my lap and made

a mental note to get after Jake later. He shouldn't be telling Sophie anything. "I have friends."

Sophie flicked her wrist as if swatting at a fly. "Maybe. But it seems that ever since your father died you've withdrawn yourself. It's not healthy."

"You don't know what you're talking about."

"Of course I do, dear. I saw you at your father's funeral. That was the day your wall came up. I saw it in your eyes."

"This is not a conversation I want to have."

"I know you don't, but it's time. It's not safe for you out here without proper training."

"I've made it this far, haven't I?"

"Pure luck, but something tells me it won't last."

I swallowed hard, remembering the dead dog and the murders.

Sophie swept her hair back. "Vykens are always watching, waiting for one of us to make a mistake. I know you think you've been careful moving around as much as you have, and that's probably what has kept you alive this long. But it's been almost a year-and-a-half and you're still here. It's not safe for you anymore."

"How do you know?" I couldn't admit she might be right.

She answered my question with a question. "Do you feel safe?"

I paused. "I like it here. For the first time since my dad died, I feel normal. I have friends, I'm in a book club, I'm on the basketball team—"

Sophie frowned. "You know how we feel about competitive sports."

"But that's just lame. I'm not trying to be better than anyone. I'm just trying to work off Light's energy. Sports help me do that."

"That's where we can help. Don't you see? You don't know

how to control the energy yet, but you can learn this at Lucent."

I shook my head. "Not now. Maybe after I graduate."

"What if that's too late? You know your mother's killer was never found. It could be stalking you now."

"Stalking?"

Sophie nodded. "Yes, stalking. That's what Vykens do. It's never a quick kill for them, especially the ones who have tasted Light and are no longer confined to the darkness. There's a very good chance your mother's killer can still walk in the day and if he can, you'd never know who it was."

"What do you mean still walk in the day? I thought once they tasted Light, they can always be out in the day."

"That's what we thought too, but years ago we found out the Light they steal is eventually snuffed out by their darkness and the Vykens have to find someone new to feed on. If the Vyken who killed your mother knew she had a daughter, then it would be looking for you. You've made yourself an easy target, Llona."

"Would I recognize a Vyken if I saw one?"

"Unfortunately, no. They are masters of deception. That's why we fall victim to them so easily. We are, by nature, very trusting. It's what happened to your mother. The Vyken who killed your mother was your father's close friend. He preyed upon your family for over a year before he finally took your mother's life. She trusted him completely."

I felt a stabbing in my heart at the mere mention of my mother's death. "It was a friend?" I whispered.

Sophie looked grim. "Yes. I tried to warn your parents. I told them they shouldn't allow others into their lives so completely, but your mother wouldn't listen. I'm afraid to say that's what caused the rift between us. She thought I was being paranoid," Sophie's voice cracked. "I should've made her listen."

The sudden rush of emotion from Sophie, and the discovery

of my mother's killer was not something I wanted to think about. At least not in front of Sophie. I cleared my throat and changed the subject. "So if there was a Vyken after me, most likely it would be an older male correct?"

Sophie wiped at her eye. "Not necessarily. Vykens have learned to manipulate Light, giving them the ability to change their appearance. For all you know, it could be your best friend at school."

"That's impossible."

"Why?"

"Because I would sense it."

"How?"

I shifted. "I don't know. I just would."

"Are you not listening? I admit you've done remarkably well with so little knowledge, but don't let it go to your head. You are not invincible. It was that attitude that cost your mother her life."

"So you're saying I can't have friends?"

"Of course not, but you have to choose the right ones: those who are like you. At Lucent there are girls your age who are going through the same things you are."

"I doubt that," I mumbled.

"What does that mean?"

"Nothing." Sophie was the last person I wanted to share my woes with. "How are we supposed to help others if we are locked away in some school?"

"Right now we are just trying to preserve our kind. And you're not locked away. The girls can come and go as they please."

I opened my mouth to speak, but she interrupted me.

"We want our kind to help others, but not until they are properly trained. Eventually you'll be placed back into society where you can help the most."

"Like serving on the boards of charities?" I mocked. From what my father had told me, Auras were rarely allowed to have hands-on experience helping others. I'd never heard of an Aura who worked in a soup kitchen, but I'd heard of plenty who helped build one. I remember my mom saying once (not too happily either) that our safety had become more important than our purpose.

"Exactly. You can still help without getting too close to others." Sophie suddenly slapped the arm of the couch. "Enough serious talk. I'm only here for a couple of days. Do you want to do something fun?"

"Like what?" I didn't think it was possible for her to have fun.

"First, let me ask you a question. What can you do with Light?"

"You mean how can I use it?"

"Yes."

"Well, I can turn lights on and off by just thinking about it. Once I made an entire gymnasium black out." I waited for Sophie's eyes to widen with surprise, but she just stared. "And I can calm people down by touching them," I added.

"Like your mother."

"I guess. And I think I'm really good at reading people, but I'm not sure if that's Light or just me."

"Could be a little of both. Anything else?"

"I have great hearing."

For some reason this surprised her. "Really? How long have you had this gift?"

I shrugged. "For as long as I can remember."

She stared through me and whispered, "Mark."

"What about my Dad?"

She shook her head. "I don't want to discuss your father right now. What else can you do?"

"Well, on full moons I'm really fast and I have great reflexes.

I think I might be a little stronger too."

"Yes."

"What's up with the full moon anyway?"

"It's when the sun's reflective light is at its strongest. This reflection makes it easier for you to take advantage of Light's powers."

"Are you saying I could have Light's energy all of the time?"

She leaned forward. "Absolutely. You just have to know how to call upon it. That's why you need to come to Lucent. We can teach you all of this." She paused. "But I'm getting distracted. We wanted to have fun. Let me show you what else Light can do." She stood up.

"Really?"

Sophie flashed a mischievous grin. "You might want to put on something warm."

Eighteen

Following Sophie's directions, I drove up the canyon as far as Jake's little car could before the snow became too deep. From there we had to travel by foot, and it didn't seem we were going in any particular direction. She'd stop frequently, look left to right, and then keep walking. I just wished she'd make up her mind because I was freezing.

The snow was at least a couple feet thick and every time I took a step, I broke through its hard crust. Sophie, however, had no difficulties walking across the snow, even though she had to have been at least twenty pounds heavier than me. She wore a white coat that covered the entire length of her body. Beneath the coat, her wispy, layered skirt fluttered behind her like a tailgating ghost. I finally called out to her to stop.

She turned around. "What are you doing sitting on the snow?"

"Apparently, I have elephant legs! I can't walk in this stuff." I moved out of the hole and took another step, but once again the top layer couldn't support my weight, and I fell through.

Sophie laughed and walked back to me.

"How do you do that?" I asked.

"Do what?"

"Not break through the snow. You walk on it like you're a mouse."

She gave me a pity smile and tilted her head. "There is so much for you to learn. I'm using Light, dear." She helped me up.

"How?"

"The best way to explain it is," she thought for a moment, "it's like holding your breath, only you can still breathe."

"That's the best way to explain it? Hold your breath but still breathe? Sounds like a bad Chinese movie to me: 'Go through the door that is not a door!'" I mocked.

"Would you stop? I'm trying to help."

I mumbled a sorry and found my way out of the hole.

"Try and imagine there is a balloon inside you, making you weightless."

"Can I fly?"

She shook her head. "You're still bound by the laws of gravity. Light is only making you lighter, almost as if you're in water. Now close your eyes and call upon Light. Imagine it expanding inside you."

"Serious?"

"How else are you going to learn?"

"Fine." I closed my eyes and concentrated. I did as she asked and pictured a balloon, but after a minute I felt like I was burning up. I opened my eyes and gasped for air.

"Well, that's one way of doing it," Sophie laughed.

I looked down. All around me the snow had melted. "Not quite what you had in mind?"

"Not really but you're learning. You just need to practice." Sophie glanced around. "I guess we can stop here, but we need to wait a little longer for the sun to go down."

"Why?"

"What I'm going to show you is much more impressive when it's dark." Sophie jumped down in my hole with me. In seconds she had warmed the rest of the snow around us until the ground was dry. "We can sit here and wait."

We sat in silence for several minutes, listing to the winter stillness. My thoughts drifted to May and how difficult it would be to not know where your ability came from. I was about to ask Sophie about her but stopped. May should be the one asking, not me.

"What are you thinking about?" Sophie asked.

"Huh? Oh, nothing."

"You can tell me."

I glanced around while trying to think of something to say. "Just how strange it is to be here with you."

She nodded. "We should've been doing things like this a lot sooner."

"Why?"

"You are so far behind other Auras. Normally it's the mothers who teach their daughters about Light, but where your mother isn't around, it should've been me."

"It's not a big deal."

"Llona," Sophie paused. "I need to ask your forgiveness."

"For what?" Sophie ask forgiveness? This had to be a first.

She looked me in the eyes. "Your mother's death was very hard on me. In a lot of ways, I blamed myself. After her death I knew I'd have to be the one to teach you about Light, but every time I saw you, I saw your mother's eyes staring back at me. It was just too difficult. I know that was selfish of me and not fair to you. You had already lost so much and here I was, not even able to be in the same room with you."

"That's pretty harsh." I had to look away.

"I know. That's why I must beg your forgiveness. I was a coward. I see that now. I promise from here on out I will be there for you like I should've been for all these years. Could you ever forgive me?"

I was extremely hurt by her confession. Why was it that everyone around me acted like my parent's death was the most devastating thing for them? Did anyone stop to consider how their death might affect their actual child? I wanted to get upset and ask her why she waited so long to finally "confess," but thought better of it. Choosing to take the high road, even though I felt like storming away, I said, "It's fine. It's in the past."

"Really? I'm so glad you said that. I feel much better now." She reached over and gave me a hug. I forced myself to return it even though I was repulsed by her sudden affection.

Sophie looked up. "It's dark enough. Wait here."

She moved about twenty feet away in the middle of a small clearing and bowed her head as if praying—concentrating was more like it. In a matter of seconds, bright lights ignited all around us. Several of them were moving but most of the lights were still. Some lights were bigger while some burst from the seams in the trees or glowed from beneath the snow. I suddenly felt like I was in the middle of space with stars all around me.

"What is this?" I asked.

"I've lit up the life forces of all the creatures around us: bugs, squirrels, spiders—you name it. Most are immobile due to the cold, so you can imagine how much more impressive this would be with warmer weather."

"It's amazing. I had no idea there were so many living things around us."

"Most of us are ignorant to life. If one can become aware of the beings around us, they have a much better chance of fulfilling their destiny."

"I don't understand."

"The future is never ours alone. Without others, our destiny could never be fulfilled. Could you imagine Superman trying to fulfill his purpose if there weren't people to save? He could never do it. And so must we be aware of those around us and never shut the door on opportunities that help us to grow and learn, no matter how difficult they seem. Only by doing this will we be able to live to our full potential."

I was speechless, to the point where my eyes filled with tears. Sophie's words, combined with life's glow against the darkness of the night, hit me hard. I'd missed out on many experiences, because I chose to shut myself off from the world. I'd gotten better, thanks to Christian and May, but I was still holding back.

"Llona? Are you all right?"

"Huh?" I blinked. A single tear fell from my eye. I quickly cleared my throat and said, "I'm fine. This is just so impressive."

"It's one of many beautiful things you can do with your gift if you will allow yourself to be taught."

Before I could think of how my next words might be received, I said, "Can we use Light as a weapon?"

Sophie's face twisted in disgust. "Light should never be used as a weapon. It is only to be used to beautify, uplift, and to comfort. Your ignorance has given you a lack of respect for Light and its purpose."

"I was just asking," I mumbled.

Sophie took a deep breath. On her exhale, the lights went out. "Come on. Let's get back."

I followed her back to the car in silence. I knew she was majorly disappointed in me, but that only made me madder, especially after her apology. How was I supposed to know the rules and etiquette of Light?

When we returned to the house, Jake was waiting for us with pizza. Gratefully, Sophie acted like nothing had happened, and other than a few comments about Jake's appearance, she was actually pretty decent. We ate dinner and played games until midnight before we finally called it quits.

The next day, Jake and I didn't break from our normal Thanksgiving tradition, much to Sophie's dismay. We left for the local all-you-can-eat buffet restaurant at eleven and didn't return until two. Sophie looked bored the entire time, but Jake and I had a lot of fun trying to see who could eat the most food. We agreed I won, but only because I had avoided drinking anything. Jake had filled himself with milk way too early. When we got home I called May and told her about Sophie.

"Do you want me to ask her about you? She might know something."

I could practically hear May thinking on the other end. "Let me do some digging first, see what I can find. If I come up empty, then I'll ask her next time you talk to her. Did you tell her about me?"

"Not at all. I'll let you do that when you're ready."

"Thanks, Llona."

After planning to go to a movie on Saturday, we said our good-byes. I walked into the living room and found Sophie standing with her suitcases.

"Are you leaving already?" I asked.

"I'm afraid it's that time. Will you please seriously consider coming to Lucent when you graduate?"

"I will, I promise."

"Good. Now give me a hug. I don't know when I'll be able to visit again."

"It was good to see you. I'm glad you came."

"Me too." She turned to Jake who was eating in the kitchen. "You're doing a great job. I mean it. Thank you for everything."

Shocked, Jake quickly wiped milk from his upper lip. "No big deal. Have a safe trip."

After she closed the door, Jake said, "That was weird."

"The last two days were weird," I added, thinking I never wanted to do it again. But little did I know there would come a time in my not-too-distant future when I'd wish to go back to those strange moments with Sophie. For there I was safe.

Nineteen

Monday morning I found Christian waiting for me at my locker.

"How was your Thanksgiving?" he asked.

"Full of giving thanks. Yours?" I avoided direct eye contact. It still hurt to look at him.

"Fine."

I removed the books from my bag while trying to ignore Christian who seemed to be struggling to say something.

Finally he blurted, "Sorry we haven't really talked lately. I've been pretty busy with football."

"No problem." I closed my locker. "I've been busy too."

"Are you going to the football rally on Friday?"

"Out at Deer Lake?" I turned to walk toward class. Christian followed.

"Yeah. We never did anything like that at my last school."

I swung my backpack over my shoulder. "I moved here just after last year's rally so I didn't go, but I hear it's fun."

"So are you going to go?"

"Not sure."

"It's supposed to be really cold, possibly even snow. I doubt a lot of people will be there."

I was getting the distinct impression he didn't want me

to come. "Are you going?" I asked.

"Coach is making us. It'll probably be lame."

"Maybe I'll come to find out."

Christian's left eye twitched. "I'd stay home if I were you. I'll tell you all about how boring it is after. Maybe I could take you out to dinner on Saturday to fill you in?"

This was getting annoying. "We'll see. I have to go to class." I walked off before he could stop me.

I'd been looking forward to math class all weekend. At first it was unsettling how spacey I became around Mr. Steele, but during the last several weeks, his class became the one place where I thought about nothing else. Today was no different. The moment I stepped foot into the room, Mr. Steele became my focus. I wish I could say I was focused on what he was teaching, but all I could concentrate on was him: the way his body moved, the way words fell from his perfectly shaped lips. It was all so mesmerizing. I always thought I was above all this prepubescent lovesick crap, but obviously I wasn't.

Before I knew it, the bell rang. Miraculously I managed to tear my eyes away from Mr. Steele long enough to gather my books and put them into my backpack.

"Llona?" Mr. Steele asked.

My heart stopped. I looked up, too stunned to speak.

"Could you stay for a minute? I need to talk to you."

I felt myself nod. I remained seated, just staring.

After all the other students exited the room, Mr. Steele sat next to me holding a folder.

"How are you doing?" he asked.

It took me a second to answer. "I'm good."

"Life at home, is it good?"

"Yeah."

"You live with your uncle, right?" He was tapping his fingers on the folder in front of him.

"Yes."

"You have a good relationship with him?"

"Yes."

"Good." He opened the folder.

"I probably don't have to tell you this, but your math grade is low."

"How low?"

He frowned. "To the point where you might not pass my class."

I sunk into the seat.

"I've been lenient this far because I know how well you did last year, and how well you're doing in all your other classes. I was hoping you'd catch on and be able to raise your grade, but it's not looking that way. Do you have someone who could help you? Your uncle perhaps?"

I nodded.

"Good because you only have a few weeks left to bring your grade up." He handed me a stack of papers. "If you complete these, I'll give you extra credit. That should help."

"Thank you," I said, feeling very embarrassed.

He stood up. "If you ever need to talk about anything, have any questions, whatever, you come see me, okay?" He patted my back and disappeared down the hall.

I slowly gathered the papers and stuffed them into my bag. I could still feel the warm pressure of his hand against my back.

"What are you still doing in here?" May asked when she saw me from the hallway.

"Mr. Steele basically just told me I'm failing. I guess I'm still in shock."

She cringed. "I was hoping this was going to be easy."

"What?"

"I have something to tell you. Sorry it has to be more crappy news, but you need to know."

"What?"

May sat down and took a big breath. "First, the girls who were with Christian and Adam at the corn maze—they're just friends. In fact, I found out one of them has a boyfriend."

"That's not bad," I said, confused.

"No, it's good. Actually, I meant to tell you that after the bad news, but I couldn't help myself." She grinned and then shook her head, bringing back her serious expression. "So the last few weeks, Christian has been harassing me about that night."

This took me by surprise. "He has? Why?"

"I guess after we left, he inspected the area and found some bone in the remains of the fire. He said he knew we were lying. Every day he's been bugging me about it and so, when he came to my house yesterday—"

"On Sunday?"

"Yeah. Anyway, I guess I just cracked. He was really putting on the pressure. I didn't know what to do."

"So you told him?"

"All I told him was that someone was playing a prank on you and shaved your name into a dead dog."

"How did you explain the fire?"

"I said I dropped a match on it. Of course he wanted to know why I'd done that, and I just told him you were embarrassed and didn't want anyone to see it."

Moaning, I dropped my head onto the desk. "Is that it?" I asked.

"Almost. He wanted to know how you found the dog."

I lifted my head. "What did you tell him?'

She shrugged. "Nothing. How did you, anyway?"

"I guess I just sensed it."

"I'm really sorry I told him."

"It's not your fault."

"So you're not mad?"

"Not at you."

"At Christian?"

"Why is it any of his business anyway? He's been acting really strange lately and it's really starting to irk me. This morning he was trying to convince me not to go to the rally on Friday."

"He was? Why?"

"Another one of the many things I don't know."

"But you have to come. It'll be so fun," she said.

"Oh, I'll be there. I'm not letting Christian ruin anything."

The night of the big pep rally on Deer Lake had arrived. It had been the perfect day. The weather had been crappy, gray and overcast, but for me it was perfect. It was a full moon, and I was feeling invincible.

May picked me up as soon as it was dark and together we drove up the mountain, following several other cars all headed to the same destination. As soon as May parked between two jacked-up trucks, she jumped out. "I'll be right back," she said.

I looked in the direction she was heading: Adam. I wanted her to come clean about liking him, but I doubted she ever would.

I moved toward a roaring fire, saying hi to several of my classmates on the way. Many of them had their faces painted and were talking about how we were going to take state. The mood in the air was one of excitement and elation. I took a deep breath and inhaled it all.

"Pretty crazy, huh?"

I turned around. Matt smiled big. His hair was disheveled, tucked beneath an oversized gray hoodie. Over it, he wore a heavy coat. Because of the full moon, I barely felt the cold.

I returned his smile. "I didn't know you were coming."

"Me neither. It's not really my thing, but I remember a certain someone telling me how this was my last year and I should have fun, so I thought I'd check it out."

"I'm glad you did." I adjusted my beanie.

"I didn't think you liked these things either," he said.

"I thought I'd take my own advice."

Matt looked down at me. "Aren't you cold?"

"Surprisingly, no."

"You are an odd one, Llona. Let's go stand by the fire."

It surprised me when he put his arm around my shoulders and guided me toward the roaring flames, which were taller than us both. I glanced up at him, but his expression was blank, and I knew he meant nothing by the gesture. I let out my breath and relaxed.

"Llona! Matt!" Tracey called. I noticed her eyes move to Matt's arm. "What are you guys doing?"

"Just trying to get warm," Matt said.

"There's hot chocolate over there." Tracey pointed to the other side of the fire. "And doughnuts."

"That's my cue. You guys want any?" I took the opportunity to leave Tracey and Matt alone.

"I'm good," Matt said.

"Me too," added Tracey.

I rounded the bonfire and was almost to the crowded hot chocolate table when I heard, "What are you doing here?" Christian stepped out from within the crowd.

"Trying to have a good time, and I'd like to keep it that way." I patted his chest twice and walked away.

"Llona, wait!" He jogged after me.

I whirled around. "What do you want?"

"You shouldn't be here."

"Why? Why can't I be here?"

"Just trust me. You shouldn't be here." He took a step

toward me, but I backed up.

"What's wrong? You used to trust me."

"That's before you became all Jekyll and Hyde-y on me."

His mouth dropped. "I have never been cruel to you."

"What's your definition of cruel?"

His eyes closed briefly and for a second it looked like he was in pain. "I didn't mean to hurt you. That has never been my intention."

"Then what is your intention?"

Christian sighed and stuffed his hands into his pockets. "I never intended to—"

"To what, Christian?"

He lifted his head and stared directly into my eyes. "To have feelings for you."

This caught me off guard, but I didn't let myself swoon. Too much had happened. "So you say you want me to be safe, but you don't want to have feelings for me? Don't the two go hand-in-hand?"

"They shouldn't. Not for me at least."

"Why?"

He glanced away. "It's complicated."

"No, rocket science is complicated. This shouldn't be."

He shrugged.

"When you decide to uncomplicate it, let me know. As for me leaving, it ain't happening. Try and have some fun tonight. I know I will." I turned around and practically pushed my way to the front of the hot chocolate line, but when I came face-to-face with Mr. Steele, who was serving the hot beverage, my anger quickly melted like an ice cube in a fire.

"You look full of energy tonight," Mr. Steele said to me in his usual velvet, sophisticated voice.

"Full of something," I agreed.

He laughed. "Maybe you should join the football game

over there, burn off whatever you're full of."

I glanced toward the lake. Several cars were parked in a big circle with their lights turned on, facing the center. The dark silhouettes of students moved within the light as they played with a glow-in-the-dark football.

"Go join them, Llona," Mr. Steele said. He was suddenly standing right behind me. I jumped. "They could use someone with your skills."

I turned around. "My skills?"

"I've watched you play basketball. You're very good."

My face reddened. Gratefully my back was turned to the fire so he didn't notice.

"Thanks," I mumbled.

Out of the corner of my eye I saw Christian walking toward us. To avoid another lecture, I quickly said, "Thanks, Mr. Steele. I think I will." I hurried away, glancing back a few times to make sure Christian wasn't following me.

I walked between two parked trucks, and just before I had the chance to ask if I could join the game, Mike called, "If you're thinking of playing, don't. We already have enough players."

Adam moved out of a headlight next to me. "We could use one."

"Yeah," May added. "You can be on our team, the winning team."

"Whatever. You're winning streak is over." Mike tossed the ball to a teammate across the field.

Even though car headlights were turned on, the darkness swallowed most of their light before it could make an impact on the game. Playing football in the dark was like nothing I'd ever done before. It gave me the ability to hide much of my speed and agility. This turned out to be very important, especially because I was playing against Mike and loved showing him up.

He was the quarterback for the other team, and it was just too easy to intercept almost every throw he tossed. His frustration was my elation. By my sixth pick, he became so upset he turned and tossed the football as hard as he could toward the lake. It landed on the ice and continued to slide away from us.

"Way to go, Mike!" someone yelled.

"Anyone bring another ball?" another asked.

I squinted my eyes into the darkness. The ball wasn't too far away. I could see it's glow partially concealed by a chunk of ice.

Behind me, another person said. "That's all we had."

"Nice, Mike. Way to ruin the game."

I turned to the group and said, "I'll get it."

"I don't think it's safe," May said.

"Of course it is," Mike blurted. "The ice is frozen over. Let her get it."

"If it's so safe, why don't you get it?" May snapped.

"Llona thinks she's all that. She can do it."

"I got it," I called and jogged to the edge of the lake.

I carefully stepped onto the ice. It groaned once but held. I stomped hard just to be sure. It remained solid. I proceeded slowly, but after several steps and no more creaks or groans, I became more confident and ended up running and then sliding several times toward the ball. Laughter erupted behind me. In a matter of seconds, I reached the ball. "Got it!"

I moved to take a step when I heard the sound of glasses clanking together. I looked around to see where the sound could be coming from. After a few seconds, the clinking changed into sort of a tearing. I wasn't nervous until I felt the ice beneath me begin to shake.

"You going to throw it back or what?" Mike yelled.

I held completely still, afraid of what was about to happen.

"What's wrong?" May called.

"The ice," I whispered back as loud as I could. "It's cracking!"

"What?"

I looked down at my feet and slowly tried to slide one foot forward. Another tearing sound. I immediately thought of what Sophie had taught me—think light-footed, think airy. I tried holding my breath, but just like with Sophie, the ice beneath my feet began to melt, further weakening it. Water pooled around the soles of my shoes. Cursed Light!

Maybe I could jump, I thought. I had enough Light coursing through me that I could probably make it. I crouched low. As I did so, I noticed Christian running up the shore toward May. I couldn't hear what he was saying, but he looked frazzled.

Placing my hand on the cold ice, I prepared to spring forward. Just as I was about to push up on my legs, the ice gave way, and I no longer had any ground beneath me to push off on. Instead of going up like I'd intended, I fell into the cold water and there was nothing I could do to stop it.

Twenty

When I was seven years old, I discovered roly poly bugs. I loved the fact that when I'd touch one, the bug would roll into a tight shell as a way to protect itself. I would find and gather as many of those bugs as I could until I'd have enough to play marbles with their hard, circular bodies. The instant one of the bugs began to relax from its shell, I'd touch it again and flick it into the other rolled-up bugs. I played this for almost an hour before my mom caught me and gave me a lecture about being kind to all creatures, especially those smaller than me.

I'd forgotten all about the bugs until I felt the frigid ice water touch my skin. The Light within me retreated as quickly as a touched roly poly bug, leaving me to struggle on my own.

"Struggle" is too positive a word. I did manage to break the surface and gasp for air. I even managed to reach out to Christian, who I saw army-crawling on the ice toward me, but that was it. It was like the cold had seized up my body like an engine in water. And what little current there was sucked me under. The last thing I heard before I felt my head sink below the dark water's edge was Christian yelling my name.

My body floated slowly beneath the ice, carried by the gentle flow of water. I attempted to claw at it, searching for any weaknesses, but my hand could barely open, let alone close down upon anything solid. The tips of my fingers simply grazed the slippery ice.

I should've tried harder, but suddenly all I could focus on was the color of my nails. They were rapidly changing to a grayish blue color that looked familiar. Then I remembered. They were the same color as my father's when I was asked to identify him at the morgue.

I'm dying, I thought. This sure was unexpected and not at all how I envisioned my death. I was supposed to die gardening in a flowerbed as a hundred-year-old woman, not as a seventeen-year-old trapped in a lake beneath inches of ice.

After a moment my hands were no longer able to move, and I became like a statue, completely still, arms outstretched. I thought a death like this would be painful, but when my lungs began to burn and I instinctively took a breath, I suffered very little. There was only the initial terror of feeling the icy water slide down my lungs, but after a few short seconds, all I felt was peace. Even my mind was completely calm. And for the first time I realized how beautiful it was underwater.

The light from the full moon just barely lit up my watery grave, giving the water a dark, mystical look. It wasn't such a bad place to die after all, I decided. The color of the water was a starry, navy blue, reminding me of the comforter on my bed at home. And the occasional fish I passed seemed to be hanging from the ice like a mobile above a baby's crib. I tried to smile but my face was frozen.

Suddenly I stopped drifting. Barely still able to move my head, I turned slightly to see a fallen tree on the bottom of the lake. Its branches had captured me in its grip. Just as well. It might be easier for them to find my body this way.

I waited patiently for my eyes to close and for darkness to claim me, but it didn't come as quickly as I expected. Why was it taking so long? I thought once water filled your lungs that was it. The end. Roll the credits. At least that's how the movies always portrayed it.

While I waited for death to overcome me, I began to hum a song I'd listened to earlier that day. It seemed appropriate for the moment, and it also helped me to pass the time.

I was only a few bars into the song when two shadows appeared above me on the ice. One of them pounded hard against the frozen surface. Probably Christian, but I couldn't be sure. Just before my eyes closed, I saw the second figure bend down and smash through the ice with one blow.

Moments later, I had the sensation of being lifted and then dragged, yet I couldn't feel anything. Several seconds after, chaotic, muffled voices began speaking all at once. I tried to make sense of their words, but my mind-numbing nausea made me feel like I'd been riding a roller coaster for hours on end. Maybe if I could throw up, I'd feel better, but I couldn't even open my eyes, let alone stimulate regurgitation.

This new sensation was worse than being underwater. At least when I was trapped in the water I could see. Extreme panic set in as I tried to see or feel anything. I half wondered if I was dead. Why else would I not be able to open my eyes or feel myself breathing? I attempted to quiet my mind so I could try and make sense of what everyone around me was saying.

Suddenly a bright flash of red tore through my brain. This is it! I'm going mad. My body was gone and soon my mind would be too. I longed for the peace that the underwater prison had given me, for I felt none of that now. Only chaos.

But then I heard it.

As clear as a town's siren at noon. Christian's voice somehow broke through the madness. "Llona! You've got to hold on. Do you understand?"

I wanted to tell him that I didn't understand, but I still couldn't move or do much of anything.

"I can't find a pulse." That was May's voice.

A whisper in my ear, "Llona. I know you're in there. Just hang on." Christian again.

"How soon until the ambulance arrives?" a female voice asked.

"Not soon enough. We need to take her to the hospital now!" This from the unmistakable Mr. Steele.

Again the female voice, "I don't think it's safe to move her. We should wait."

"She hasn't broken anything. She's only frozen," snapped Mr. Steele.

"He's right," Christian said, and I felt my body being lifted again. "Let's take my car. She can lie in the back."

"I'm coming with you!" May called.

"I'll drive," Mr. Steele added.

I heard the back door of Christian's SUV open. My body was hoisted up and then laid carefully down. The car started.

"I hope you don't mind if I break any speed limits," Mr. Steele said. I'd never heard his normally cool and confident voice so anxious before.

"I don't care. Just get us there fast," Christian said.

I still couldn't feel anything. Shouldn't I at least feel myself breathing? I heard what sounded like fabric tearing.

"What are you doing?" May asked.

"I'm taking off her wet clothes. I need to get her body warm," Christian said.

"At least leave her bra and underwear on," May suggested, for which I was very grateful.

"I will. I'm just trying to save her life, May."

"Do you have to be undressed too?" May asked again.

"She needs body heat. Now will you lay off?"

May sniffled.

"What are you doing?" Christian said.

"I want to hold her hand," May said.

"Hang on!" I heard Mr. Steele yell. We must have swerved sharply because I heard May grunt and something like metal crash nearby.

Christian whispered again, "You've got to hold on, Llona. Please. You're too strong to go out like this." He paused when his voice began to quiver. After a deep breath, he continued, "I never told you, but the first time I saw you, I thought I was looking at an angel. You were walking to school wearing a white T-shirt and jeans. You'd taken off your hat when you thought no one was looking and your hair fell down your back like wings unfolding. I think this was one of the rare times I saw you as your true self."

If I could talk, I would've been speechless.

"Do you feel a pulse?" May asked.

"Um, I think so," Christian said, but the way he said it made me nervous. His tone was that of a grown-up telling a child a cut isn't that bad when in actuality, a bone is sticking out their flesh.

"We're almost there," Mr. Steele called back.

"Come on, Llona. Don't let go of your Light," Christian breathed into my ear.

I froze. I completely froze. Or I should say my mind froze; my body couldn't have been more frozen. Christian had used the word Light. And he hadn't said it in a weird spiritual sort of way either.

I heard the screeching of tires. "We're here!"

This is when things really became crazy. I heard car doors opening and closing. I felt myself being jostled around and then Christian barking orders to hospital staff. There were lots of voices I didn't recognize, asking all sorts of questions. I tried to listen to them all, to distinguish one voice from another, but something strange began to happen. The only way to describe it is I felt my body begin to separate, followed moments later by a bright light that slowly began to fill the dark space in my mind.

I hadn't been able to focus on most of what was happening around me, until I heard this conversation: "She's surprisingly warm for being pulled out of a frozen lake."

"I agree, but I still can't find a pulse. Ron, can you?"

"No. Is the defibrillator ready?"

"Almost."

"Ready."

"Clear!"

A strange humming sound, followed by a loud thump.

"Again," someone shouted.

I heard someone else curse.

"Clear!" Thump sound again.

"Nothing, Doctor."

Silence.

"What? No! She's still alive," Christian yelled. He sounded further away than the others.

"Get him out of here," a deep voice said.

There were sounds of scuffling and then the sound of something crashing into a wall.

"You have to believe me. She's still alive!" Christian said again.

I wanted to scream that he was right, but even as I thought it the Light in my darkness grew dimmer. That, coupled with the sudden feeling of floating, had me worried.

"I'm sorry, son, but there's nothing else we can do. By the looks of her, she's been without oxygen for too long."

"No!" Christian was furious. "Try again. She's still alive!"

Then Mr. Steele, "How do you know, Christian?"

"Because there's still Light," he blurted. "She doesn't have much longer. Please! We can save her."

I then heard more scuffling followed by more shouting. It sounded like a fight had broken out. Someone yelled, "Call security!"

"Save her!" Mr. Steele called.

I tried to pay attention, but I began to drift off. The peaceful feeling had returned.

"Hang on, Llona," Christian said.

I felt my body jerk and then heard a sound like bones breaking. I think they were mine.

In a quieter voice, Christian said, "Don't let go of the Light and you will live. Just stay with me."

I wasn't sure what he meant by saying "hold on to the Light" until I saw the light begin to fade away like a retreating sunset. I didn't want this to be the end and something told me the moment Light disappeared, I would too. As peaceful as it was, I didn't want to die.

"Don't leave me," I shouted at the retreating light. "I want to live!"

"Come on, Llona. Open your eyes," Christian said, his voice tense.

In my mind I imagined my eyes opening. Not calmly, but violently. I pictured everything I could think of to pry them open: crow bar, knife, scissors, anything that would tear them open.

"Open your eyes," I screamed at myself over and over until, finally, my eyes opened.

Twenty-One

"A MAN IS NOT COMPLETELY BORN UNTIL HE IS DEAD."

I was dead, but now I am born again. I don't think my experience is exactly what Benjamin Franklin meant when he wrote the words, but I was born again. Not in the spiritual, found God sort of way, but I felt different. A strange sort of excitement for life, and I knew I'd never be the same again. I was going to fight. I didn't know how, didn't even know if it was possible, but somehow I was going to find a way not to be vulnerable anymore. The Light inside me seemed to leap at my new determination as if it too were ready to fight.

"Llona?"

Christian came into focus. *Christian.* Christian knows. He knows about me.

"How?" I asked him.

"She's alive," I heard someone call.

Within seconds, Christian was pushed away, and I was swarmed by doctors and nurses. They asked me all sorts of questions, but I couldn't take my eyes off Christian. I kept having to move my head around to see him through the many people who were bombarding me. I had to know how he knew.

"Do what they ask," Christian whispered from across the room, but I heard it as clear as if he were shouting. And then he was gone.

I collapsed into the bed, suddenly very aware of how badly my chest hurt. I cried out in pain.

"It's your sternum," a doctor said. "It's going to be sore for awhile. And you probably have a few broken ribs too. How does the rest of you feel?"

"Other than being sore, I'm cold." And suddenly very self-conscience. A sheet had been pulled up to my shoulders, but I still felt very exposed.

"Here's a gown," a nurse said. "I'll go get you another blanket."

The doctor stared down at a chart in his hands. "You are quite the miracle girl. We thought we'd lost you. If it wasn't for that determined young man, we probably would have."

I nodded. "How long do I need to stay here?"

"At least overnight."

"I need to call my uncle."

"I believe someone already has. Are you ready to be moved?"

"Where to?"

"Fourth floor."

I nodded. A couple of nurses wheeled my bed into the hall and into an elevator.

My new room was very simple, a mini version of the ER, but at least it was private. After the nurses situated me and left, May was the first person in. She gave me a big, but gentle, hug.

"How do you feel?" she asked. Her eyes were red and swollen.

"I'm okay."

"I thought you were dead."

"That's what I keep hearing."

"What happened?" She sat at the foot of my bed.

"I went after the football and the ice cracked. I guess this is what I get for being cocky and trying to show Mike up."

"Kind of a severe punishment, don't you think?"

I sort of smiled. "Where's Christian?"

"Getting dressed."

"Huh?"

"He didn't have a shirt on."

"So what happened after I fell into the ice?" I wanted to put the sounds I'd heard with some sort of picture.

May shook her head. "It was crazy. We were all watching you on the ice when Christian came running up to me. He was totally freaking out, saying you shouldn't be out there when all of a sudden you fell. Everyone started screaming, but Christian ran after you. I thought he was going to get to you in time, but then you just disappeared. Christian looked so panicked I thought his head was going to pop off. He was staring down at the ice like he could see through it or something and then he started moving around. That's when Mr. Steele came to help."

"Mr. Steele?"

May kept talking, "And then Christian stopped moving and dropped to the ground. He started pounding on the ice as hard as he could. He was saying something, but I couldn't hear what from the shore. Then Mr. Steele did something that, now that it's over and I can think about it, makes me totally fall in love with him."

"What?"

"With one blow, he punched through the ice and grabbed you."

"That was Mr. Steele?"

"Yeah. He pulled you out and then Christian carried you to his car." May lifted her hands. "Now don't get mad, but something happened."

"Like what?"

"To keep you warm, Christian undressed you. But I told him to keep your unmentionables on."

I smiled. "Good."

"I helped a little too," she said.

"What do you mean?"

"I held your hand and warmed you up. At first, I was afraid I'd light you on fire, but luckily that didn't happen."

"Yeah, lucky."

"I just focused really hard on not letting the full extent of my powers go. And I think it worked, because by the time we got to the hospital your skin didn't feel like ice anymore."

"Thanks, I appreciate it. So what happened in the hospital?"

"More craziness. I'm surprised nobody got arrested."

"What do you mean?"

"When they brought you in, you didn't have a pulse. The doctors tried shocking you, but nothing worked. They finally said you were dead. When Mr. Steele heard this, he punched a whole in the wall."

"He did?"

"Yeah, it was weird. And then Christian didn't stop yelling that you were still alive. The doctors were trying to push him out of the room when all of a sudden Mr. Steele starting fighting everyone. He shoved a doctor across the room and punched another."

My eyes grew big. So that was the scuffling I'd heard.

"And then he told Christian to go and save you and he did."

I shook my head. "Bizarre."

"I know, right?"

"Where's Mr. Steele now?"

She shrugged. "I don't know. Once they said you were alive I didn't pay attention to much else."

There was a knock at the door. Both of us turned our heads.

"Come in," I said.

Christian walked in wearing my favorite black shirt of his. "I'm glad you're alive," May said and squeezed my hand. "I'll leave you two alone. Can I come see you tomorrow?"

"Of course." My eyes didn't leave Christian's. He moved to the side of my bed and pulled up a chair.

As soon as May was gone, I asked again, "How?"

"I can't explain now, but I will. I promise. You're uncle's on his way up. I just wanted to make sure you're okay."

"I'm fine."

"How's your chest? I'm sorry I hurt it."

"Don't apologize. You saved my life."

Christian's eyes moved to the dark window and then back to me. "It's still a full moon. You should feel better tomorrow."

I stared at him, mouth gaping. "How do you know all this?"

He placed his warm hand over mine. "Tomorrow. I promise." He was silent for a moment, head bowed, and then, "This is going to kill me to leave you tonight."

"Then don't."

"Jake will want to be with you."

I sighed, knowing he was right. Jake was probably freaking out.

"I owe you an apology," I told him.

"For what?" It was his turn to be surprised.

"I should've listened to you and gone home."

"No, it was selfish of me to ask you not to come. It's just easier for me when I know you're home, know what I mean?"

I shook my head. "Not at all."

"You will, but it doesn't matter anyway. I could never have predicted what happened tonight."

"Were you expecting something to happen?"

"Yes."

"What were you expecting?"

"Definitely not you falling through the ice."

"Then what?"

The door opened suddenly.

"Llona," Jake cried. He rushed to my side. "Are you okay?"

"I'm fine, Jake, just tired."

"Are you sure?"

I nodded.

"What happened? The doctor said you fell through some ice, and they had to revive you."

"That pretty much sums it up."

"What were you doing on the ice?"

"It wasn't her fault, Mr. Reese. She was just getting the football for everyone. They told her it was safe."

Jake scowled. "Since when did you start trusting teenagers?" He then turned to Christian. "And when did you start calling me Mr. Reese?"

Christian shrugged. "Sorry, Jake."

"Well, I'm just glad you're okay. I would never have forgiven myself if something happened to you."

Christian stood up. "I'll leave you two alone. Llona, I'll come see you tomorrow."

"Thanks, Christian. For everything," I said, wishing he didn't have to go. He seemed to be thinking the same thing.

"Christian, do you mind if I have a word with you out in the hall?" Jake asked.

"Of course not."

As soon as they left the room, I turned on to my side with great difficulty. A few minutes later, Jake returned.

"What was that all about?" I asked.

"I just wanted to tell him thank you for saving you. I heard what he did. He's one of a kind, you know that?"

"I do."

"You know what's really strange? He reminds me of your father."

"Really?"

"Yeah, I can't put my finger on it, but he has this whole hero/protector thing about him."

"I know what you mean."

Jake stared at me; his eyes dripped with concern. "Are you comfortable? Can I get you anything?"

"I'm good. Super tired though."

"I'll let you get some sleep. Do you mind if I sleep in the chair? The nurse said it folds out into a bed."

"That would be great. I'd love the company."

*   *   *   *   *

I don't remember falling asleep or Jake getting his bed ready, but suddenly I was wide awake. I wasn't sure what time it was, but it must've been well into the night by the looks of things. The lights outside my room had been turned down, and faint sounds of beeping were coming from down the hall.

I rolled onto my back, surprised how much better I felt. I closed my eyes to go back to sleep, but the feeling in the room inexplicably changed. It felt heavy, almost suffocating. I opened my eyes only to find myself instantly paralyzed, unable to move any part of my body. Even my head remained trapped by an invisible force.

My eyes circled what I could see of the room, searching for the source of my current predicament. I found the problem at the foot of my bed. For there stood the tall shadow of a man. I couldn't see his face, but by the hostile feeling in the room I knew whoever it was meant me harm.

I tried to scream, tried to move, but my body wouldn't respond. Fear gripped me, but it wasn't fear that had paralyzed me. It was something in the air, physically pressing down on me until I felt I might be crushed.

The figure moved closer. It was an unnatural jerky movement, much too fast for a human. It jerked again; this time moving only a foot away. The shadow made no sound. It was as quiet as the dead and its presence was just as disturbing. Its head cocked to the side as if it were analyzing me. I still couldn't see its face, but as the shadow began to lower itself to me, its eyes looked as if they were growing smaller until they were two black circles with an even blacker center.

I attempted to scream again, but nothing came out. I focused every ounce of strength I had on trying to make any sound, but my efforts were wasted. In that moment I knew I couldn't do it alone. I called upon Light, imagined its power filling my entirety. It responded instantly until my whole body tingled. Finally, I sat up, mentally flipped on the lights, and opened my mouth. Erupting from my lungs was the kind of scream you only hear in horror films.

"What is it? What's wrong?" Jake cried, looking as if he'd just heard a gun go off.

"Is everything all right?" a nurse asked as she rushed into the room.

My heart beat out of my chest and beads of sweat dotted my forehead. "There was someone in my room," I gasped.

Jake looked around. "Where?"

"Standing next to me. Just a second ago."

The nurse moved into the hallway. "I didn't see anyone come in, and I've been here all night."

Jake placed his hand over mine. "Do you think it was a nightmare?"

"No! It wasn't a nightmare. He was here."

"Who?"

"I don't know, but someone—not nice." I'd wanted to say a Vyken, but didn't want to scare Jake. For some reason the very name seemed to terrify him more than it did me. How I knew it was a Vyken, I couldn't be sure. I'd never met one before, but by its unnatural movements and the way it had affected me, what else could it have been?

"Would you like a sedative, dear?" the nurse asked. Her tone reminded of the book *One Flew over the Cuckoo's Nest*.

"No, I don't need a sedative." They didn't believe me. I collapsed into bed. Christian would've believed me. I glanced over at the clock and sighed. 4:27 a.m.

"Try and go back to sleep, Llona," Jake said, his voice soothing.

"I won't be able to," I mumbled.

"What if I promise to stay awake? I'll watch TV or something."

"Really?"

"Sure."

For some reason I did feel safer knowing he'd be awake. I turned over, tucked the blanket under by chin, and closed my eyes. Before I fell asleep, I said a silent prayer, hoping that whatever Christian had to tell me would somehow help protect me. If Christian knew about Light then there was a good chance he knew about Vykens.

Morning greeted me with an onslaught of different doctors who poked and prodded at me like I was some newly discovered jungle insect.

"It's remarkable," my excellent hearing heard one of them say from down the hall. "Dr. Adams said she must've been clinically dead for at least fifteen minutes."

"Someone must've made a mistake. She'd be brain dead if that were true," a female voice replied.

"Go ask him yourself. Or better yet, read her chart. See if you can make sense of her lab results."

Their voices trailed off, leaving me to wonder what was wrong with me. This was the first time I'd ever been to a hospital. In fact, it was my first time seeing a doctor. I never thought it would be a problem until now. I needed to get out of here and quick before they decided to seal me off in some giant petri dish.

As soon as Jake returned from getting breakfast at the cafeteria, I blurted, "It's time for me to go."

His mouth gaped open. "You can't go yet. The doctors are still running tests."

"No more tests. I'm fine."

"Llona, please. Let them make sure everything is normal before they release you."

"But I'm not normal. Did it ever occur to you that my tests might show something strange?"

"Why would they?"

"Why wouldn't they? I'm an Aura. I don't know how that changes my physical make up, but I already heard a couple of the doctors talking and something's not right. You need to get me out of here."

He nodded. "All right. Do you want to wait until after breakfast? The cart is just down the hall."

"No. Let's just go."

"Okay. I'll send a nurse in to get that thing out of your arm, and then I'll get the paperwork to get you released."

"Thanks, Jake."

After the nurse left the room, I dressed and tied my shoes. Christian was right. I did feel much better thanks to the moon. The only thing that didn't feel better was my sense of impending doom. I only hoped that whatever Christian had to tell me would ease my mind.

Several minutes later, Jake returned holding a stack of papers. "All clear to go."

I zipped up my coat. "Sorry to put you through all this."

"It was an accident, nothing more. I'm just glad you're okay."

I tried to smile and averted my eyes. Me falling into the lake had been an accident, but what had happened afterward wasn't. A Vyken had tried to kill me, and I knew he wasn't going to stop until I lay as still as my mother had in her mahogany coffin.

Twenty-Two

When we returned home, I walked straight to my bedroom and closed the door. The mirror on the opposite wall reflected my image, and I shook my head in disgust. All I was, was an illusion. I kept myself hidden beneath a hat, I ran at the first sign of trouble, and most of all, I denied the power of Light. It was a strength that could protect me if I learned how to use it. And not the way my aunt wanted me to. Surely Light could be used for more than creating beautiful things and making people feel good.

I would start right away, I decided. I wasn't sure how, but somehow I would learn to use Light offensively and defensively.

I'd barely finished breakfast when the doorbell rang. I was hoping it would be Christian, but instead Heidi walked in. She gave me a hug and asked how I was. I gave the usual answer, then faked being tired and disappeared to my room again. It's not that I didn't want to see her, I just didn't feel like talking about what had happened and I could tell she was dying to ask.

I lay down in bed and put headphones on to drown out any sounds coming from the living room. I was sure Jake was filling her in, and I didn't care to relive it again.

I thought about the Vyken being in my hospital room and

couldn't help but shiver. I'd almost been killed by a Vyken. I wondered if my mother had been as frightened and helpless as I had. I turned over, letting my mind ask questions it would never have answers to.

Suddenly I felt a gentle touch on my shoulder. I opened my eyes and rolled over. Sitting on the bed next to me was Christian. I don't know why I did it, but all of a sudden I burst into tears and threw myself into his chest. His arms came around me, holding me tight.

"It's okay. Everything's all right now," he whispered as he stroked the back of my hair.

I cried for several minutes until I finally forced myself to sober up. I had so many questions that needed answering and blubbering wasn't going to get me any closer to the truth. I pulled away and wiped my eyes. "Sorry," I mumbled.

"It's okay. How do you feel?"

"My body feels great, but my head is a mess."

"I'm sure you have a ton of questions."

I nodded.

"Then ask."

I took a deep breath and then let the air out slowly as I tried to decide which question to ask first. I began with what I thought would be the simplest one to answer. "Who are you?"

"I'm your assigned guardian."

I opened my mouth to laugh, but he said it with such a serious expression that I quickly closed it again. "My what?" I asked again, thinking maybe I'd heard wrong.

"Your guardian."

"Like a godfather or something?"

He shook his head. "No. I was assigned to be your guardian by the Council, the same Council your aunt sits on."

He stopped me when I started to ask another question. "Before you bombard me with more questions, let me explain.

Every Aura, except for you of course, is assigned a guardian at age twenty when they leave Lucent Academy. The guardian's duties are to protect their wards from Vykens. We serve for three years and then are transferred to a new Aura. I've been training to be one since the age of ten under the direction of my father who is also a guardian."

"Is that why your father doesn't like me, because he's sick of Auras?" I asked.

"It's not that he doesn't like you, he's just big on following the rules."

"What rules?"

"I'll get to that. But first I want to tell you our history."

I swallowed.

"The first guardians were an elite group of men, specifically chosen by Auras for their bravery. The Auras blessed these wise men with special abilities so that they could help protect them from Vykens."

"What kind of abilities?"

"We're faster and stronger than normal humans, but nothing too crazy. Just enough to put us on an equal playing field with a Vyken. It takes a lot of hard work to get to that level, but when we do we get to teach the upcoming generation of guardians until we're assigned to an Aura. When I turned eighteen, I was assigned to you."

"Woah!" I interrupted. "You're already eighteen?"

"My birthday was in the summer."

"How did you get into school?"

He looked away, embarrassed. "I told them I was held back in the first grade." His eyes turned to mine. "It was the only way I could keep an eye you! No guardian has ever had a ward as young as you before."

"Why?"

"Because at your age, they're at Lucent where they can be

protected. They don't need a guardian until later."

"Surely there are other girls out there who have chosen not to go to Lucent. I can't be the only one."

"As far as I know, you are. And if for some crazy reason there is a girl out there who doesn't know she's an Aura, the Council has ways of finding her. It takes little convincing to get them to go to Lucent, especially when they start feeling Light."

"I don't get why everyone makes such a big deal about Lucent," I said.

"Don't knock what you don't know. Those girls learn a lot."

"Like what? Like how to grow flowers and light up the dark?"

"There's more to it than that. You have no idea how far behind you are."

"I'm not behind," I mumbled.

"Your mother went to Lucent."

"What do you know of my mother?"

"Everyone knows, or has at least heard of, your mother."

"Why's that?'

"She went against the Council—the same Council her sister, your aunt, sat on. It was a big deal back then. In fact, people still talk about her. They use her as an example of what not to do."

"But my mother was never anything but kind to everyone she met! What could she possibly have done that was so horrible?"

He paused before answering, and I noticed that when he did, he wouldn't look at me. "She married her guardian."

"My father was her guardian?"

He nodded. "It's strictly forbidden for guardians to become involved with their wards, let alone marry them."

"Why?"

"A guardian cannot effectively protect their ward if they're in love with them. Their judgment becomes clouded."

"Is that what happened to my father?"

"I don't know. Just like your mother, no one knows the circumstances behind your father's death. He was one of the best guardians so everyone was surprised when he died."

I frowned. "My father died in a car accident."

"What?" His eyes widened. "You don't know?"

"Know what?"

"Your father was killed by a Vyken. The council suspects by the same Vyken who killed your mother."

"How could I have not known about this?"

"Your aunt was probably trying to protect you."

I shook my head. "But why didn't Jake tell me?"

"Maybe she convinced him not to. She can be very persuasive."

"Even so," I said, but my mind interrupted me by suddenly putting together two pieces of what was once a difficult puzzle. "So my father was my mother's guardian and they fell in love," I repeated slowly, my mind processing the words. I looked up at Christian. "That's why you've been acting strange and staying away from me."

"I was never away from you, just out of sight, but yes. I found myself"—he struggled to find the right words—"caring for you more than I should."

I shook my head in disbelief. Everything made sense now: his constant yo-yo behavior, his stalker-like movements and that bizarre kiss.

"I'm sorry for putting you through all my emotional crap," Christian began. "I know it was hard on you. It just took me awhile to convince myself that all we could ever be is friends."

"You've convinced yourself?"

He stood up. "Please don't look at me like that. This has been the hardest thing I've ever done in my life. Every time

I look at you, I just want to—"

I leaned forward. "Yes?"

He lowered his eyes and sighed. "Can we talk about something else?"

I was about to press the issue, when my eyes caught Christian's reflection in the mirror. Specifically, I focused on his ear. "Do guardians have awesome hearing?" I asked.

His eyebrows raised. "Yeah, how'd you know?"

"I guess I inherited it from my dad."

"But you're a girl. No offense, but it's always been a guy thing."

I shrugged. "I guess I won the DNA lottery."

He was about to say more but stopped. "What's this?" He picked up my mom's old letter from my nightstand.

I forgot I'd left it out. I quickly snatched it away. "It's nothing. Just a letter my mom left for me when she died."

"Then why wasn't it signed by her?"

In addition to fast reflexes, apparently Christian was also a speed-reader. "Okay, maybe it wasn't from her, but I like to think it was. She was always doing strange things like that."

"How did you get it?"

"It was left on my bed in the arms of my favorite teddy bear."

"That doesn't make sense. Let me see it again." He held out his hand.

I reluctantly handed it to him. His eyes read over it several times. "Llona," he said. "What happened to you in the cornfield? Wait. Not just in the cornfield. Tell me everything strange that's happened to you lately."

I swallowed hard, trying to remember the first time I felt afraid. "Well, it started at the beginning of the school year. I thought I was being watched through my window. Was that you?"

He shook his head. "I never watched you close-up, only from a distance."

"So you're a long-range Peeping Tom?"

"What else has happened?"

I sighed. I thought it'd be difficult to tell him everything, but once I started I couldn't stop. I told him about the person in the woods calling my name the night I'd jumped into the river, the shadow in the tree, and my feelings about the shoe and the murder at my car. I explained my odd feeling in the cornfield before I found the dog. And finally I told him about last night and the Vyken at the foot of my bed. "I was so scared, Christian. I couldn't move. Why couldn't I move?"

Christian's reaction surprised me. Without warning, he embraced me to his chest. I was pressed so tightly against him that I could hear his heart beat racing.

"You have to leave. Tonight! Go to Lucent with your aunt. You'll be safe there," he said.

I pushed him away. "What? No! I'm not leaving. That's ridiculous. You're my guardian. Can't you protect me?"

"Obviously I can't. The Vyken has gotten too close and seems to know you too well." He shook his head and stood up. "My first ward and I can't even protect you."

"How do any of the other guardians do it? They can't watch their wards 24/7 either."

"They don't need to. Those other women are older and have been trained properly. They know how to make themselves almost invisible or run away if needs be. And they've also learned to communicate telepathically with their guardians in case of an emergency. Our situation is very different from the others, don't you see that? I can't keep you safe." He paced the room frantically.

"Can't you give me a crash course in how to do all that?"

He threw up his arms. "Come on, Llona! I can't teach you that stuff. My training was completely different from Auras."

I thought for a minute while Christian stared out the

window. He skin was pale and I thought he might throw up. All of a sudden the solution came to me like Einstein's $E=MC^2$ formula. And the more I thought about it, the more I knew it was the right decision. I could feel Light burning my skin in agreement.

I moved quickly to Christian. "I know this might sound crazy, but I want you to teach me what you know. Teach me to fight."

He stared at me. "You can't be serious."

"Really. I'm tired of running, and I'm tired of feeling like a victim. You've taught others to fight. Teach me."

I glared at him when he started laughing.

"What's so funny?" I asked.

"The whole idea of it. Auras can't fight. It's not in their nature."

"I think I'd know what's in my nature and what's not, and I'm telling you my nature wants to fight."

He walked away from me. "This is crazy. Not only is the whole idea absurd, but I'm sure there's a rule somewhere that says it's forbidden."

"Why?" I followed him across the room.

"Because! It's not like there are a bunch of Auras out there. You need to be protected. You have no idea how important they are." In a much quieter voice he said, "You have no idea how important you are."

"Christian—"

"Please, Llona. Go to Lucent where you'll be safe."

A knock at my bedroom door made him step away.

"Llona?" Jake asked. The door opened. "Some of your friends are here to see you."

Behind him, May, Matt, and Tracey rushed in. Tracey gave me a hug followed by May.

"You don't look like you almost died," Matt said as he

too wrapped his arms around me. When he let go, his arm remained on my shoulders. "You really scared us last night."

"Sorry," I said.

He hugged me again. "I'm glad you're okay. The world wouldn't be the same without you, Llona Reese."

I noticed Christian grimace and turn away.

"You sure got here early, Christian," May said. "Did you even leave her last night?"

"Of course. She needed rest."

"Thanks for saving her," Tracey told him.

Matt chimed in. "Yeah. I heard it was pretty amazing. Quite the drama ER scene."

"It was nothing." Christian still looked upset from our earlier conversation. He moved over to me. "I have to get going, but I'll come back soon, okay?"

I nodded.

After Christian left, my friends insisted on ordering pizza and watching a movie. The movie, some low-budget comedy, turned out to be more entertaining than I thought it'd be. We laughed the entire way through, as we couldn't help but make fun of the cheap filming and the inflated acting skills of the no-name actors. By the time they left, my spirits had been lifted, and I had this incredible feeling that everything was going to work out.

I wasn't about to go to Lucent, not when I had only six months left of school, but I also didn't want to make things more difficult on Christian. I meant what I said about learning to fight and if he wasn't going to teach me then I'd find someone who would. The training wouldn't be near as good as it should be, but at least Christian would know I was serious.

When Jake returned home from lunch with Heidi, I told him my brilliant idea.

"I'm serious," I cried when Jake started laughing.

"I think it's a great idea," Heidi agreed. "I took Tae Kwon Do for three years when I was younger."

"You did?" Jake asked, clearly impressed.

"Yup. My father wanted to make sure I could protect myself if I ever needed to. You should let her do it, Jake. That would be really cool of you."

"I agree, Jake. That would be really cool of you." I grinned.

He shook his head. "You know your aunt would never approve of it."

"She doesn't have to know," I said.

"I don't know, Llona."

"Not to be all defiant, but I am going to be eighteen in a few weeks and then I can pretty much do whatever I want."

"Come on, Jake," Heidi said as she nestled up to him. "Let her do it."

His eyes narrowed. "All right. What harm could come from it?"

Heidi cheered. "You're going to love it. It's such a workout. I don't know if I'd do karate though. Do more of mixed martial arts, that way you learn everything. There's a place not far from here."

The doorbell rang. Christian was back.

"Hi, Jake, Heidi," he said.

"Christian, I think you'd agree," Heidi said, turning to him suddenly.

"With what?"

"That Llona should take a martial arts class."

"A what?"

Jake spoke first, "Llona suddenly has a desire to learn how to fight. Ridiculous, huh?"

Christian chuckled. "Sure is, but I'd let her do it. I bet she quits after two weeks."

"I will not!"

"Why do you think she'll quit?" Heidi asked.

"Because Llona doesn't have fight in her."

"Apparently, you don't know me very well," I snapped.

"We'll see."

Heidi glanced down at her watch. "I have to go, but I'll come by tomorrow. Llona, I'm really glad you're okay. I care about you a lot." She gave me a quick hug.

When she left, Jake disappeared into his bedroom, leaving me and Christian alone. We both remained still, listening only to the steady tick of the clock until I asked, "So where did you go?"

Christian sat down at the kitchen table. "I was clearing my schedule for the next little while."

"Why?"

"You should know why."

"Because of me?"

"Of course because of you. I can't pretend like I'm a high school jock anymore. You are and always have been my priority."

"Not for long. Once I learn how to fight, you won't have to protect me."

A mocking grin spread across his face. "We'll see."

Twenty-Three

I was determined to prove Christian wrong. When Monday came, I decided to go visit the dojo Heidi had told me about. I was more than ready for it, especially after the crazy day I'd had at school. I'd never had so much attention in all my life. First everyone was shocked that I was even there and then after the initial shock, they bombarded me with questions about what'd happened. Luckily, Christian and May protected me from most of it.

In math, I'd wanted to thank Mr. Steele for helping me, but a substitute was teaching instead. I was disappointed, but figured I could thank him the next day. I took advantage of his absence and learned as much as I could. With all the extra credit I'd completed, I almost had my grade up to a C.

As soon as the last bell rang, I was out of there. I didn't even bother saying good-bye to May or waiting for Christian, whom I knew would be upset. But I didn't worry too much. He knew where to find me.

The dojo was like I imagined: white walls, mirrors, red and black mats. I walked in on a children's class already in progress. They looked to be around eight years old. I watched the mini ninjas for a minute before I headed to the office to discuss classes.

A short, bald man with an egg-shaped head, and the body

of a tree trunk explained that a coed class had started a few weeks ago, but he would let me join if I promised to work hard to get caught up. I easily agreed, but when he told me the cost I almost choked.

"These aren't your typical fighting classes," he said in a deep voice. "Many of our students go on to fight professionally. I know the cost seems steep, but I guarantee you will learn many different fighting techniques and will be able to hold your own against an opponent in a matter of months."

"Is that a promise?"

He stuck his hand out for me to shake. "If you work hard, absolutely."

Satisfied, I completed all the necessary paperwork.

"You can begin today if you'd like," he said.

The moon was still partially full so I knew I had enough energy to start right away. "Today's good."

"Great. I'll have a uniform ready for you. See you in an hour."

I left feeling empowered, but my jubilance was short lived. Outside, Christian leaned against his car.

"So you're serious," he said.

"I told you I was."

"I give it two weeks."

"You've already said that. Thanks for the vote of confidence." I unlocked my door.

"I have no doubts that you are physically capable, but not emotionally. You'll see. You won't like fighting."

My face grew hot. "You have no idea what I'm capable of."

"Do you? Be realistic. Fighting's not for you."

Before I could stop myself, I balled-up my fist and punched him in the gut. He doubled over, sputtering for air.

"If fighting's not for me, then how come that felt so good?" I jumped into my car and drove away before he could respond.

I'd only made it a few blocks before I saw his SUV appear in my rearview mirror following me home. He practically tail-gated me the entire way.

As soon as I pulled into the driveway, he was right behind me, jumping from his car. "Okay, you made your point. You do have some fight in you. How about we make a deal?"

"What kind of deal?"

"If you stick with your classes for three weeks, then I'll start teaching you what I know."

"Really?"

"Sure. Why not?"

"Won't you get in trouble?" I asked.

He shrugged. "We'll deal with that later. This is about what makes you safe. If taking these classes makes you feel safer, then so be it. But in the meantime, I'm going to be with you as much as possible."

A few months ago, I would've loved to hear this, but now I found it annoying. Probably because I knew the only reason he wanted to be with me was because he was my guardian. "You don't need to be with me all of the time. I've made it this far in life. I'm pretty sure I can make it the rest." I was half kidding, but he didn't laugh.

"You're not taking this seriously."

I opened the front door. "Oh really? So I'm learning to fight only to better my physique?"

"Your physique hardly needs to be bettered," he said. Instead of leaving, he plopped down on the couch. "No, I think the real reason you're doing this is because you want to prove that you can handle everything on your own. Your whole life you've taken care of yourself, and now all of a sudden you find you're in a situation you can't control and it's driving you crazy."

"You might be partially right, but I am serious about fight-ing. And I really believe it's what Light wants too."

"We'll see." He propped his legs up on the coffee table. "When does Jake come home?"

"Not for another hour, but I'll be gone when he gets back."

"Where are you going?"

"My classes start tonight."

"I'll take you and pick you up. We'll go out for ice cream afterwards."

"Deal."

*   *   *   *   *

My first martial arts lesson was a lot harder than I expected. The instructor had a thick Asian accent, and many of the students already had several years of training. I was glad when the class finally ended. The instructor told me I did well, but I think he was just being kind.

"How did it go?" Christian asked when I walked out.

"Don't ask," I said.

"Already throwing in the towel?"

"Not in this lifetime."

After ice cream, he drove me home. Just as we were pulling up to our house, I noticed a strange car parked in the driveway.

"Who's that?" Christian asked.

"No idea. It's not Heidi." I jumped out of the car and made my way inside. My heart stopped when I saw who was sitting on my favorite spot on our living room couch.

Twenty-Four

"LLONA, LOOK WHO CAME BY TO SEE HOW YOU'RE DOING," Jake said.

I stared, mouth open, head spinning.

Mr. Steele stood up. "I hope it's okay I dropped by. I couldn't make it to school today. How are you feeling?"

I squeaked out the word, "Better." Pull yourself together, I told myself.

"We were really worried about you. It's a good thing Christian was there. Everyone else had given up on you." Mr. Steele looked at Christian. "You making sure she takes it easy?"

"Yes, sir, as best I can."

"Llona just got back from fighting lessons," Jake piped up.

I shot him an angry look.

Mr. Steele raised his eyebrows. "Is that so? So much for taking it easy. What are you learning?"

"Nothing yet." I could feel my legs growing weak. Why did he have to be so good-looking? I moved to the couch to sit down before I collapsed.

"She thinks she can fight," Christian said in a mocking tone.

Mr. Steele smiled. "You will make a worthy opponent for someone one day."

I managed a smile.

"So where were you today, Mr. Steele?" Christian asked.

"Remember the doctor I punched?"

"Yeah, that was great."

"He wanted to press charges, but I convinced him not to."

"What a moron," Christian said.

"We worked it out. So when do you start playing basketball, Christian?" Mr. Steele asked.

I stared at Christian. I had no idea he'd made the team.

"Actually I decided not to."

"Really? How come? I heard you were their star player."

Christian's face reddened. "There are a lot of good players. I'm just giving myself a break for awhile, you know, to try and get my grades up."

"Are you sure there's not another reason you might want some extra time?" He glanced in my direction.

Christian didn't miss a beat. "That's just one of the perks."

Mr. Steele stood up. "I should be going. Thanks for letting me come by, Jake." He looked over at me. His eyes seemed to burn into mine, forcing me to look away. "I'm glad you're alive, Llona."

As soon as he left, Christian turned to me. "Why is it that every girl goes gah-gah over him?"

Jake laughed.

"Isn't it obvious?" I asked.

Christian snorted. "I don't see anything special."

Jake opened the front door. "I'm off too. I'm meeting Heidi for dinner. I'll be back soon. You guys want me to bring you back anything? Chinese?"

"That's okay," Christian said. "I'm going to fix something here."

As soon as Jake left, Christian went into the kitchen and began moving about as if he'd grown up there.

"Why didn't you tell me you made the basketball team?" I asked.

"What does it matter?"

"I feel bad you had to quit."

"I didn't have to. I wanted to." He turned the burner on the stove to high and placed a pan on top.

"But I know how much you love sports."

He shrugged. "I didn't come back to school to be on a team. The only reason I did it before was to blend in. We were afraid if you knew who I was, you'd run away again. You like tomato soup?"

"Sure. I still feel bad, though. Maybe if you'd teach me to do some real fighting, I won't need you as much."

He smiled. "I hope not."

*   *   *   *   *

The next couple of weeks blurred together. I continued training and actually began to feel like I knew what I was doing. My movements were more fluid and didn't seem to be so forced. Even Christian seemed impressed with my progress.

I kept up with basketball, even though the coach told me she'd understand if I couldn't finish the last couple of games, given what had happened to me and all. But I insisted on finishing the season, especially since we were undefeated.

As for Christian and I, we became inseparable. Everyone at school thought we were a couple. At first I tried to tell them we were just friends, but after awhile I realized it was easier to let them believe what they wanted. Christian didn't care one way or the other, but it sort of bothered me because we had the appearance of a relationship but none of the perks. It was as if Christian had lost all interest in me except to be my protective big brother. But I couldn't shake my feelings for him as easily as he had for me.

Because of this, I tried as best I could to find time away from him. It was simply too hard to be near him without longing for more. In addition to the dojo and basketball practices, I convinced Matt to change the book club to once a week instead of once a month. I knew Christian wouldn't ever join because of Matt. For some reason Matt really bothered him though he'd never tell me why. I also considered getting a job, but couldn't quite bring myself to give up my weekends.

A week before Christmas break we had our state basketball championship game. I'd never been so nervous! All my friends came, including Jake and Heidi. The moon was only partially full, but it was enough to keep me from embarrassing myself.

We were down by a basket with only one minute left in the game. The opposing team had the ball and was making a break for it. Leah attempted to steal it from a mammoth redhead, gratefully slowing her up while the rest of us posted beneath the basket. The redhead attempted to pass the ball, but Leah knocked it away. Our eyes all widened as it headed out-of-bounds.

With only seconds left on the clock, I knew I couldn't let the other team gain possession or the game would be over. As if a surge of adrenaline, Light exploded into my muscles, and I sprinted as fast as I could to the sidelines where I made a mad leap into the air. I didn't care that it happened to be where the other team was sitting; I only kept my focus on the ball. Just before I started falling, I slipped my hand under it and flipped it hard to Leah, who had the awesome foresight to run toward our basket. With only a few seconds left, Leah caught the ball and shot a three-pointer while I crashed into several girls. I quickly stood up in time to see the ball go through the hoop. The crowd erupted into cheers, and I, along with the rest of the team, rushed on the court to embrace Leah. It was the most amazing feeling!

"That was such an awesome save!" Leah shouted at me over the celebration.

I just smiled and congratulated her and the rest of team.

It took a long time for the crowd to die down, but when it did, my friends found me and celebrated with us. Christian whispered in my ear, "Good job, but wasn't that cheating?"

I looked at him, shocked. "It's not like I can control what I'm doing!"

"Well, you will soon, and then you can't use that excuse anymore." He grinned. "Good job, Llona. I'm proud of you." He wrapped his arm around my shoulders, and I was happy.

*　　*　　*　　*　　*

Christmas day began like every other Christmas. I woke up to the smell of bacon and pancakes, mingled with the sweet aroma of Jake's special hot chocolate. We always ate breakfast together before we opened our presents and this year was no different except for one thing: there was an unexpected knock at the door.

Jake tossed me an angry look. "Is that Christian?

"If it is, I didn't invite him."

"Doesn't he have a home?"

I stood up to answer the door. Like we both thought, it was Christian. He held several packages in his arms.

"Merry Christmas," he bellowed in a pretend Santa voice. He walked by me into the living room. "I come bearing gifts."

Jake couldn't help but smile. "Whatcha got there?"

"Nothing big. Just my way of saying thank you for putting up with me the last several weeks."

"Sounds more like a payoff to me," I said.

"Don't be so grumpy. I've got something for you too."

Christian handed a big box to Jake along with several small packages. "You first, Jake. You've had to put up with me the most."

"I doubt that," I countered.

"Thanks, Christian." Jake slowly unwrapped the big present first. He was only halfway when he began to squeal. "You have got to be kidding. Tell me this isn't what is really in the box—no, wait—tell me this *is* what's in the box."

"What is it?" I asked.

Christian's grin couldn't have been bigger.

Jake turned the box around to show me.

"What is it?" I asked again.

"It's the latest gaming system! It's not supposed to be released for another few months. Who did you have to kill to get it?"

Christian laughed. "My dad pulled some strings. It's technically a beta version, so you might come across some weird bugs."

Jake stared at the box. "I can't believe it."

"Open the others," Christian urged.

He didn't have to ask twice. Jake tore into them and laughed every time he discovered a new game for the console.

"I'm going to set it up now." Jake stood up and darted off to his room.

"What about my present?" I called after him.

"I'll open it later," he yelled back.

"Great, Christian. You ruined Christmas." I stormed off to my room.

"Maybe this will make it better," he said from behind me.

"You can't buy *me* off so easily." I was about to shut my bedroom door, but he blocked it with his foot.

"Come on, Llona. Just open your present. Please?"

I let the door open a little. "If I do, will you promise to go afterward? We were just starting to open our presents. Of course, what I got Jake will seem like kitty litter compared to what you just got him, but still."

"Look, if you still want me to go after opening this, then I will, sort of."

"What's that supposed to mean?"

"I'll just be outside, keeping on eye on things."

I sighed. "Whatever." I held out my hand.

Christian handed me a small square box that wasn't wrapped.

"I really wished you wouldn't have," I said as I opened it.

Inside was a silver necklace with what looked like a narrow dog tag hanging from its chain. I pulled it out and tried to read the inscription. "It's beautiful. Thank you. What does it say?"

" 'Endure to the end' "

I looked at it closer. "Endure to the end," I whispered. The metal tag had been etched in a circular pattern reminding me of the symbol for eternity.

"Will you put it on me?" I turned around.

He took the ends of the necklace, and, after pushing my hair to the side of my neck, fastened it.

"Why did you choose that inscription?" I asked.

His hands moved to my shoulders. "I know I don't act like it all the time, but you have no idea how much you mean to me." He swallowed. "I need you to endure, to do all that you can to see that you live a good, long life. I couldn't bear it if anything were to happen to you."

I felt his body move close to mine. In one swift motion, I turned around and stared into his eyes. Any thoughts of him thinking I was like a sister were suddenly erased. He was looking at me with such passion that I wondered how he was able to hide it for so long. He leaned his forehead against mine and very slowly his hands moved up to my waist. My lips parted and air escaped. The sound must've startled him because all of a sudden he froze and closed his eyes. His jaw muscles bulged.

"I'm going to go set up a game or something," he said and walked away.

"Can it be Twister?" I called after him.

He didn't answer.

The rest of the day went without incident between me and Christian—much to my dismay. I felt stupid giving him my present after he'd given me such a considerate gift. All I gave him was a jersey from his favorite football team and a pink sugar cookie—his favorite snack food. We played games for awhile, watched a movie, and ate way too much. Around six, Jake got called into work because of some computer glitch, leaving us alone.

I enjoyed it, but after twenty minutes, Christian began to pace and then inexplicably said he had to go too.

"Do you really have to?" I whined.

"Yeah." He stood up and glanced around. "Where did I put my jacket?"

"Um, I think it's in my room. I'll get it." I stood up and walked down the hallway. "I wouldn't want you to stay here any longer than you have to," I said under my breath.

"What did you say?" he called after me.

I ignored him and opened the door to my room. The light from the hallway let in just enough for me to see Christian's jacket on top of my dresser. I moved in to grab it but noticed something on my bed. It was a box wrapped in black paper with a red ribbon on top. Christian must have left it as a surprise. I smiled. He wasn't really leaving after all. The whole "where's my jacket" thing was just a ploy to get me to find another present.

I picked it up, removed the lid, and frowned as my brain tried to process what was lying in the box. At first I thought it was a small stuffed animal—a teddy bear perhaps. I reached in to touch it, but when my fingers felt the course white hair, I knew there was nothing synthetic about it.

The box dropped from my hands and as it hit the floor, the limp body of a dead rat flopped out.

White mouse.

White dog.

And now a white rat.

He'd been with me since the very beginning. Just then a dark figure appeared at the window. Instinctively, I screamed. When I heard Christian rush down the hallway, I quickly kicked the box and the dead rat under my bed. When I glanced at the window, the shadow was gone.

"What's wrong? What happened?" he said, the moment he entered the room.

I flipped the light on. "Nothing," I stammered, trying quickly to gain control over my nerves. "I thought I saw a mouse." There. That wasn't too far from the truth.

"A mouse? It sounded like you just saw death."

I swallowed and forced a smile. "Death, mouse, same thing."

Christian moved to the window and peered into the darkness. "Where is it?"

"Um, I think it ran into the closet."

Christian opened the closet door and pushed aside several shoes. "I don't see it now."

"It's probably long gone. It was a fast little bugger."

"Do you want me to stay?"

Inside I yelled yes, but I heard myself say, "No. I think I can handle a mouse."

"Okay then." He pulled his jacket on.

I followed him to the front door, all the while trying desperately to think of something that would get him to stay, but came up empty. I knew the moment I saw the rat and the shadow at my window, I couldn't tell Christian. He'd insist I go to Lucent. I couldn't go to Lucent, especially now. I was finally learning to take control of my life by learning to defend myself. I'd never get this opportunity again, and the last thing

I wanted was to be dependant upon a guardian to feel safe for the rest of my life.

At the door, I said, "It's been three weeks, Christian. You said I'd quit, but I haven't. You owe me."

He nodded and reached into his pocket. "I was wondering when you'd bring that up."

"You're not going to back out, are you?"

"No. A deal's a deal." He removed his hand from his pocket and revealed what looked like a watch. "Here's your first lesson. Give me your wrist."

"This may surprise you, but I already know how to tell time."

"This isn't a watch. It's a heart monitor." He latched the black-looking device tightly to my wrist.

"I don't get it."

"For the next twenty-four hours, this monitor will determine your base heart rate. After that it will automatically set itself to beep if your heartbeat goes over your base rate. The goal is to always remain calm and keep your heart rate normal. If you can do that, you'll be able to think your way through tough situations and this is what will save your life. Once you master this, then I will teach you what I've been taught."

I examined the monitor. "How long did it take you to do this?"

"Months."

"Months?"

"It shouldn't take you as long. Use your Light to help keep you calm. It should be easy. Light loves being at peace."

"Then what's wrong with me?"

"What do you mean?"

"How come I like to fight?"

He tilted his head, thinking. "I don't think you like to. I just think life has put you in a position where you feel you have to fight to survive."

Just then Jake's car pulled into the driveway.

"Want to go to a movie tomorrow or something?" Christian asked me as he opened the front door.

"We'll see. I'm feeling pretty tired," I said, as I searched the black sky for the moon.

"Get some rest then."

"See you."

Later that night, with glove in hand, I carefully dumped the rat in a white bag and stuffed it in the bottom of the kitchen garbage. I wasn't about to dump it outside and risk the chance of coming face to face with a Vyken. I don't know if that even mattered anymore. A Vyken had entered my house. While I was home. And he knew where my room was. That means whoever was stalking me was definitely an acquaintance and possibly a close one.

After washing my hands, I locked all the doors and windows then slipped a carving knife under my pillow. All these precautions didn't make me feel any safer.

I'd like to say things became better the next several weeks, but they didn't. First there was the annoying sound of Christian's dumb heart monitor going off every time I breathed heavy. The teachers were constantly getting upset at me, but after I politely explained that I had to wear it per the doctor's orders, they left me alone.

It was a lot harder than I thought trying to remain calm. It would go off even when I wasn't stressed. Like one time Matt put his arm around me to walk me to class like he always did, but suddenly my heart rate went up, and off went the annoying alarm. I couldn't figure out why; I didn't like him like that and I know he didn't like me either. We were just friends. I guess I still wasn't used to being touched.

Whatever the reason, Matt became good practice for me to remain calm and keep my breathing slow and steady. I was beginning to get really good at it—during the day. Night was a whole other story.

Almost every night I was visited by the same dark figure outside my window. He'd appear out of nowhere for just a few seconds and then be gone, but lately his visits were becoming more frequent. And it was like he knew when I was in my room no matter how quiet I was or how late the hour.

I didn't have blinds on my windows, nor did I want any until now. I loved having a view of the mountains. It made me feel like I was a part of them, but now the openness made me feel vulnerable.

The nightly visits by shadow man only made me train that much harder. I asked my martial arts instructor if I could join the advanced class held just after mine. He said I could as long as I was able to keep up. I not only kept up but started to excel in it too. I found I could use Light to predict my opponent's moves, making my blows more effective. But even more amazing, I was able to fight and still maintain a normal heart rate.

But at night, the beeping sound of the monitor often woke me up, and I'd only have to look to the window to know the source of my anxiety.

"What do you want?" I whispered loudly one night. But even as I finished my sentence, he was gone.

After that I started sleeping on the couch in the living room. This made all the difference in the world. In only a week's time of fighting hard and keeping my heart rate normal, I began to feel more confident. So when Jake told me he had to go away for the weekend on a business trip, I wasn't concerned at all. In fact I was so confident, I decided to sleep in my own room again, just to prove I wasn't afraid.

My favorite late night talk show had just ended. I locked all the doors and mentally turned off the porch light. I tried not to be nervous as I made my way down the hall to my room, but with every step my anxiety grew. Before I even got there, I knew what I would face. It was as if I could feel his presence, waiting.

I stopped just before entering my room. No more. I was going to put an end to this once and for all. I rushed to the garage and flipped on the light. It took me several minutes to find what I was looking for. I found it buried behind several boxes: black paint. I grabbed the rest of the painting supplies and headed back to my room. This time I didn't feel the anxiety I'd felt before. Shadow man was gone.

I turned the light on in my room and worked quickly. In less than ten minutes, my entire window had been painted black. I stepped away from it, satisfied. And for the first time in weeks, I finally fell asleep peacefully in my own bed. That is until 2:21.

Twenty-Five

My eyes focused on the green, glowing light of the clock. It took me a moment to realize the heart monitor was beeping. Along with my heart racing, came labored breathing. The air felt heavy, pressure mounting with every second. I sat up and tried to inhale. The feeling was so powerful—much like it'd been in the hospital—that I half expected to see a Vyken standing in my room.

I didn't want to, but my gaze turned slowly toward the window. My body followed until I was standing next to my bed, facing the painted glass. He was behind it; I had no doubts. Count to ten and he'll be gone, I told myself. I managed to get to eight before I took a step toward the window.

I was losing control.

As much as my mind fought against the pull, my body moved on its own accord. The sound of my heart beating was louder than the beeping monitor. A cold sweat broke on my brow, and my hands became ice cold. When I was only inches from the window, I stopped and stared into the blackness. I could see nothing beyond it, but I could feel him as close as if he were standing next to me.

The last of my bravery shattered to pieces when the paint directly in front of me began to peel back as if a claw were scraping it away—on the inside of the glass. I watched in horror as five thin stripes of black paint fell to the carpet. Again the invisible nails scraped at the glass, leaving a clear slash mark in its wake. It sounded like nails on a chalkboard; a violent chill rocked my whole body.

One last time the invisible hand clawed off paint, leaving a narrow view to the other side. What I saw melted my insides. A bloodshot, yellowed eye peered in at me as if I were a mouse in a hole.

I begged myself to move, to do anything, but I could only stare. Not until I felt the icy touch of something invisible touch my shoulder did I finally react.

Using all the strength I could muster, I called upon Light's energy. I focused every part of me on lighting up the house. Immediately, all the lights including the back porches lit up, taking with it my shadow man.

I moved quickly, grabbing my coat, shoes, and keys, and then bolted outside to my car. I pressed on the accelerator as hard as I could. The sound of the tires squealing against the wet pavement probably woke the neighbors, but I didn't care.

By the time I reached Christian's house, I was crying hysterically as I banged on the front door. That's not how I wanted to react, but I'd never been touched by something so dark and evil. The unclean feeling lingered on me like a bad dream.

Gratefully it was Christian who answered the door. I threw myself into him without thinking. His arms came around me and he held me tightly, making me feel safer than I'd felt in weeks.

He waited for me to calm down and catch my breath before he finally asked, "What happened?"

I opened my mouth to speak but then realized the heart monitor was still going off. "Get this stupid thing off me," I cried as I tried to tear it from my wrist.

Very gently, Christian turned over my arm and pushed a button on the side of the monitor, silencing it. "What happened?"

"I—" I began, but stopped suddenly. "You need to teach me to fight, and not the normal crap I've been doing. I need the upgraded version with all the perks." I stepped away from him.

Instead of answering, he took me by the hand and guided me into the living room.

"Before we do anything else, I want you to sit down and tell me what happened."

"You mean what's been happening." I took a deep breath and collapsed into the sofa.

Christian sat opposite me. In a calm, but strained voice, he said, "Please explain."

I hesitated, but only for a moment. I thought I'd be able to handle everything. I thought I was stronger. Obviously, I wasn't.

I couldn't look him in the eyes as I told him all that had happened, beginning with the rat on Christmas. In fact, I avoided looking at him all together. His bare knee became my focal point. When I finished telling him what happened tonight, my eyes moved to his suddenly clenched fists.

"So you see, I have to learn what you know and fast. I don't want to be scared anymore," I whispered.

He was silent for several moments, then, "This is all my fault. It's my job to protect you, and I've failed. I will call the Council in the morning and have someone else assigned."

I looked up at him, aghast. "You can't be serious. You haven't failed."

He shook his head. "But I have. I should've been watching your house longer. I should've set up a tighter security system. I shouldn't have been such a moron!"

"You installed a security system?"

"Just on the doors and windows."

"When?"

"Before you moved in."

"I thought it was from the old owners. I didn't know it actually worked."

"Obviously it doesn't—not how it should anyway. I had no idea a Vyken could get to you like that." He visibly shuddered. "I'll need to report this. Other guardians should know."

"No. You can't! If you do, my aunt will tell my uncle, and they'll all force me to leave. I'm not leaving. There's only a few months left of school."

"School isn't important. Your life is."

"This isn't about school. It's about not running. You said you'd teach me. I did what you asked and even wore your lame beeping machine. And I think I got pretty good at it."

"Except for tonight."

"Well, yeah. I was touched by something inhuman. Who wouldn't freak out?"

"I'll admit you've gotten better. And what you've been able to do with your fighting has far surpassed what I thought you were capable of, to the point where it's a little unnerving."

"Why?"

"Because Auras supposedly aren't capable of fighting. And even if they were, the Council doesn't allow it. If they found out, you and I would be in a lot of trouble."

"What is so wrong with me trying to defend myself?"

"Because you weren't meant to fight."

"Who knows what I'm meant for? Is my destiny already written somewhere?"

His shoulders sagged. "Look, I'm not saying I agree with it, I'm just telling you what I've been taught."

"If you don't agree, then teach me." I tried to keep from yelling, but I could hear my voice losing control.

After a moment, he said, "Fine. We'll start tomorrow. You can stay here tonight."

The dark cloud above me lifted. "Really? Won't your dad care?"

"He's at the same convention as Jake." He stood up. "Come on. I'll show you to the guest bedroom."

My legs felt like bricks as I made my way up the stairs. If it wasn't for Christian's hand on my back, encouraging me, I might not have made it. But no matter how tired I was, I was still afraid to be alone.

"Is something wrong?" Christian asked, when I remained in the doorway.

I turned around. "I don't mean anything by it, but could you stay with me?"

He nodded. "Of course."

I slowly slid under the covers and pulled them to my chin. Our eyes met briefly before Christian lay down on the floor next to the bed. Within a few minutes, my mind began to drift, but before I wandered too far into dreamland, I heard Christian whisper, "I'll get him, Llona. I promise."

Twenty-Six

"ALL OF OUR LESSONS WILL START WITH A FIFTEEN-MINUTE yoga session," Christian began.

"Really? Yoga? You never struck me as the tofu-loving sort," I joked. We were in Christian's basement, which had been converted into a miniature basketball court/training room. The giant room was every teenager's dream, and I could tell by the worn mats that it had been used plenty.

After Christian had picked me up from the dojo, he'd wanted to give me a rest before training. Six months ago I would've taken him up on the offer while the moon was barely a sliver, but ever since I decided to fight, I found I had much more energy, regardless of the moon.

"Yoga will get you in the right frame of mind. Everything I teach you will require you to be calm and collected. Do you think you can handle that?"

"Bring it on, Yoda." I crouched low into the Eagle Pose.

*   *   *   *   *

Christian was right about yoga. After just a few days of training, I was already more focused. Yoga helped me become more at one with Light, giving me added strength and agility.

This was a new feeling and gave me much-needed confidence.

Although I was learning a lot during the day, nighttime was still difficult. I was often anxious, almost to the point of hyperventilating. After the Vyken's visit at my window, Christian had installed a more sophisticated security system surrounding the perimeter of our home. He also promised to watch our house throughout the night. I refused, as I couldn't see how he could maintain school too, but he assured me it was what he was trained to do.

My clock flipped to 3:00 a.m. I sat up straight, breathing hard from a lingering nightmare. I slipped out of bed and moved to the window, which had recently been stripped of the black paint. Christian thought it would help my anxiety if I could see outside and be able to see him not far away.

I looked out the window and smiled. Sitting in his usual spot, half way up the hill, was Christian, a blanket wrapped around him. The light from the moon encased every part of his tensed body as he stared in the direction of my house. His eyebrows were pulled so tightly together, they shadowed his eyes.

I moved the curtain back until I found the recently installed security keypad. I pushed a few buttons and a green light appeared. As quietly as possible, I opened the window and began to climb out. Christian was by my side before my bare feet could touch the cold ground.

"What's wrong?" he asked.

"Nothing. I just wanted to see you."

He shook his head. "No. You need to stay inside." His face looked pale, making the dark circles under his eyes stand out like a raccoon's.

"You can't keep doing this," I said.

"Doing what?"

"Watching my house like this. You're going to collapse."

"I'll be fine. The last thing you should worry about is me."

My eyes found his. "Impossible."

"Go back inside."

"Give me your hand first."

"What?"

"Just do it. Please?"

He slowly lifted his hand. I gently closed my palm over his, shut my eyes and concentrated. In a matter of seconds I felt Light ignite between us. I transferred what I could without making myself too weak in the process. I opened my eyes. "How do you feel?" I asked, dropping his hand from mine.

He swung his arms backwards and turned his head back and forth. "Much better."

"Good. I'm not sure how long it will last though."

"What did you do?"

"Gave you some of my Light."

"But won't that make you weak?"

I shrugged. "A little, but you needed it more than me."

"Don't ever do that again." He stepped away.

"Christian?"

"Go back inside, Llona."

"I was just trying to help."

"I know, but I don't need it."

"Sure you don't, Hercules," I said and turned around to climb back in the window. If he wouldn't let me help my way, then I'd find another way.

*   *   *   *   *

Sure enough, after just a few weeks, the dark circles under his eyes seemed permanent. I decided something needed to be done about our current arrangement and there was only one person who could make it happen.

"Can we talk?" I asked Jake after breakfast.

"Sure. What is it?"

I swallowed. "There's something I've been meaning to tell you."

"Sounds serious."

"It is, sort of. I mean, we have it taken care of. In a way."

"Have what taken care of and who is 'we'?"

"You know Christian—"

"Yes, I know him." He leaned forward.

"Well, there's something you don't know about him." I tapped my hand on the table. Why am I so nervous?

Jake waited patiently.

"You see, Christian and I are close. We're bonded in a way that most other couples aren't and our current arrangement is making it difficult on us."

Jake's eyes widened, and he began to shake his head. "No. Not me. This can't be happening."

"What?"

With a grim expression, he said, "Adoption is always an option."

"What? Why would we—Oh, Jake! No that's not what I was going to say."

I laughed so hard I thought milk would come shooting from my nose.

"So, you're not pregnant," Jake guessed.

"Hardly. Christian and I haven't even kissed." Not in my book anyway.

"Then what are you talking about?"

I decided to just blurt it out to prevent any more miscommunication. "Christian's my guardian."

Jake grew quiet.

"Jake?"

His head lowered.

"What's wrong?" I asked.

When he finally lifted his head, his eyes were wet. "Your father was your mom's guardian."

"I know."

"Did Christian tell you?"

I nodded. "How come you told me my father died in a car accident?"

"Do you know how he really died?"

"I know a Vyken killed him. That's about it."

Jake wiped at his eyes. He suddenly looked ten years older. "After your mother died, your father became obsessed with finding Lander."

"Who?"

"Lander. He was Mark's—your father's—friend who turned out to be a Vyken. He was a manipulative jerk—even I liked him."

"How did they meet?"

Jake leaned back in his chair, remembering. "They met at the logging factory where your father worked in Oregon."

"I remember living there, but I don't remember a Lander."

"Really?" Jake seemed genuinely surprised. "You spoke to him many times. You must've been what, four or five?"

I shrugged, thinking nothing of it. "What happened?"

"Your father wasn't like your mother. He didn't let people into your lives very easily, but after a long time he came to trust Lander. He befriended our family like a wolf in sheep's clothing. All of us were fooled.

"Then one early morning while your father was out of town, Lander called saying he had a flat tire. Your mother woke me up and told me she was leaving to go help him since Mark was gone. Instead of going back to sleep after she left, I got out of bed. The sun was just coming up, and I wanted to take advantage of being able to play video games unsupervised."

I shook my head.

Jake continued, "I had just barely started playing when you woke up screaming." He swallowed. "I couldn't get you to stop. You just kept screaming over and over for almost two hours. I finally called Mark to tell him what was going on. He could hear you screaming in the background. When he asked where your mother was and I told him, he completely freaked out. He knew something was wrong.

"He told me he was on his way home and to turn on your mother's favorite music to calm you down. Luckily it worked." He paused and took a deep breath. "By the time your father came home, the police were already at our house. They found your mother's body in the middle of the street. I tried to talk to Mark, but he went immediately to you."

This was the first time I'd ever heard this story, and I had to bite the inside of my cheek to keep from crying. "And my father? What happened to him?"

"Like I said, he became obsessed with finding Lander. He quit his job and began searching full time. He chased him all over the country."

"That's why we were moving all the time," I said, remembering how horrible it was. We were never in a place longer than a few months.

"Yes. It was a rough time for both of us. I begged Mark to let me come with him, to help him, but he refused. He said I needed to be there for you. Besides, I hardly had his abilities, but I would've given my life for him."

"Why couldn't he just let it go?" I said. "Why did he have to leave us to avenge her death?"

Jake stared at me. "You think that's what he was doing?"

"Wasn't it?"

"He was doing it for you. Once your father found out that Lander was a Vyken and had killed your mother, he knew you'd be his next target. Not right away, but eventually. He

234

was trying to save your life."

My voice was so quiet I barely heard it. "I had no idea."

"I'm glad we had this talk then. I would've told you sooner had I known you were angry with him. You were always his priority."

Very slowly, my eyes met his. "How did he die?"

"We don't know. My guess is he found Lander and they fought. He must've lost because his body was found in almost the exact same position as your mother—two puncture wounds in the neck."

"Do you think Lander will come back for me?" Deep down I already knew the answer, but I didn't want to associate a name to the faceless creature who haunted me at night.

He sighed. "It's a fear I have every day. I'm not like your father. I can't protect you like he could. These last several years I've trusted you to know when you don't feel safe. That's why I never argued with you when you said you wanted to move. I had to trust you knew what's best. I also knew Sophie had people checking up on you occasionally, but I had no idea she had assigned you a guardian. And Christian? I just thought he was your boyfriend this whole time."

"Hardly," I said.

"Isn't he kind of young to be one?"

"Sophie thought a guardian posing as a student would be best to keep an eye on me."

"How old is he?"

"Eighteen."

"Huh," Jake said as he tried to digest what I'd told him. "Then why the dramatics? What's going on between you two?"

I took a deep breath. "There's more, but you have to promise not to tell Sophie."

"I can't do that."

"But if I tell you and you tell her, she'll make me go to

Lucent early, and I don't want to do that. For the first time in my life, I feel in control. I don't want to leave."

"How about I agree to listen and then we'll work something out, but I can't promise anything."

I considered this. If I didn't tell him, then Christian might pass out from exhaustion. There's no way he could make it another few months at the rate he was going. As much as I didn't want to leave, I couldn't watch Christian suffer any longer.

With my mind made up, I told Jake about the Vyken coming to my window at night and how Christian had been guarding me ever since. "It's killing him, Jake. I tried to get him to stop, but I think he feels responsible or something."

Jake nodded. "It's how your father was. Look, Llona, this is serious. Have you seen the Vyken during the day?"

"Not that I know. Do you think it could be Lander?"

"It very well could be, but coming to your window doesn't sound like his style. He would want to get to know you. Do you remember anything about his looks?"

"No, but it's always been dark. And besides, that wouldn't matter. Vykens can change their appearance, so Lander could pretty much be anyone I know."

"Wait, what? Since when?"

I shrugged. "Since Sophie told me."

"I had no idea. I'm not in the loop on all the Aura gossip. The rules in your world seem to change all the time. Knowing this, it's probably best if you do go to Lucent."

I lowered my head.

"That being said," Jake continued, "You are different. You're not like other Auras, not even like your mother."

"Really?"

"Your mother was strong, but she was also careless. She lived her life with no regards to the future. That's not how you are. You're so much more careful. And you're not afraid to fight. Maybe I won't make you leave." He rubbed the back of his neck, frowning. "Let me think about it though."

My face lit up. "You mean it?"

"We'll see, but I am worried about Christian."

"I think we can help him."

"How?" Jake asked.

"First, you have to have an open mind. Second, you can't freak out."

"Just spit it out," he said.

"Let him stay here at night. He can sleep on the couch, and I'll be in my room. That way if there's a problem, he'll be right here. He can get his sleep and still be close enough to protect me."

The hand that was rubbing the back of his neck moved to his temple. I think I was giving him a headache. "That may work, but I don't want any unnecessary contact between the two of you, if you catch my meaning."

"Not gonna happen. It's against the rules."

"Rules can be broken. Remember your father and mother?"

"But Christian's not like that. He takes his position very seriously."

"So did your father, but when it comes to matters of the heart, rules don't matter."

I placed my hands flat on the table and stared at him. "I promise. It won't be a problem. Besides, other than me leaving, this is the best way Christian can keep me safe without killing himself in the process."

Jake stared into the distance while he tapped his fingers. I waited patiently for him to decide—for a second.

"Come on, Jake. I promise nothing will happen."

He turned to me. "All right. He can sleep on the couch, but I'm going to come up with some strict rules."

I threw my arms around him. "Thank you!"

I jumped up and opened the front door, but Christian's car was already gone. He usually left at dawn to get ready for school, but sometimes, he'd come back. I guess I'd have to tell him at school.

Christian wasn't in first period and when I couldn't find him in second, I began to worry. As far as I knew, he'd never missed a day of school. I tried calling him, but he didn't answer his cell phone. After third period, I faked sick and drove straight to Christian's house. His SUV was parked in the driveway.

As soon as I jumped out of my car, I saw Mr. Knight leaving the house. I was half tempted to dive behind my car and hide, but he had already spotted me and was walking toward me with an expression that said, "Wait until I get my hands on you!"

He moved so close I had to back into my car just to leave a little space between us. "Hello, Mr. Knight. How—"

"This is your fault." He raised a finger at my chest. It might as well have been a gun.

"Excuse me?" I asked.

"You think you're more special then the rest of them? That you don't have to follow the rules?"

"I'm sorry, sir, but I don't know what you're talking about."

His eyes twitched and his nostrils flared. "Christian got hurt protecting you last night."

Twenty-Seven

My heart sunk into my stomach. I placed my hand on my car to steady myself. "Is he okay?"

"If you would've gone to Lucent like all the others, this would never have happened. I knew Christian should have declined a guardian position for someone so young and inexperienced." Spittle from his lips sprayed my face. I resisted the urge to wipe it away.

"Is Christian okay?" I asked again.

"He will be."

"What happened?"

"He broke a rule. That's what happens when you start feeling beyond what a guardian should feel for a charge." He shook his head. "You are just like your mother, careless and thoughtless. And I don't care what difficult circumstances the Council—or should I say your aunt—thinks you have. You are just like the rest of them and should have to follow the same rules. They made a mistake allowing your mother to do whatever she wanted, but they're making a bigger mistake allowing you to do the same thing."

My head snapped up like a struck bow. "I don't care what you think about me or my mother. I just want to see Christian."

He stared at me for what seemed an eternity before he

finally stepped out of the way.

As I walked off, he called after me, "Think about someone else for a change."

In my mind, I imagined myself giving him the bird.

I opened the front door without knocking. A maid or servant—or whatever the rich call them—asked, "Can I help you, miss?"

"I'm looking for Christian."

"He's upstairs. Third door on the left."

I bounded up the stairs and threw open the door. The bedroom was so opposite from the rest of the house I wondered if I'd entered the wrong room. Other than a bed and dresser, there was no furniture. The walls were bare except for a shelf that held an encased, autographed football. I quickly forgot about the oddness of the room when my eyes found Christian lying in bed. My heart broke.

"What are you doing here?" Christian asked. It was difficult to understand him because he was trying to speak through two swollen lips.

I didn't answer. I moved to his bedside and very carefully touched his swollen face. His chest was bare except for a white brace that wrapped itself around both of his shoulders, making him look like he was wearing a cop's gun holster.

"Shouldn't you be at school," he said, and turned away from my touch.

"I am so sorry."

Christian struggled to sit up. "For what? You didn't do anything. I was the moron who got hurt." He grimaced as he shoved an extra pillow behind his back. "It looks worse than it is. I'll be fine in a couple of days." He paused. "Will you say something? You're making me feel like Frankenstein."

"What happened?" I finally asked.

He attempted to sigh, but his breath caught in his chest

and he gasped for air. "Stupid ribs," he mumbled.

I took hold of his hand.

With his head down, staring at my hand, he began, "Last night at around three, the Vyken came. He was on the mountain ridge above your house just standing there, staring. When I stood up, I caught his attention. I thought he'd run, but he just kept staring. And then the strangest thing happened. His body began to shift and his figure changed until it was you I saw standing on the ridge. I knew it was you because of your long, light hair. It was blowing all crazy in the wind."

"How could it have been me?"

"Well, not you, of course, but he'd made himself look like you."

"How's that possible?"

"It's the first time I've heard of it. I mean, I know Vykens can change their appearance after drinking an Aura's blood, but I didn't know they could do it multiple times." He shook his head. "It's crazy."

"Then what happened?" I asked.

His eyes met mine. "If you were anyone else, I wouldn't tell you this, but I think you can handle it."

"What?"

"After a minute, your blonde hair became blood red. And then your face . . . you had no eyes, only black holes." He moved his hand out from under mine, and then grasped my arm tightly. "And then your head fell off."

"Wow," I said, taking in what he'd just told me. "So what did I do next, you know, with a broken neck and all?"

"That's what you want to know? I knew you'd be able to handle it, but I didn't think you'd act so nonchalant about it."

I took hold of my head and moved it around. "My head works just fine. What you saw was just an illusion. What's the point of getting upset over something that didn't happen?"

"Because the Vyken was showing me what he's going to do to you."

I shrugged. "I already know he wants me dead. Now I know how. Maybe I'll start wearing a metal neck brace or something."

"This isn't funny. Why aren't you taking this seriously?"

I took a deep breath. "You're right. It's not funny, but if I start thinking about how a Vyken wants to snap my neck, I'll become a raving lunatic. I need to have a clear head about this, stay unemotional. Isn't that what you have been trying to teach me?" I smiled at him.

"Maybe I need to stop being such a good teacher."

"So finish your story. How did you get hurt?" I asked. I needed him to get my mind off the image he'd planted. The truth was—I was terrified.

Christian continued, "After his psychotic transformation, I lost it. I charged after him, determined to kill him. I chased him through the mountains for almost an hour. I was so intent on getting to him that I wasn't paying attention to my surroundings. I lost my footing and fell down a steep ravine and ended up looking like this. It was one of the dumbest things I've ever done."

"What rule did you break?" I asked.

"Huh?"

"Your father. He said you broke a rule."

"It's a dumb rule to begin with. You see, we're not supposed to pursue a Vyken. We are always supposed to stay with our charge."

"And wait like sitting ducks?"

"Like I said, it's a dumb rule, but a rule nevertheless."

"Actually, it's a good rule." I dropped my head. "Your father's right. This is my fault."

"No, it's not. I just made a bad decision."

I wasn't listening. "As much as I don't want to, I think it's time I went to Lucent. At least if I was there you'll be safe— and me too. It's selfish of me to stay."

"No. Things are different now." The lines in his face pulled tightly together. "I have to tell you something. When you first started learning to fight, I really believed you wouldn't be able to do it. It isn't that Auras are weak or anything, they're just," he struggled to find the right word, "too pure or something. Fighting is supposed to be a conflict of their nature. But then you came along and destroyed that whole theory. You have learned more these past months than a guardian does in five years. You're fast, strong, logical, unemotional; well, most of the time."

I smiled. "I'm still a girl."

"I'm very aware of that. Too aware."

My cheeks burned.

"I don't want you to go yet, Llona. There's so much more I want to teach you—to see what you're capable of. Maybe we could change things for the better."

"How?"

He leaned toward me, wincing. "I've never liked the idea of sending Auras to a private school where they learn to blend in and mask their gift just so they can stay hidden. I think we need to have people out there hunting and killing Vykens, making it possible for Auras to really make a difference in this world. Can you imagine what Auras could do if they weren't afraid to be who they really are?"

I considered this. It would be an amazing world to have Auras like my mother around who knew how to defend them- selves. I remembered the tale my mother used to tell me about how wonderful the world was when Light didn't have to hide.

Christian chuckled. "Wouldn't it be great if Auras could just use their powers and hunt Vykens?"

My head snapped up. "But they did!"

"What?"

I spoke fast. "The story my mom used to tell me, like every night. She said Auras—" I lifted my hands and made the air quote gesture—"used Light's power to fight against the Vykens. They fought against them. Used their powers, Christian. I'd always get mad at my mom for telling me the same story over and over, but now I can see why she did. She wanted me to know the truth! She wanted me to know what Light's capable of!"

Christian looked thoughtful. "I don't know. The Council's rules are strict, and they've been around for hundreds of years."

"But surely there are others who think the rules are lame."

"Some, but they are very careful who they voice their opinions to. Years and years ago, like in the thirties or something, there was a strong movement to hunt Vykens. They even had an Aura fighting with them."

"Serious?"

"Yeah. I guess she was pretty amazing and even managed to kill some Vykens."

"What happened?"

"She was eventually killed. When this happened, anyone who followed her was brought to trial before the Council. The group was quickly disbanded, and they all faced harsh punishment."

"Like what? It's not like the Council are police or anything. They can't put you in jail."

"No, but they have other ways. Like they can ostracize you from your own. Basically make you a leper. Not very many Auras go against the Council. Take your mother for example. She didn't have any Aura friends. Your father too. They were completely cut off."

I laughed out loud. "Like they cared, especially my mother. She had more friends than anyone I've ever known. I highly doubt this bothered her in the least."

"It probably didn't, but for most Auras this can be very frightening. If you don't obey the rules of the Council, then there's no one to teach you, no one to protect you. Your mother was lucky her husband was a guardian, otherwise she would've been left defenseless."

"How come I have one then?"

He paused. "Not to make you feel bad or anything, but the only reason you were assigned a guardian is because your aunt is on the Council."

"So your dad was right," I whispered.

"You may have gotten special treatment, but I can promise you no other Aura has been through what you've gone through. I think you deserve it."

"I don't deserve anything."

His hand tightened on mine. "You deserve to be happy and feel safe. I'm sorry I haven't done a better job of making that happen."

"You've done great. But it has got to stop."

He shrugged and lifted one corner of his mouth, showing the dimple in his cheek. "It's just the way it is."

"Not any more. If I'm going to stay here until the end of school, and you're going to stay my guardian, then our arrangement needs to change."

"And what would you suggest?"

"Jake said you could sleep at our house. On the couch of course," I said.

"Really?"

"It's a great idea. You'll be close enough to know if there's a problem, and you'll be able to get a lot more sleep."

I expected him to give some kind of resistance, but instead, he surprised me by saying, "That would make things easier."

"Yes, it would. Do you think your dad will care?"

"Not at all. It will probably be easier on him, knowing I'm indoors instead of out. You sure Jake's okay with this?"

"Totally, but only as long as you promise to keep your perverted hands off me."

He smiled. "I'll try, but it'll be hard."

I touched his face again. "Is there anything I can get you?"

"Not now, but after school you can bring me back one of those fat sugar cookies with pink frosting and a glass of milk."

"Deal." I stood up and turned to leave.

"Wait! One more thing, Llona."

"Yes?"

"If what I'm about to ask you makes you feel the least bit uncomfortable, then I want you to pretend I didn't say anything, okay?"

"Um, okay."

He took a deep breath before he said, "I want you to start using Light as a weapon."

Twenty-Eight

What? I was still saying "what" in my mind hours later while sitting in last period. It was useless trying to concentrate on the teacher's words. I just couldn't get over what Christian had asked me to do. It was one thing to train my body to fight, but to ask me to use Light as a weapon was entirely different. Not that I wouldn't use Light as a weapon if I could, quite the opposite. If I thought it were possible, I wouldn't be wasting my time and energy teaching myself to become what I hoped would be a secret ninja warrior.

Use Light as a weapon? I'd gone over the possibilities in my mind so many times, but I still couldn't see how it could be done. I took my pencil and began to write down all the things I knew Light could do. So far all I'd been able to do with it was turn the lights on and off, make others feel cozy inside, melt snow, and make a flashlight turn on without batteries. And Sophie could light up hidden life in the forest and walk on top of deep snow.

As for my mother, I remember she used to create these smooth light balls and would circle them above my bed at night like a baby mobile while she sang me to sleep. That was probably the most impressive thing I'd ever seen Light do.

I glanced over my list. So far it looked like the only weapon

I could use against a Vyken was to either make him feel special or light up an area around him. Terrifying, I know. I crumbled up the paper and shoved in into my backpack. This was going to be tough.

It was late, later than I wanted it to be, but I had to wait until Christian came in and fell asleep before I could experiment. Every night I waited for the inevitable sounds of sleep to fill the house before I tried manipulating light. For some reason I felt self-conscious doing it in front of him. Even the thought of showing him my Light made me feel like I was undressing. I knew he wouldn't care, but using it just felt too personal.

I opened my bedroom door quietly and listened for any sounds coming from the living room. All the lights were off and everything was quiet. Jake had gone to sleep hours ago. There was a chance Christian wasn't quite asleep, but by how silent everything was, he'd be close. Christian had a tendency to toss and turn if he wasn't asleep, and I heard none of those movements now.

Like Christian had promised, he'd recovered from his wounds more quickly than a normal person—a perk to having great genetics. Within a couple of days, he began sleeping on our couch. He'd come over around 11:00 p.m. and leave at sunrise. Most of the time I pretended to be asleep when he showed up. I thought it would be easier on everyone, especially Jake. I could tell he still questioned his decision, but I never did. The improvement in Christian was worth it.

I quietly closed the door and drew the curtains. Lying down in bed, I stretched out my hands. In a matter of seconds a light burst from my palm. It had taken me days to get to this point, and longer to shape it into a tight ball I could maneuver around the room.

For several minutes I used my hands to compact the light

into a usable form. I found if I didn't do this, the moment the ball crashed into anything it would dissipate like fog. However, if I compacted it enough, the ball would actually bounce off hard objects. The night before, I'd gotten it to ricochet off the walls in my room like a pinball machine. It was sort of fun, but still nothing that would frighten, let alone hurt, an attacker.

With the ball finally tight enough to manipulate, I raised it up and let it hover in the air. What could I do to make it fearsome? But after ten minutes of me doing nothing, the ball began to dissipate. Frustrated, I started over.

I concentrated hard and lifted a newly formed light-ball into the air. Instead of focusing on how to use it as a weapon, I let my thoughts wander to the dark shadows of my mind. It was a place I normally wouldn't dwell in, but tonight I lingered within the anger I'd kept hidden for so long. I let my desire to hurt and mangle the Vyken fill my whole being until every nerve hummed with violence. It was the cruelest I'd ever felt in my life.

Before I realized what I was doing, the light-ball flew from my hands and crashed into the wall opposite me. I gasped and moved to examine it, but before I could, Christian flung open my door and snapped on the light.

"What's wrong? What happened?" he said. He looked surprisingly alert, like a hunting tiger.

"Congratulations. You win the lightest sleeper award," I blurted.

"Huh?"

"I just tripped, very quietly I might add." Christian stared at me with a blank look so I continued. "I was on my way to the bathroom, but I tripped on that shoe." I pointed to a turned over shoe by my bed. I was suddenly glad I'd decided not to clean my room earlier.

Christian picked it up and examined it.

"It's not going to tell you anything, Christian. Shoes are funny like that. Can I get by you?" I actually did need to use the bathroom now.

"Yeah, sure."

I did my business and then returned to the room. "Can I go back to bed now?" I purposely turned off the light when I saw Christian getting closer to the hole in the wall.

"You sure everything's okay?" he asked.

"Daisies and bunnies." I climbed into bed.

He waited a second before he said, "If you need anything, you know where I am."

I faked a yawn and mumbled, "Uh-huh."

I waited ten minutes before I dared slide out of bed again. I re-created a light-ball, but this time it was purely for vision sake. I held it up to the hole in the wall. The dry wall was caved in where the ball had struck. I stuck my finger in the depression. It didn't go in as far as I would've liked, but at least it did damage. I was finally on to something.

*   *   *   *   *

It was a cold, wet morning. An unexpected spring storm had rolled in overnight, drenching everything. With it came warmer temperatures. I stared outside and watched the rain slowly disintegrate a pile of plowed snow in the school parking lot.

"Llona? Earth to Llona."

I glanced over, blank-faced. The English teacher was staring at me. Several of the students snickered.

The teacher's thin lips twisted open. "When you are done daydreaming, could you please go to the office?" She waved a yellow slip in her hand.

"Right. Sure." I quickly stuffed my book into my backpack

and stood up. I kept my head down as I made my way out of the classroom.

As soon as I was free from my teacher's stare, I picked up my pace. I'd never been called to the office before and it made me nervous. But my nervousness quickly changed to anxiety when the secretary behind the desk told me my uncle was waiting for me outside.

Jake should be at work. Why would he be here? I wrapped my arms around my light jacket and stepped into the rain. I was glad I'd decided to wear a beanie to school today. The rain was coming down harder, and I would've been twice as cold if my hair was wet.

I looked around for Jake's car. Nothing. I was about to walk through the parking lot to see if I could find him when Christian's black SUV pulled up. He rolled down his window. "Hop in."

"What are you doing?"

"Skipping school and taking you with me."

"So there is no Jake?"

"Nope."

I smiled. "What did you have in mind?"

"Get in and I'll tell you."

"I think you're ready for our next training exercise," he told me once I was in the car.

"Can't it wait till school is over?"

He shook his head. "Nope."

"How come?"

"You'll see. Be patient."

"Yes, Master Yoda."

Christian turned toward his house and drove up the hill.

"There are clothes for you in the back."

"Can't I change at your house?"

"We're not going to my house."

I frowned. "Then where are we going?"

"We're training outside today."

I glanced out the rain-streaked window. "In this weather?"

Christian motioned his head toward the back of the car. "Hurry and get changed. I don't want to waste any time. And you can't wear your beanie." He turned up the radio before I could protest.

I sighed and climbed in the backseat, deliberately bumping the rearview mirror toward the ceiling.

"I wasn't going to peek," he said over the loud music.

"Yeah right, pervert," I joked. I couldn't see his expression to tell if he knew I was kidding or not. Sometimes he took me way too seriously.

Just when I finished changing, Christian turned onto a dirt road and into a canyon. It was not one I recognized. "I've never been here before," I said.

"It's not that popular." He shut the car off in the middle of the road. "Now as soon as we get out, I'm going to move fast, and I want you to keep up. It's going to be cold and because of the rain you won't have much footing."

I peered out the window and up to the dark, cloudy sky. "Not to be a party pooper or anything, but the moon just barely came out last night. I don't think I have the energy for this." Fighting was one thing but even thinking about a hard run made me tired.

"It doesn't matter what cycle the moon is in. You still have Light in you regardless of what time of the month it is. You just have to learn to access it."

"Easier said then done, my friend."

He turned to me. "Llona, you are the most competitive person I've met. Do you really want me to waste you?"

He knew me too well. "I didn't say you would waste me," I backpeddled. "I just said it would be harder than usual." That was the understatement of the year, but I wasn't about to tell him that.

"Just follow me and concentrate. Ignore all outside stimuli. Sometimes it helps me if I play a song in my head." He placed his hand on the door handle. "You think you can keep up?"

I wanted to adamantly say no, but instead I said, "Bring it on!" I couldn't turn down a challenge like that.

Christian bolted out the door. I moved to join him but fell as my foot slipped on wet mud. I looked up just in time to see Christian disappear into the woods. I groaned and stood up. Here goes nothing.

I took off after him, slowly at first. I could barely see him in front of me, sprinting up a steep trail. The cold wasn't as distracting as I thought it'd be, but the rain was horrible. It drenched my hair in a matter of seconds, and I kept getting distracted from having to wipe it out of my face. Only when I started humming the same song that had been playing in the car earlier, did I start to focus.

Once I eliminated the cold and the rain as a distraction, I concentrated on finding the dormant Light inside me, which proved to be very difficult while running. I was running fast but not nearly fast enough to keep up with Christian. Already I couldn't see him anymore.

"Not on my watch," I whispered to no one.

I forced my legs to push faster with longer strides until I thought they'd collapse from exertion. It wasn't until I reached complete exhaustion that I felt a burst of light explode throughout my body. My muscles immediately filled with its energy— the same energy I felt on a full moon, if not more. Air moved more freely into my lungs and my vision became clear. Even my hearing became more focused. I could hear Christian's footsteps not far off. I was not as behind as I thought.

I raced after him, fully sprinting now. In less than a minute

I was right on his tail. He turned around, grinned, and then started running faster. He'd been holding back.

I adjusted my speed to keep up with him, making me a little winded, but not much. Without warning, he moved off the trail and straight into thick underbrush, still traveling at the same speed. I followed, but quickly found I had to adjust the way I'd been running. Not only did I have to concentrate on blocking out the cold and rain, but now I had to concentrate on where I stepped and moved. The uneven ground was never the same and at every turn, branches reached out as if to grab me.

At first I was really nervous as I ran through the forest, trying to avoid disaster with every step, but without being aware of it, my mind begun to take visual snap shots of the surroundings. This gave me the ability to know exactly where I was going to step next. Several steps ahead, in fact. It was as if I was able to see into the future just enough to know my next move. The moment I realized this, I started having fun. I felt like a freerunner again, but this time I didn't have to worry about who may be watching.

I caught up to Christian quickly and couldn't help but beam when I saw the surprise in his face. This time it was my turn to grin. I kept pace with him even though I felt I could pass him if I really wanted to.

I continued to follow him up the mountain. The closer we came to the top, rocky terrain and huge boulders replaced the once dense forest. I was completely soaked by this time and every time I turned sharply, my wet hair slapped me in the face, stinging my cold skin.

"Just up ahead," Christian called.

I couldn't imagine where he was taking me. All I could see was more rocks and what looked like a steep drop-off up ahead. Off to my left, my eyes locked with a mountain goat. It quickly bounded off in the other direction. Smart goat. I would leave too if I saw two crazy people running this high in the mountains in the middle of a storm.

Christian stopped on a flat slate-like rock formation just before the drop off. "We're here," he said.

I stopped next to him. "Where exactly is here?"

"The place where we're training today." Lightening cracked overhead. I looked up into the rain. "I'm glad my shoes have rubber on them."

"I've been waiting for a day like this for a long time," he said while stretching his legs.

"One that can kill you?" I walked over to the edge of the cliff and looked down. It must've been at least a hundred feet to the bottom.

"You've been fighting really well, but you need a more realistic environment. Where I've been teaching you is too easy and too safe. It's not like the real world."

I turned around. "And this is?"

He ignored my question. "You did well keeping up with me," he said. "I thought it would take a lot longer for you to figure out how to work Light on your off days."

I pushed the hair away from my face again. "Me too. I wish I would've known about that sooner. It sure would've saved me a ton of embarrassing moments."

"But you needed those moments."

"For what? To feel even more like an outcast?"

"It's through hardship that greatness is born. You don't know how different you are from other Auras. Most of them have lived a privileged life, never knowing how to work hard or sacrifice for others. They've been surrounded by a wall at Lucent, pampered and treated like royalty. I used to think that's where they belonged because of their sacred nature, but after meeting you and seeing what you're capable of, I realize there's a whole other side to Auras that's being ignored. You guys could do so much good if given the opportunity. Of course, if I were to ever mention any of this to anyone, it would be considered blasphemy."

"Maybe we could change their minds?" I offered.

Christian stared into the distance. His face and eyes looked strangely dark beneath the shadows of the storm clouds. "Maybe," he whispered. He turned to me suddenly. "You ready to fight?"

I rolled back my shoulders and cocked my head side to side. "I'll go easy on you."

I was going to trash talk more, but before I could, Christian swung his right fist at my jaw. I easily ducked and returned the blow. He sidestepped it and did a backwards kick to my head. I caught the kick midair and flipped him hard backwards, forcing him into a somersaulting flip. He landed expertly into a crouched position.

"Good," he said, voice low. "Now faster." He lunged for me again.

We fought against each other: two warriors pushing each other faster and harder with every step. Neither one of us could overcome the other. That is until thunder exploded, shaking the whole mountain. For a split second I became distracted, giving Christian just enough time to swipe my legs out from under me. I fell hard against the rock beneath us. In a mock pro wrestling move, Christian slapped his elbow and fell down upon me with a huge grin. "You're mine!"

"Now what are you going to do with me?" I teased.

"Nothing I want to do." He stood and helped me up. "Let's cool down."

Following his lead, I maintained various yoga positions, while the storm above gradually subsided. It was oddly empowering being on top of a mountain in the middle of a storm. My heart beat from within my chest, yet my mind was as clear as the sky on a cloudless day. I felt at one with the world.

After our bizarre, yet invigorating meditation session, I sat down on the ledge, my legs dangling over.

"Do you have to sit so close?" Christian asked

I looked down into the gully below. "I guess not." I slid back several feet. Christian sat next to me and peered up into the overcast sky.

I decided this was the perfect time to ask him about May, indirectly of course.

"Can I ask you a question?" I asked.

"Sure."

"Have you ever heard of a human who has the ability to use fire?"

I expected him to give me a strange look, but he didn't. Instead, he said, "Of course. They're called Furies. How do you know of them?"

"Something I heard once," I said, telling a half truth. "Where do they come from?"

"I don't know their history too well, but like Light, fire has become a part of certain humans. Furies aren't too popular among the Auras, though."

"Why?"

"It's the fire within them. It craves power and domination. Eventually the lust becomes too great to control and their hearts turn black like Vykens."

"So they're bad?"

"Not all of them. In fact there's a Fury who sits on the Council with your aunt. He's a mean sucker, but he knows the line between right and wrong."

The rain had finally stopped, and in the distance the sun began to push through the clouds. I could feel its warmth against my skin.

"I was going to tell you that night," Christian said suddenly.

"Huh?"

"That night I was late. I was going to tell you everything about me."

"What happened?"

"When you left your house, I followed you up the trail. But we weren't alone. There was someone else there that night. I turned directions and pursued them to make sure whoever it was, wasn't a threat. At the time, I didn't think it was a Vyken."

"Why wouldn't you?"

"Honestly, when the Council assigned me to you, they said it was 'for precautionary measures only' and it was also at your aunt's insistence. They said Vykens don't prey on young Auras. They like the blood of a stronger, more experienced, Aura. Supposedly it gives Vykens more power," he paused. "I'm telling you this because I'm beginning to doubt a lot of what the Council has taught me."

"Why?"

He stared off into the horizon. The deep lines in his forehead told me how conflicted he was. "I've been taught all my life that Auras couldn't fight, but you proved that wrong. I was told Vykens can't change their appearance multiple times, but obviously they can. I was told Vykens are super strong and fast and that's it—no other abilities, but that isn't the case. One touched you from a distance and somehow took control of you. It's like they're getting stronger. And all this after they told me the chances of a Vyken coming for you were slim, but now one is hunting you, torturing you. I feel like I've been lied to. And there's something else."

"What?"

"After the second murder, I spoke to the head of the Auran Council. I told him about what was happening and he said not to worry. He said the murders were a coincidence.

A coincidence? If the same thing were to happen to an older Aura, they would've moved her far away. This whole thing just doesn't feel right."

Because I didn't know what to say, I asked, "So when you asked me to meet you in the woods that night, why didn't you tell me the next day who you were?"

"I was going to, but when I showed up at your house the next morning, you were mad or sad—I couldn't be sure which."

"Right," I said, remembering.

"I was afraid if I told you, you'd move away. I realized then that I'd have to earn your complete trust."

"Good call." I shifted positions. Something he had just said nagged at me. "Christian?"

He looked over at me. "Yes?"

"If you don't trust the Council, maybe I shouldn't go to Lucent this summer."

He shook his head. "No, you should. There may be some inconsistencies in what they're teaching, but I can't be sure. I need to do more research before I accuse them of anything. No, you definitely need to go. You'll learn a lot there. You've been too sheltered out here."

"Won't I be sheltered there?"

"Only from a life you already know. You need to go learn about the life you know nothing about, like Furies. In a way you're lucky. It's not always good to know what's really out there. Some of them will terrify you."

"Like what? Wait. Never mind, I don't want to know yet."

"You'll learn soon enough. Once you go to Lucent in the summer everything you know will change."

"Including you."

A few seconds passed before he said, "I guess so."

I wanted to talk more of the future and hopefully find something positive in it, but before I could, he said, "I'd better get you back."

That night I focused more on my light bullets, and with the moon's cycle no longer affecting my strength, thanks to Christian's very dangerous, yet highly effective training on the mountain, it came much easier. In a matter of days, I had them piercing through just about anything. And it couldn't have come at a better time, because I couldn't shake the feeling that something big was coming. The tick-tock of death's clock was growing louder.

Twenty-Nine

"I HAVE TO ASK YOU SOMETHING," CHRISTIAN SAID AS HE swung a balled fist in my direction.

I ducked and countered it with a high kick to his face. "Is it personal?"

He caught my foot—"I don't think so."—and flipped me hard backwards.

I completed the back flip and landed on my feet. "Would you say your question is a C-SPAN question, or more of an MTV red-carpet question?" I attempted to kick him again, but he ducked.

"I would say somewhere in the middle."

"So it's a David Letterman question."

He stopped. "Can I just ask?"

I plopped down on a blue mat. I loved sparring at Christian's house. There was a ton of room and it smelled a lot better than the dojo. "Go for it."

He sat down next to me and pretended to tie his shoe even though it was already tied. "Prom is coming up and I know you're going to be asked by a bunch of guys, but it just wouldn't make sense for you to be on a date and have me stalking you the whole time." He took a big breath. "I think it will be a lot easier if—"

"Are you asking me to prom?" I teased.

"Yeah, but I understand if that would be too weird for you."

I didn't hesitate. "I couldn't imagine going with anyone else."

His eyes met mine and he smiled. "Good. Then it's a date—a protection date—I mean."

"Right. A protection date, like on the movie *Bodyguard*, right?"

He frowned as if trying to recall the movie.

"You know, Kevin Costner has to protect Super Singer Whitney Houston, which he does, but not without falling madly in love her. That kind of date right?"

He grinned. "I think we're way past that. Come on, let's get some dinner."

I accepted his hand and followed him out of the room. I would've given anything to have him mean what he'd just said, but I was all too familiar with his teasing tone. I could cross out any chance for romance at prom. It would be just me and my friend Christian. Yippee.

*   *   *   *   *

"That doesn't surprise me," May said after ingesting a sub sandwich. "I knew Christian would ask you. I'm just surprised he didn't do it months ago."

"Why's that?" I crumpled up my garbage and stuffed it into the fast food bag. Instead of going inside the crowded restaurant, we had decided to eat in May's car.

"Because it would drive him crazy to see you with anyone else. You've seen how he gets when you're with Matt."

"But it's not because he's jealous or anything. Christian doesn't like me like that. He's just overly protective."

May shook her head. "I don't buy it. I see how he looks at

you. I'd give anything to have Adam look at me that way."

May had liked Adam for a long time, but other than a few casual dates, he didn't seem too interested in her. "Why don't you ask Adam to prom? We could double."

"I can't ask him. That's going against tradition." May tilted the rearview mirror to inspect her makeup.

"Since when do you care about tradition?"

She held still, staring at herself in the mirror. "You're right. I don't. I think I will ask him. What's the worst that could happen?"

"That's the May I know. We should see if we can get Matt and Tracey to come too," I suggested.

"Oh, that girl has it bad for Matt. What a perfect idea."

And so the ball was in motion for the perfect prom setup. True to her word, May asked Adam that very day. He accepted so easily that I began to wonder if maybe he did like her.

Matt was another story. He had no desire to go to prom with anyone.

"Llona," he told me the next day at lunch. "I attended a bunch of school activities this year thanks to you, and I admit I had fun, but prom?"

"What's the big deal?"

He laughed. "When I think about prom, all I picture is the prom scene from *Napoleon Dynamite*."

"That's not how it's going to be. At least I don't think so," I said.

"Sorry, Llona, but I'd rather chew glass."

"But I know someone who really wants to go with you."

"You do?"

"Are you really that blind?"

"Huh?"

"I may be breaking a friend's trust, but I think this situation warrants the breach." I looked around conspiratorially. "Your secret admirer's name starts with a 'T' and ends with 'racey.'"

"Tracey," he said a little too loudly. He lowered his voice. "Tracey? Really?"

"Absolutely. She's liked you all year."

"Huh. I would never have guessed."

"Did you even try?"

"No. The last thing on my mind was a relationship with anyone."

"You don't have to have a relationship with her, but you could make her dreams come true."

"If her dream is to be asked to prom, then I don't want to go. I want someone with a little more ambition than that."

I should have realized those were the wrong words to use. "I was exaggerating, Matt. It's hardly a lifelong dream of hers. In fact, did you know she's been accepted to Stanford? She wants to be a lawyer."

"Really? I didn't know that. I wonder why she never told me?"

"She's not the type to brag."

"Tracey." He said her name quietly as if considering the possibility.

"Just think about it, okay?"

He nodded, staring off into space.

After school, a beaming Tracey found me at my locker.

"You'll never guess what just happened."

By her smile I knew exactly what had happened. "What?"

"Matt just asked me to prom."

"That's so wonderful." I gave her a hug. "We should make it a triple date: me and Christian, you and Matt, and May and Adam."

"Absolutely."

*   *   *   *   *

Two weekends before prom, all of us girls decided to go dress shopping. When I found out the theme for prom was "Once upon a dream," the image of a perfect dress came to mind. The problem was it was only in my imagination. It was a light blue, almost white, lacy dress with a hint of sparkles. It's what I imagined a fairy to be wearing if I ever saw one.

By the third store I finally found a dress I thought I could modify. May and Tracey were surprised I picked it because it didn't look that great, but I saw it's potential. One of the lessons my mother had taught me was a person could find potential in anything—or anyone—if they were looking for it.

May had found a long, elegant red gown that made her look like Scarlett O'Hara, and Tracey had bought a green dress that flattered her eyes. We had an amazing time, laughing and sharing as only friends do. I knew our trip together would go down as one of my most memorable high school moments. Little did I know, however, that something much more memorable in the most horrific and devastating way would make remembering any good times in high school challenging.

THIRTY

ON THE DAY OF PROM, ALL SIX OF US LOADED INTO CHRISTIAN'S SUV and headed to the Paint Gun Exploratorium where we played paintball for hours. I had so much fun that I considered shooting guns as my next hobby. Christian quickly shot down my idea, no pun intended.

After paintball we ate a fancy lunch together at Christian's house and played games. This proved valuable because it was then I discovered his Achilles' heel. Christian stunk at games, specifically card games, and I was very happy to take advantage of this weakness.

When we finished messing around, Christian drove us girls back to my house. He waited for them to pile out before he stopped me. "I'll be back in about an hour to pick you up," he said.

"We can just meet at the dance like everyone else."

"No. I'd feel better picking you up, if that's okay."

I nodded. "You know, I think I'm going to make it."

"Make what?"

"The end of the school year. Not to be a rain cloud on this perfect day, but I kind of thought I'd end up dead."

His eyes turned dark. "Don't say that."

"But things are better now and I don't feel that way

anymore. Maybe the Vyken knows I could kick its butt and it ran away scared."

"I don't think so." He looked away, a thoughtful expression on his face. "I have a feeling it's waiting."

I wanted to disagree with him, to scold him for being a pessimist, but the truth was I'd been feeling the same way. "Everything is going to be fine. You'll see."

His eyes returned to mine. "I hope you're right."

"I hope my dress covers it," Tracey said while looking down at her thigh. A bright purple paintball bruise the size of a baseball peeked out from beneath her shorts.

"It should. I don't think the slit goes that high," May told her.

"Do you want some ice on it?" I asked her. I felt pretty lucky ending up with only a couple of bruises. Poor Tracey had several.

"No, I can barely feel it." She paused. "I hope the dance isn't too lame. I want Matt to have fun."

"He will," I assured her as I pinned up her hair.

"Do you have any mousse, Llona? I forgot to bring mine," May asked.

"I don't, but Jake has some," I said and left the room to get it.

"What do you use for your hair then?" May called after me.

"Nothing."

"You will tonight," Tracey called. May laughed, and I had to wonder what they were up to.

I didn't have to wait long. Within twenty minutes my hair looked like a princess's right out of a Disney movie, tiara and all. It looked incredible, but they'd used so much hair product that it felt like a brick was sitting on top of my head.

"Wow. Thanks guys. It looks really good. I just hope I don't sprain my neck," I said while turning my head back and forth.

"You'll get used to it," May said, fluffing her hair. We had put May's hair in curlers. It made her look different, beautifully so. I couldn't wait to see her in the dress she'd chosen.

"So I'll see you guys in a couple of hours?" Tracey asked.

"Sure thing. Don't be late."

Tracey disappeared, followed shortly by May, who gave me a hug before she left.

I couldn't have been happier. I had awesome friends, a great relationship with my uncle, and sort of a boyfriend—well, okay, I'm stretching the truth. Christian and I couldn't have a relationship, but when he looked at me I knew there was something more.

I carefully pulled my silver-blue dress over my stiff hair and looked at myself in the mirror. The dress hung off my shoulders by an almost invisible strap. The material was so sheer it looked like a spider had spun a web all around me. The dress flowed outward from my waist mimicking a waterfall from a melting glacier.

In a matter of months I'd completely transformed myself. I wished Jake could be here to see me, but he wouldn't be back for a couple of days. He and Heidi went to Park City on their first getaway alone. Jake had seemed nervous, and I wondered if maybe he was going to propose.

A knock at the door tore my gaze from the stranger in the mirror. Before I could get to the front door, Christian walked in and froze.

"You look—" He breathed a heavy sigh.

"I know, I know, my hair looks like the Matterhorn ride at Disneyland."

He took a step toward me. "No, it's beautiful. You're beautiful."

"You don't look so bad yourself," I said. He really did look amazing dressed in a black tux and his hair slicked back. He reminded me of a movie star on Grammy night—except for the strange, almost painful expression. "What's wrong?"

He moved one more step until he was standing right in front of me. "I thought this would be easier," he said.

"Easier than what?" I asked.

"Than watching you from afar with someone else. I shouldn't be your date." His eyes met mine.

"What's the big deal? We hang out all the time together and you're always Mr. I-don't-even-know-you're-a-girl. Just keep playing that role. You're good at it."

"I'm tired of that role."

"You're the one that created it."

"It's the rules, Llona."

"Right, the rules." I placed my hand on his chest and gave him my most encouraging smile. "You can do this, Christian. I'm leaving in two weeks and then you'll never have to see me again. You won't have to be tortured anymore."

He looked away. "I guess you're right."

I wanted to scream at him that, no, I wasn't right. The thought of not seeing Christian again was enough to make me double over in pain, but he acted so cavalier about the whole thing that I forced myself to think of something else.

"Let's have fun tonight," I said. "It's been such a perfect day. I don't want anything or anyone to ruin it, okay?"

He nodded and smiled. "It has been perfect, hasn't it?"

"The best. Now let's go before I throw a beanie over my princess-do."

*   *   *   *   *

Christian held my hand as he led me into the magically transformed high school gym. At least I think it was the gym. The walls had been covered in black material; bright lights peeked from holes like stars in the night sky. More lights covered the ceiling and in the corner of the room, a single bright light had been made to look like a full moon. Navy blue and white sheer material draped gracefully across parts of the gym and clusters of real pine trees were spread sporadically throughout. It was like walking through a setting of Shakespeare's *A Midsummer Night's Dream*.

"And the award for the best prom decorations goes to Highland," I breathed.

"Someone sure went all out," Christian agreed. "This is a hundred times better than my last prom."

I stopped. "You went to prom?"

"Yeah."

I waited a few seconds before I said, as casually as possible, "Who'd you go with?"

Christian grinned. "Jealousy doesn't become you."

"I'm not jealous, just curious."

"Right." We stood in silence for a minute, looking around the gym, until I couldn't stand it anymore.

"What did she look like?" I said. "Again, just curious."

He laughed hard. When he finally stopped, he held his hand to my face. "You are the Taj Mahal and she was my grandfather's shed. There is no comparison."

This satisfied me, for the time being anyway. It wasn't until just now that I realized how much I didn't know about his past. He could've had lots of girls before me. I closed my eyes tight to get the image out of my mind.

"Let's dance," he said suddenly and pulled me onto the dance floor.

"Shouldn't we wait for the others?" I asked.

"They'll find us."

The song playing was a fast pop song by a female singer I didn't recognize, but that didn't surprise me. This wasn't my type of music, but it was much easier to dance to then my twisted, dark favorites.

When the song ended and another began, a much slower one, Christian didn't ask, he just pulled me close to his chest and wrapped his arms around me. Together our bodies swayed as one to the beat of the music. I raised my head until our cheeks touched. His five o'clock shadow scraped against my skin, sending a pleasurable chill up my spine. A sigh slipped from my throat just as he tilted his head. His lips grazed my neck and his hands tightened on my back, pressing my body against his.

At this moment I knew exactly what he wanted, for it mirrored my own desires. We wanted to be together, without feeling guilty, without having to worry about the rules, without having to worry about the consequences. Whether we'd admit it or not, we were two teenagers in love.

My head lifted until our eyes met. He leaned his head toward mine and his lips parted just barely. I lifted on my toes to meet him halfway and closed my eyes.

"Hey guys!"

The words were like the sound of two trains crashing together, forcing Christian and I apart. We both opened our eyes and stared at each other. He gave me a weak smile. I didn't return it.

Christian turned away from me, but kept his hand on my back. To Matt and Adam he said, "Where's the girls?"

"Late, I guess," Adam shrugged.

"You look great, Llona," Matt said.

"Thanks. You look good too." Matt was the type of man who was born to wear a tux. It looked natural on him, like a second skin. "So do the decorations exceed your expectations?" I asked.

Matt glanced around. "I must admit, it's not what I'd

expected." He looked back at me and then to Christian. "Could I have one dance? Would you mind?"

Christian visibly tensed but, ever the gentleman, he said, "If it's all right with her."

"Of course." I reached for Matt's hand.

"Come on, Christian. Let's get a drink," Adam said, playfully shoving Christian forward.

"I can never tell what's going on between you two," Matt said, once we began to dance.

"That makes two of us."

"So what are you going to do after high school?" he asked.

"Not a hundred percent sure, but I think I'll go to the same school my mother went to."

"Where's that?" he asked.

"New York."

He seemed taken back. "New York, huh? "

"Far, right? What about you? Are you still going into politics?"

"That's the plan. And I won't be too far. D.C. is only five or six hours away."

"So you got the internship?"

He nodded.

"Congratulations! That's so cool. Are you going to attend college there too? Or just do the summer intern thing and then come back?"

"I'm still trying to decide. I did get accepted to NYU. Maybe I'll come keep you company." He smiled.

"That would be awesome." The music, another slow song, was suddenly having a hypnotic effect on me. I closed my eyes and relaxed more fully into Matt.

"Are you okay?" he asked.

His voice sounded miles away. Before I had a chance to answer, he stopped moving, reached into his pocket, and pulled out a vibrating cell phone.

"It's from Tracey." He flipped open his phone and read the text message. "Odd."

"What?"

"She says she's at your house. And who's Angel?"

"Huh?" I took the phone from him. The message read, "At Llona's house. With Angel." I read it over and over until I thought my legs might give out. My Angel. The letter. My mother's letter. No—not my mother's letter. Her killer's letter. And now he was back for me.

"Llona?" Matt asked.

"I have to go," I said barely above a whisper.

"Where?" I heard Christian say behind me.

"Tracey's at her house," Matt told him.

"Is May with her?" Adam asked.

Matt shrugged.

Because I was about to fall, I forced my legs to move—away from them.

Christian caught up to me. "I'll drive."

I didn't respond, not because I didn't want to, but because I couldn't. I was afraid if I opened my mouth, I'd throw up.

This was it. This was really happening. Somehow I'd convinced myself that nothing was going to happen, that I was finally safe. But the Vyken was just waiting for the perfect day. And it had been the perfect day—up until now. I quickened my pace. Tracey was with him. Tracey was with that monster. I whimpered.

Christian stopped me. "What's wrong?"

"I don't have time to explain. We have to hurry!" I kept walking. Why was I walking? As soon as I stepped into the night, I began to run. Stupid high-heeled shoes. I quickly abandoned them in the parking lot.

"Llona, stop!" Christian said when he caught up to me.

"Open the door," I said when I reached his car. He quickly unlocked it and hopped in the driver's seat.

"What's going on?" he asked.

I told him about the message. "It's him, Christian. He has Tracey."

Christian stepped on the gas. "It's going to be okay."

"No, it's not." The sinking feeling in my gut told me my life would never be the same.

"Stay here," Christian said when he drove his SUV into my driveway.

"Not a chance. She's my friend." I jumped out of the car and rushed through an already open front door.

Christian grabbed me roughly and whispered, "Wait! You can't rush in there. Keep your mind clear so you don't end up dead."

He was right. I took a deep breath and tried to focus.

"I'll go in first," he said, stepping in front of me.

He moved slowly into the darkened living room. I heard him feel for the light switch. When the lights wouldn't turn on, he said, "Can you turn them on?"

Mentally I tried, but it felt as if I was being blocked. "No, I can't."

"Stay close."

The house was completely black except for a faint light glowing from my bedroom. We slowly made our way toward it.

"Do you feel anything?" Christian asked.

"Actually I don't. I don't think he's here."

Christian pushed open my door, and, like me, seemed to be trying to figure out exactly what we were looking at.

On my bed, sitting with crossed legs, was Tracey in her green prom dress; her head cocked to the side. A single lit candle on my nightstand cast dancing shadows across the room. They were the shadows of the dead. I recognized them immediately and stepped forward.

Christian grabbed me. "Don't!"

I pushed his hand away. "Tracey?" There was something around her neck. A red scarf? I reached to touch her.

"Llona, no!" Christian cried.

As soon as my hand touched her shoulder, Tracey fell backwards on my bed.

Not a scarf.

A slit throat.

Thirty-One

SOMEWHERE BETWEEN THE LIVING AND THE DEAD EXISTED A world for those who belonged in neither. It was a dark and lonely place, not meant for hope, love, or joy. It was a place I'd been to before when I'd lost my parents. I didn't think I'd be back so soon.

"Llona! Get up. We have to call the police." Christian was tugging at me. In a daze, I stood up. Tracey was with the dead now. And her wide open, accusatory eyes told me it was my fault.

I heard Christian speaking into his phone. My address. He was telling someone my address.

His hand pressed against my back. "Llona," he said as gentle as a summer breeze. "The police will be here in a few minutes. Let's go wait in the garage."

I turned to follow until I saw a letter resting between Tracey's crossed legs. I picked it up.

"What is it?" Christian asked.

I opened it and read quietly: "I've come back for you, Little One. I told you I would." I crumpled the paper and walked out. Christian followed behind.

Inside the garage, Christian gently took hold of my shoulders. "I wish I could comfort you right now, but we don't have much time. The police are going to be here in a minute. Do you understand what I'm saying?"

I stared out into the cool night.

"As far as you know this was a random killing. There was a miscommunication and Tracey thought we were meeting here. She just happened to be in the wrong place at the wrong time. Are you listening to me?"

I must have nodded because he didn't say anything else. He just stared with me, holding my hand.

When a police car arrived, Christian walked out to meet them. I watched from the dark garage as he told them what happened. His body was stiff and his expression emotionless. I couldn't understand how he could talk about it without shutting down.

When he led them into the house, I followed, but stopped at the doorway while he showed them to my room. A beeping sound on the kitchen counter drew my attention. My cell phone. I flipped it open. One new message. A text message in bold letters read: "All the world's a stage and May's about to fall off."

I calmly placed the phone back down. I could hear Christian still talking in my room, while a second policeman moved into the hallway to make a phone call. No more people were going to die because of me. This ends tonight.

I turned to sneak outside, but a second patrol car pulled into our driveway. I moved back into the house and, while the cop in the hall had his back to me, darted into Jake's room. After removing the screen from his window, I jumped out. I didn't care about the silent alarm that was probably going off in Christian's pocket. By the time he got here, I'd be long gone, propelled forward by years of anger and pain.

I let Light guide me. It seemed to know exactly where to go quicker than my brain. When I realized I was headed in the direction of the high school, I knew exactly where the Vyken held May.

I circled around the school, away from the boisterous prom scene several buildings over, and threw open the doors to a pitch-black auditorium. They shut behind me like the lid on a coffin.

A bright spotlight flipped on; its stream of light raced to center stage, capturing a tied-up May in its beam. I scanned the area. There was no one else, but by the spinning sensation beginning in my head, the same feeling I had in the cornstalks, I knew a Vyken was nearby. The only way this was going to end, for better or worse, was to face him. The moment I was born, my life had been set on this path. It didn't matter if I was ready or not, it would all be over soon. My only goal was to help May escape it alive.

I began the long walk down the slanted decline to the stage. I was surprisingly calm. I didn't even try to be quiet when I walked up the steps to May. There was no point.

May's head was slumped forward, but not in an unnatural way like Tracey's had been. I breathed a sigh of relief when I saw her chest rise and fall.

I took a step to untie her when all of a sudden the spinning in my head reached a whole new level and I stumbled. It was like I'd been hit with a poisonous dart, but it was a familiar poison. I tried to remember Christian's training with the heart monitor.

"You are a vision," I heard a familiar, smooth accent say.

I fell to my knees. Relax! I inhaled deeply.

Behind me, Mr. Steele laughed. "It's remarkable the effect I have on you. It's as strong as it was when you were a child. I wish it would've been the same with your mother, but her senses had long been shut off."

My mother. I had to clear my mind. All this time, I'd

mistaken the dizzy, weak-like feeling I had around Mr. Steele for silly puppy love when in actuality he was a Vyken. How many more mistakes would I make?

Mr. Steele moved in front of me, blocking May. Dressed in an old-fashioned tuxedo, his normally slick black hair was messy and lay partly in his eyes. He would've looked perfect except for part of his right sleeve had been burned. My eyes moved to May.

"Of all the Auras I've hunted and killed," he began. "You've been the most fun. Your lack of training has made you reckless and unpredictable. I've found it so refreshing."

Struggling to stand, I concentrated on getting rid of the nauseating effect he had on me.

"It was wonderful playing games with you—the shoe, the nightly visits, the feel of your skin," he paused, licking his lips. "Actually, I rather enjoyed killing the mother of the boy who painted you. He tarnished what's mine to destroy, so I tainted his heart." He walked behind May and stroked her hair. "But you had your own surprises, didn't you? What a rare treat it was to find your best friend is an undiscovered Fury."

I stood up, legs finally straight. Behind my back, I concentrated on creating the tightest ball of light I could, the size of a bullet. I made as many as my hands could hold while he continued to talk.

"I remember the first time I saw you so innocent and full of life as most children are. You were with your mother when I discovered you. It was merely by accident. Ella had no idea you two were being watched."

At the sound of my mother's name I froze.

"She was taking you for a walk through the Redwoods, and I remember thinking how strange it was that a mother would be with a child all alone in the dark woods. But then she did something remarkable. Would you like to know what she did?"

I searched for my voice but had none.

"She became transparent, invisible. I watched as you walked right through her. I knew then how extraordinary my find was. Only a powerful Aura would be able to do something like that." He sauntered across the stage, arms behind his back as if he were strolling through Central Park. "It didn't take much to maneuver my way into her life. She was so naïve and trusting, making for an easy kill." He turned to me. "I could've done the same to you—become your best friend. Imagine all the fun we could've had: sleepovers, sharing secrets, silly boy talk. And just when you're feeling warm and fuzzy, wham!" He clapped his hands together. "I rip your head off. But my desires were overruled, hence all the scare tactics. I had to force your Light to develop early."

I hadn't heard most of what he'd said. I was still stuck on the part about my mother. I'd become so angry that Light burned inside me, making him lose his grip on my consciousness. Finally, I could think clearly. "You killed my parents," I said.

He clicked his tongue. "Control your temper, Little One. I only did what comes natural to me. If drinking milk was forbidden, would you be angry at a babe sucking at its mother's breast? And as for killing your parents, I only killed your mother. I did taste your father, but I did not kill him."

"If not you, then who?" I demanded.

He stared at me thoughtfully, then said, "The shadow that always watches but can never be seen. He saved me the night your father caught up to me. You should've seen Mark's face when he thought he was finally going to avenge your mother's death and save the future life of his precious Llona. But Mark failed to see the shadow from behind until it was too late. The shadow snapped his neck as easily as one snaps their fingers." Mr. Steele snapped his fingers, startling me.

"Show me your true self," I said, wanting desperately for him to shut up.

He tilted his head. "And why would you want that?"

"So I can see the real face of who I'm going to kill." I quickly formed three more tight balls behind my back.

"I can see I no longer have an affect on you. You are right. There is no need to keep up this illusion." He waved his hand in front of his face. "But are you sure you want to see the true face of evil? I was one of the first created. We were made from the darkest parts of man's mind where greed, lust, and murder wait in ambush for that one small moment when man becomes weak."

His perfectly clear complexion suddenly cracked, revealing a black interior.

"We let this darkness turn our hearts and minds black by the sins of those who claimed to be righteous."

A large chunk of skin fell from his face.

"We would not exist but for these hidden secrets."

He reached up and tore off the remaining flesh. Beneath was a black face, if you could call it that. Where there should've been a nose was an empty hole, but when he turned his head, pieces of bloodied flesh still clung to the inside of his skull. His leathery skin pulled tight over abnormally high cheek bones, but around his mouth, the wrinkled skin bunched up into black nodules, forming a lumpy, grotesque bottom lip. His top lip was missing.

All this was horrible enough, but it was his eyes that were the most frightening. Seeing them directly, without Mr. Steele's mask, filled me with the worst kind of dread and horror I could imagine.

Images began to appear in my mind of twisted, broken, dead bodies; murderers killing for the sheer joy of it. I quickly closed my eyes to block the disturbing, soul-sucking images from my mind.

The Vyken laughed. "Evil will not be ignored."

I collapsed to my knees, trying all I could to mentally block the gruesome images. I gulped for air several times and my heart felt like it was going to beat out of my chest. The pain was excruciating. Murders, rapists, thieves—I saw it all in vivid detail. It was more than any person should have to endure.

All I could do was focus on the good in my life. I thought of my friends, of Christian and Jake. I thought of my devoted father, remembered him: the time he took me fishing and had hooked his finger, or when he bought me an Easter dress, but it was two sizes too small. I easily forgave him because of his smile. My mother used to say he stole his smile from a sunray. Slowly, the barrage of toxic images began to fade.

My mother. I thought of her now, of what she must have endured. She'd gone against everything she'd been taught, to follow her heart. Friends surely had been lost and her name ruined, but she did what she thought was right. Suddenly my mother was someone I wanted to be like.

Before I realized it, the image of my mother had completely taken over the disturbing images. The same creature that had taken my mother's precious life now thought he was going to destroy mine. Never.

I clenched my fists, head down, almost touching my bent knee, and then summoned all of Light's power. I stood up and stared the Vyken directly in the eyes.

"Bravo!" he said.

In one swift motion, I threw each individual light bullet in his direction with an amazing force. He dodged the first few, but was not quick enough to avoid them all. One grazed his cheek, cutting through his calloused skin. Another tore through his arm.

The smirk on his face disappeared when he touched exposed flesh. He brought down his blood-tinged fingers and examined it. "You are full of surprises. I may have underestimated your abilities, but no matter. Let's get to it, shall we?"

I moved to attack him, but before I could take a step forward, he appeared in front of me swinging a fist. His hand connected with my head, and I flew back several feet. I wasn't sure what was worse: the pain or the sheer shock of being hit in the face. I never knew how degrading it was to have your face smacked. It made me feel small and insignificant. I quickly stood up, despite the pain, to show he couldn't have power over me.

He attacked me again, but this time I was ready. I ducked beneath his blow, spun around and kicked him hard in the back. I moved to kick him again, but he caught my mid-air kick and twisted my foot hard. My body followed until it was stopped by the cold wood floor of the stage. I gasped for air.

"You are truly unique, Llona," he said, as he walked around me. "An Aura who fights? Ignores the Auran Council? Rare, indeed! Of course the Vykens should be grateful you are a rarity. I can only imagine how our kind would dwindle if the Auras ever realized their true powers."

In less than a second I created another light bullet, bigger this time. While he was still speaking, I rolled onto my back and tossed it at him. He attempted to move out of the way, but the bullet tore threw his other arm. This time he cried out.

I jumped up and punched him in the face. I could tell by the look in his eyes that he felt as disgraced as I'd been only moments ago. Now we were on a level playing field. I had the ability to hurt him and he knew it.

My confidence was short-lived, however, when his fist flew up faster than I thought possible, connecting with my jaw. My eyes rolled to the back of my head, and I felt my body complete an almost perfect back flip.

Gratefully, Light's power helped me to remain conscious,

enabling me to land on my feet. I continued to fight with a ferocity that, if I could have foreseen, would've frightened me.

Together we became an angry mosh pit of fists and kicks, twisting to a tune heard only by enemies who wish to destroy one another. Its beat was loud in my head and it pushed me on, harder and faster to destroy the creature who had taken all that I held dear.

I became oblivious to everything else in the room. My only focus was the Vyken in front of me who fought for an entirely different reason. His determination stemmed from greed, corruption, and a desire for insatiable power. Mine was for the love of my family and friends.

The more I hurt him, the more I was spurred on, until I began to feel something foreign and dark take hold of my mind. This new feeling gave me pause and I hesitated in both wonder and fear. The Vyken took advantage of the moment and struck me hard across the back of my head. With his second blow, I fell to the ground. I pushed myself up on all fours, but my movements were too slow. He kicked me in the stomach, forcing me onto my back. In a fraction of a second, he was on top of me, straddling my body.

He breathed heavily a few times before asking, "I do have one question. How ever did you get away from Christian? I really hoped he could be a part of this."

I was too busy trying to get my vision back to answer him.

When I didn't respond, he continued, "Like May here, Christian too was a surprise. I never thought the Council would assign someone so young to be a guardian, but I guess it shouldn't have surprised me. They never were good at making smart decisions."

"How did you know?" I finally gasped.

He leaned into me, inches from my face. "That night at the hospital when he kept insisting you were alive. I thought

Christian was crazy for trying to save you when you looked like death himself, but then he'd said the word 'Light' and that's when I knew. He was your guardian. Only a guardian would be able to sense their ward's Light. After that, I did all I could to make sure he'd save you."

He smoothed back my hair with his cold hand. "I was going to take you that night, you know. The discovery of a guardian protecting you shook me up a bit, but looking back I'm glad I didn't. Having him teach you to fight has been well worth it." He leaned in even closer until I could feel his putrid breath on my cheek. "When I'm done with you, he will be next."

The thought of him harming Christian spurred me into action. I grabbed his head between my palms and commanded Light into my finger tips. Instantly, his flesh melted beneath my burning hands, and he fell over screaming. I rolled on top of him and repeatedly punch him in the face. "You will never hurt me or anyone I love ever again!" I screamed.

I managed to hit him several times before he caught my fist and squeezed hard. I stifled a cry.

"Enough of this." Lightening quick, he stood up from beneath me, taking me with him. His calloused fingers gripped my neck, stopping air from passing to my lungs. In my face, he said, "This fight is over. Do you understand? You have lost and now your blood will become mine."

His hand jerked my head to the side, exposing my neck. All attempts to free myself were useless, and I could see now he had only been toying with me before.

My struggling body reminded me of a gazelle after it's been captured by a cheetah. It always made me mad to see how easily the gazelle would give up after struggling for just a short time, as if it knew it didn't have a chance. I didn't think I had a chance either, but I wasn't about to stop fighting.

"Hold still, Little One. It will hurt less." He lowered his

head to my flesh, then paused. "Never mind, struggle. I want you to feel pain." His head struck forward like a viper and his teeth pierced the skin of my neck. The pain was terrible, far worse than I could've ever imagined. And every attempt to push him away only made his cold teeth drive further into my flesh.

Was this what my mother had endured? A painful death? All the good she'd done, all the people she'd helped and then to be killed by this evil monster. Was I really going to let my parent's legacy be destroyed? I was all that was left. My mother used to tell me I was destined for great things—finally, I believed her.

Blood flowed down my arms and dripped to the floor. Beyond the blood, I knew Light was next to be drained, and after that there'd be nothing left. Already I could feel Light struggling to contend with death's darkness.

I opened my eyes and squinted into the stage's bright lights. Its warmth fell upon me, racing against my skin as if it were trying to tell me something. I blinked slowly and in that second had a moment of clarity. The assembly—when I'd drained the school's gym of light. I could expel light, but could I draw it into me just as easily?

Using the last of my strength, I began to suck the light from the room and into myself, hoping it would fortify my weakening Light. The stage lights flickered until they went out entirely. I reached further, mentally draining the surrounding area of power: the school, the neighborhood, all of it until I could contain no more. I was so full of light that my skin felt like it would burst from my frame. My body stiffened and my head snapped back as light spilled from my eyes and mouth.

The Vyken struggled to unlatch himself from my neck. He squirmed and tried to push away, but Light's grip was tighter. It snuffed out his darkness and as more light flowed from me, I felt him become weaker. A loud tearing sound bounced throughout the auditorium as the body of the Vyken began to come apart. He continued to crack and peel until his whole body became a pile of silver ash. What once was a vessel for absolute evil was now nothing more than a pile of dirt at my feet.

Thirty-Two

I REMEMBER IT WAS FREEZING COLD THE DAY MY MOTHER DIED, but that didn't stop me from going into our backyard to swing on our rusted metal swing set. The chilly fall weather nipped at my face; it was a welcome distraction from the somber mood in the house. Something had happened, something bad and I had a strong feeling I didn't want to know what. I saw my father when he came home that morning. His eyes were red and puffy and so when he called my name, I ran. My father never cried.

I jumped on the swing and pumped my legs as hard and fast as they'd go. I didn't even slow down when my father came outside, hands stuffed in his pockets.

"I need to talk to you, Llona. Can you stop?"

I pushed harder. My body lifted a few inches off the seat of the swing when it was at its highest point. A little further and I could touch the sky.

"Llona, please stop. I need to talk to you about your mother."

"Mom will be here soon. She's taking me to the park." I reached my hand to the sky.

"No, Llona."

I blocked the empty sadness I heard in his voice, and raised my other hand to the clouds. With neither hand on the ropes,

I lost my balance and fell from the swing. I expected to hit the ground, but my always-quick father caught me in his arms and cradled me to his chest.

"I'm so sorry, Llona," he cried, tears spilling on top of my hair. "I couldn't protect her. I lost her. I'm so sorry!" Over and over he apologized while he rocked me back and forth.

It seemed I'd stared an eternity into the sky while lying in his arms. One single moment in time lasts an eternity when you realize you've lost someone you love more than life. I'd had too many of these moments to all of a sudden be experiencing another one.

But this moment was different from the others. This time something inside me had died. I felt whatever it was flow through my blood like a poisonous virus, and I wondered if I was dying.

I used the last of the borrowed light to lighten the auditorium, and then I collapsed to the stage, the dust of the Vyken only inches from my face.

Just then the doors of the auditorium flew open and Christian rushed in. "Llona!" he called. He was at my side before I could raise my head.

"Llona?" I felt the warmth of his hand on my back.

"Get May," I managed to say.

He moved away from me and untied May. Very carefully he laid her down and examined her. I slowly moved into a sitting position.

"I'm calling an ambulance," he said and pulled out his phone.

"Is she going to be okay?"

"I think so, but we need to be sure."

While he called 911 and explained our location to the operator, I swept my long hair to the side of my neck, covering the two puncture wounds from the Vyken. For some reason they made me feel dirty, and I didn't want Christian to see them.

As soon as he said good-bye, he returned to my side. "You look like you got the crap kicked out of you."

"You should see the other guy," I mumbled.

Christian tensed and glanced around. "Where is the Vyken?"

"You mean Mr. Steele?"

Christian was silent, then, "Mr. Steele was the Vyken?"

I nodded.

"I should've known," he said.

"How?"

Christian's jaw clenched. "Where is he?"

"You're standing on him."

"What?" He looked down and stepped to the side of the silver ash. "You killed him? How?"

"Long story."

He shook his head. "That's impossible."

"I was well trained, I guess."

He knelt down, his expression granite. "Do you know how dangerous that was? Why did you leave me back there?"

"This was my problem. I wasn't about to get anyone else killed." The thought of Tracey, dead on my bed, filled me with great sorrow. I slumped my shoulders. "I got her killed," I whispered.

"It wasn't your fault. It was the Vyken that did this, no one else. Do you understand?"

I nodded my head because I knew that would make him feel better, but deep down I would always blame myself. Everything that had happened tonight could've been prevented if only I would have left. My selfishness had caused her death.

Christian's arm came around me. "Everything will be all right. Trust me, okay?"

I nodded again.

"I hate to do this now, but the police and ambulance will

be here any second. You have to know what to say."

"What do you want me to say?"

Christian glanced around the room. "Tell them the truth except for the part where Mr. Steele is a Vyken and you killed him. Since we can't produce a body, we need them to think he got away."

"What about May?"

"She probably doesn't know much. I'll try and talk to her as soon as she's awake."

"She knows everything."

"What do you mean everything?"

"I told her what I was."

"Why would you do that?" he asked.

I wished I could get angry, but there was no more fight left. "I needed a friend and so did she. She knows what it's like to be different."

"Different as in a social outcast or different as in 'special' different?"

I raised my eyes to meet his. "Like me different. She's a Fury."

Christian stared at May. "A Fury? This whole time and no one knew?"

"She didn't know who she was—still doesn't really."

A deep voice echoed from the hallway, "Hello?"

"We're in here," Christian called.

Two EMTs and one police officer rushed in. Christian bent his head and whispered in my ear. "This will all be over soon."

*   *   *   *   *

It was the day of graduation. It was supposed to be a day filled with hope for the future, but as I looked around I saw only grief and sadness on the faces of my classmates. Tracey was dead. She had been one of them and had been murdered by someone we had all trusted. Mr. Steele had not only taken Tracey, he'd killed a part of our innocence.

I glanced back at May, sitting two rows behind me. She gave me a weak smile and nodded her head. The big purple bruise on the side of her face had finally faded, but I could see in her eyes that what happened on prom night affected more than just her face.

That night Mr. Steele had sent May a text from Tracey's phone telling her to meet Tracey at the auditorium. When May showed up and saw Mr. Steele and not Tracey, she didn't think anything was wrong. She assumed Tracey was late. But as their conversation progressed, and Mr. Steele's behavior changed from being a teacher to more of an obsessed stalker (she said he was asking all sorts of personal questions about me), she decided to leave. That didn't sit well with Mr. Steele, who then threw her into a wall.

Using the only way she knew to protect herself, May tried to set him on fire by just thinking about it, but instead, nearby chairs burst into flames, burning the sleeve of his suit. Mr. Steele had been so shocked, that he paused, giving her an opportunity to run, which she didn't waste. However, it was only a short moment before he'd caught up to her. He had planned on killing her that night, but because she used her ability, he had spared her for some future use we would never know.

One positive thing to come out of all this was it had spurred May into finding out more about herself. The very next day she had called Sophie and told her everything. And although Sophie lacked the compassion that was probably needed for that conversation, she was completely honest in telling May the history of Furies, how she could learn to control fire, and what the future may hold for her. When Sophie extended her an invitation to attend Lucent with me where she could study under an elder Fury, May readily accepted.

I couldn't have been happier May was coming with me. The last thing I wanted right now was to be in new place all alone.

I glanced up into the bleachers, way in the back, to where Jake sat with Heidi. Next to him, I spotted Christian wearing a baseball cap and a heavy jacket despite the warm weather. He was supposed to be incognito, but to me he stood out like a WWE wrestler at a Girl Scout convention.

Since the Vyken had been discovered and killed, the Council no longer felt Christian needed to be my guardian, nor pretend to be a senior anymore. That's what Sophie told me anyway, but the next day a man four times my age showed up and said he would be my "escort" until I left for Lucent.

Personally I think Christian was removed from being my guardian because the Council thought he'd failed somehow. He was the one that should've killed the Vyken, not me. That's exactly what Sophie had said anyway.

I wouldn't realize the consequences of what I'd done until much later, but for now I was glad I had killed the Vyken. Maybe too glad. There was a dark part of me, hidden deep within, I felt growing like the stretched shadows of night when the sun sets across the horizon. It frightened me, but I reasoned it had something to do with what I'd endured, and given enough time it would go away. I hoped.

Graduation seemed to last forever, and I could tell by the looks of those around me they agreed too, especially Matt who was sitting a few rows in front of me. A couple of times his head dropped back like he had fallen asleep. I felt particularly sorry for him. He took Tracey's death pretty hard as he blamed himself. He should've picked her up like a normal date, he had told me. I tried to convince him it wasn't his fault, but when a person feels both guilt and grief, only on their own can they find their way out of the suffocating black hole of depression. Believe me, I know.

Finally, the last speaker finished and the principal asked us to stand while he gave us some final words of wisdom. When it came time to throw our hats into the air, some of us did, but most of us just quietly took them off. And just as quietly, we left the gymnasium and high school behind.

Outside, Jake gave me a dozen roses. "I'm so proud of you," he said, giving me a hug. "Your parents would be proud too."

"Thanks. Is Christian still here?" My escort wanted to take May and I to the airport as soon as possible.

"He said he'd see you back at the house," Jake said.

"Llona?" a familiar voice asked.

I turned around. "Matt. How are you doing?" He had already changed out of his graduation gown. He had dark circles under his eyes, and I wondered how much sleep he was getting.

"I'm okay. I just wanted to say good-bye and wish you well." He pulled me in for a tight hug.

"So you're off to D.C., huh?" I said when he finally let go.

"Looks that way. You know it all seemed so important before, but now—I don't know."

I took his hand. "It is important. You are important. You are going to do some amazing things in life."

He glanced away. I followed his gaze. In the distance dark storm clouds lined the horizon. I squeezed his hand, knowing what he was thinking. "That is not your future. You will be happy again soon. I just know it."

He looked back at me. "I shouldn't have left her alone," he said.

"It wasn't your fault." The empty sadness in his eyes broke my heart. I did the only thing I could. With just a thought, I transferred my calming Light from my hand to his. The lines in his face relaxed. "You'll call me, right?" I asked.

He nodded. "Take care of yourself, Llona. There's no one else like you."

It was my turn to hug him.

After we said our good-byes, I jumped in the car. May was waiting for me in the back.

"You ready for this?" I asked her.

"So ready. Finally we won't feel like freaks any more. It's going to be great."

I wish I could agree with her, but something told me where we were going wasn't going to be as wonderful as May wanted to believe.

After our lame escort, who reminded me of Mr. Bean, dropped May off to finish packing, we approached my house. Christian's car was parked in the driveway.

Doppelganger Mr. Bean turned around. "You're all packed, yes?" He dabbed at his face with a perfectly white, ironed handkerchief.

"Pretty much. Give me ten minutes."

He blew his nose. "We're on a time table."

"I know. I'll hurry." I jumped out of the car.

The moment I walked into the house I knew it was empty. I looked out my bedroom window to find Christian standing outside, his back to me. By his rigid stance I could tell he was upset.

I joined him. "Christian?"

He turned around and forced a smile. "Happy graduation!"

"Right. What are you doing out here?"

"Just thinking."

"What about?"

Christian nodded his head back toward the house. "You ready for this?"

"I guess. I still wish it was you taking me. Mr. Bean-wanna-be is creeping me out."

"He's not that bad."

"He carries a hanky."

Christian smiled, but couldn't laugh.

"So where are you headed?" I asked.

He shrugged. "Not sure yet. They'll probably send me back to Oregon to train younger guardians again. I doubt I'll get another ward assigned to me for awhile after the way I screwed up."

"Screwed up? You saved my life. More than a few times, if I remember correctly."

He was silent for a moment. "Mr. Bean's probably waiting for you, huh?"

"He can wait." I didn't want our good-bye to be rushed.

"I'm glad May's going with you. It makes me feel better knowing you won't be alone."

"Me too, but it will be weird not seeing you. I've gotten used to having you around."

"I know what you mean." The sadness in his eyes reflected my own.

"I wish you could come with me," I complained again.

"Against the rules."

"Pesky rules."

"Yeah."

Silence again.

"You can at least call me right?" I asked.

"It's frowned upon."

I let out an exaggerated sigh.

Christian took my hand. "Don't worry. I'll call and you can call me. We just can't be too open about it." He pulled me into a hug.

I inhaled deeply, wanting to always remember his smell.

"You have no idea how much I'm going to miss you," he whispered.

"Not as much as I'm going to miss you," I whispered back.

I closed my eyes and tried not to think of the pain I felt growing in my gut. A hook ripping open my insides would've felt better than having to say good-bye.

After a moment, he let go and stared at me intensely. "Take care of yourself. And trust your instincts. If something doesn't feel right, it isn't." He let go of my arms. "Call me when you get there, if you can."

"I will."

He turned back toward the house. Was he really just going to leave? As he moved further from me, air caught in my chest, and I didn't think I'd be able to breathe. I wanted to cry out to him, beg him to stay. My eyes filled with tears.

Christian made it to the screen door before he stopped.

My heart skipped a beat.

His white knuckles gripped the handle and his muscles tightened. "Screw the rules," he said. He turned around and in about three steps was across the lawn and taking me into his arms. He lips pressed upon mine passionately.

Finally, the first kiss I had dreamed of. I wrapped my arms around his neck and pulled him even closer. The kiss lasted less than a minute but in those seconds I knew exactly how Christian felt about me.

When he released me, he breathed, "I don't know how I'm ever going to let you go."

"It's just temporary," I said, more to convince myself. "We'll see each other again. We have to."

"We will. I'll make sure it happens." He smiled down at me.

"Promise?"

"Promise." He kissed me again, lightly.

This time when Christian left, my heart didn't feel as heavy. He had made me a promise, and he wasn't the type to break it. I would see him again.

I walked back into my room and moved to grab the suit-cases off my bed, but stopped in front of the mirror. After glancing around to make sure I was alone, I moved the side braid away from my neck. Very faintly, beneath heavy foun-dation, two red marks stared back at me accusingly. The bite marks hadn't healed. They remained a permanent fixture on my body, reminding me daily of what'd happened.

I wish it was just the bite marks that remained. The dark-ness the Vyken's poison had left inside me couldn't be con-cealed by foundation. I'd tried to ignore its presence, pretend it didn't exist, but very subtly I felt it changing me despite my best efforts.

At the sound of a knock on my door, I quickly moved my braid back in place.

"Are you ready?" the Mr. Bean look-alike asked at the door. His nose was bright red.

I looked at myself one more time in the mirror. Ready? How could I be ready for a future I didn't know? One thing was certain, however. I had survived.

SPECIAL SNEAK PEEK

FRACTURED SOUL

BY

RACHEL McCLELLAN

COMING SOON FROM SWEETWATER BOOKS

ONE

PEOPLE TOLD ME LIFE WOULD RETURN TO NORMAL, BUT HOW could it after you've killed someone? Or something. Life would never be the same again, apparently starting with my new dorm room.

"Why does it smell like blood in here?" I dropped my duffle bag on the perfectly made bed. The pink flowered bedspread wrinkled its way out of perfection.

"This room is practically brand new," Sophie said.

I looked under the bed. "I don't think so." Where was the smell coming from? "Did a butcher live in it before?"

"What about a butcher?" May asked, when she walked through the door.

"The butcher who killed a cow in my room." I unzipped my bag.

"Huh?"

Sophie frowned. "Really, Llona. You have such an imagination." She turned to May, her long ruffled skirt followed. "Did you find your room satisfactory?"

"I did. And thanks again for inviting me here."

Sophie placed a hand on her shoulder. "Lucent's glad to have you."

"When's dinner?" I asked. I thought they'd feed us on the plane, but all I got was peanuts.

"In about ten minutes," Sophie said. "Why don't you get settled and then come on down when you hear the chimes? Do you remember where the dining room is at?"

"Um, first floor, all the way at the end," I said. Sophie had given us a quick tour on the way up. There were so many rooms, I was surprised I'd remembered.

Sophie smiled. "Good. I'll see you girls down there. Oh, and by the way, Llona, even though Auras aren't normally unkind, just remember that they are still teenagers trying to discover who they are."

"What's that supposed to mean?"

"You've been on the outside your whole life," she said. "They might view you as different."

I threw up my arms. "Fantastic. So I was a freak before and now you're saying I'm a freak here too?"

"No, it will just take a while for the girls to get to know you. And I'm sure once they do, they will love you just like I do."

Uh-huh, sure, I thought. Cause that's how teenagers are. I turned my attention to my bag so she wouldn't see me scowling. It was amazing how easily adults forget what it's like to be a teenager.

"Try not to be late, girls," Sophie said before she closed the door.

May jumped onto my bed. "Can you believe this place? It's like right out of a fairytale. I feel like a princess!"

I forced a smile and shoved clothes into the nearest dresser.

"What's wrong?" she asked.

I stopped moving. "Nothing, really, yet everything. I'll get over it." I crinkled my nose. "Except for this awful smell."

"What smell?"

"You really don't smell it?" I opened the closet doors. The walk-in closet was bare except for a thin layer of dust covering the wood floor.

"It might smell a little musty," May offered. "Do you really think the girls will be mean to us?"

I shrugged. "Probably not to you. From what I hear, Furies are a rare find. I'm sure they'll treat you like the diamond you are!" I dropped onto the bed next to her.

May laughed. "You sound just like your aunt."

"This place is going to take some getting used to."

May nodded.

"How are you doing?" I asked her suddenly. She had been very quiet on the flight over, but I didn't dare ask her what was wrong in front of our Mr. Bean-like bodyguard.

May looked down. I followed her gaze. Her fingers traced the floral pattern on the quilt. "For some reason I thought I'd feel better putting all this space between us and Highland, but I almost feel worse. It's like I've run away or something." May looked at me, searching for understanding. "Does that make sense?"

"It does. It feels like we're betraying Tracey by being here. We get to live our lives while she's stuck six feet under. She shouldn't have died." Beneath the pillow on my lap, I dug my nails into my palm. It was my fault she'd died. My selfishness had left her dead, May injured, and many others depressed. The image of Matt's face when I'd said good-bye came to mind.

"Are you going to call Christian tonight?" May asked.

I think she thought by bringing up his name, I'd forget about what happened, but I would never forget, or forgive. But I could pretend for everyone else's sake. I forced another smile. "I'll try. I have to call Jake to let him know I made it okay, and if I don't have someone standing over me, then I'll try to call Christian."

"I can't believe they won't let you talk to him," May said.

"Oh, I can talk to him, but it's," I quoted with my fingers, "frowned upon."

May chuckled and stood up. "I better finish unpacking before we have to go downstairs. Come grab me when you're ready."

After May shut the door, I opened the window to let the fresh air in. I was looking forward to the cooler New York weather. I don't think I could have handled sunny and warm at this point in my life. There was nothing sunny about it.

A screen prevented me from seeing the full scope of Lucent. I traced its edges until I found the latch to remove it. I popped the screen out, slid it under my bed, then returned to the window. Leaning out as far as I could, I scanned the area.

My room was located in the right wing of the great restored mansion. There was one more floor above me and three below. When we had first arrived, I was in awe at the size of the school, but now looking at everything from this high in the air, Lucent seemed even bigger.

The sun had almost set, taking the shadows of trees and buildings with it. They stretched long and thin, crossing into each other until they blurred into the forest just beyond a tall, rock wall surrounding the school.

Behind the main building there were three more almost as big. From one of them, a steady line of people, most of them looked like students, headed toward the building I was in. That's a lot of teenagers, I thought and took a deep breath. Just then one of the girls' heads turned up in my direction. I quickly ducked back in my room and away from the window.

Already the fresh air was making a difference on the smell. Either that or I was getting used to it. I sat down at the vanity and ran a brush through my long hair. Maybe someone at Lucent could show me how to change it, I hoped. I was tired of its blonde, almost white, color. I always thought

I'd look better with brown hair, like May's.

A tinkling sound, as if someone had waved a magical wand, chimed. That must be the bell Sophie had talked about.

I swept my hair to the side of my neck and examined the two small holes where Mr. Steele had bit me. They were still there, no better than before. The red, swollen edges around the wounds made them look like eyes. I quickly applied concealer. I hated the way the stared at me, accusingly.

After I pulled a pink beanie over my head, I headed across the hall to May's room. She opened the door before I got there.

"What's with the weird chimes?" she asked.

"I don't know, but if I have to hear that every day, I think I'll go crazy."

"I know, right?" May turned to her mirror and readjusted her hair. She was wearing a different outfit, it looked brand new, and she had reapplied her makeup. She must be nervous, I thought. I never considered how hard this must be for her. May was a newly discovered Fury, which meant she had the ability to manipulate fire. She had guarded her secret for so long that to all of a sudden be surrounded by people who know your secret might be overwhelming.

"You're going to fit right in, don't worry." I wrapped my arm around her shoulder. "Come on. Let's go be the new kids."

We were almost to the end of the hall when a door opened and four laughing girls appeared, but when they saw us they stopped. As we passed, May said, "Hi, guys." They said nothing. Just stared like we were a new zoo exhibit.

Just before we turned the corner, my exceptional hearing heard one of them whisper, "I can't believe they put her in that room. I bet she's dead by the end of the month."

ABOUT THE AUTHOR

RACHEL MCCLELLAN WAS BORN AND RAISED IN IDAHO, A place secretly known for its supernatural creatures. When she's not in her writing lair, she's partying with her husband and four small children. Her love for storytelling began as a child when the moon first possessed the night. For when the lights went out, her imagination painted a whole new world. And what a scary world it is . . .